PRAISE FOR

STRESSED IN SCOTTSDALE

"Once again Marcia Fine presents a breezy slice of life through Jean Rubin. As Rubin navigates her life while tending to the needs of her demanding family, life in upscale Scottsdale reveals its own obstacles. She learns how to achieve serenity with some major shifts in attitude and firm choices. Side-splitting fun!"

—*Gail Fisher, columnist & author*

"… examines environmental issues with a sharp eye. Fine pokes good-hearted fun while bringing the issues of clean air and water to the forefront. I was thoroughly entertained."

—*Lee Robert, singer/songwriter, Executive Director of Earth Friends Wildlife Foundation*

"Marcia Fine has brought us the third antic-filled, laughter-inducing novel of Jean Rubin's frantic life. It's funny and possibly too true; you may find chuckle at the habits and foibles you recognize in yourself and neighbors scattered among her characters. Welcome to the posh life of fashionistas and would-be socialites and the havoc around them. Take it with a grain of salt. Remember: satire exaggerates…"

—*Barbara Lacy, journalist*

"'Stressed in Scottsdale'? Surely that's an oxymoron. Award-winning author Marcia Fine's tangled socio-political spoof of 'stress' set in this sunny, chic resort yields an enjoyable read, laced with relevant themes, keen attention to details and razor-sharp humor."

—*Deborah Hilcove, BelVista Publishers, LLC*

Wry, witty, and right on target!"

"Stress Tip: When it's 108 degrees, your kids have stopped listening to you, your mother wants to wear all her costume jewelry at the same time, and you can't seem to get rid of that nagging knot in between your shoulder and neck, it's time to read *Stressed in Scottsdale!* Fine's book sheds light on all those zany characters that make up this great desert landscape called Arizona."

"Marcia has hit it out of the ballpark again! This satire will hit a nerve. More importantly, it sends the message that we are not alone in our struggles to find balance while meeting our family obligations."

"Another winner from an author who reveals what happens in a community called Scottsdale. Outrageously clever truth?"

"An entertaining and smart read! Jean is witty, fun and just the kind of friend you want to cheer for!"

"I love the character of Jean Rubin. She is as real as a hot Arizona summer!"

"… dry heat setting with feisty humor. An entertaining read!"

"Fine raises serious issues about marriage, our relationships to offspring, parents and the environment. It's a realistic insight into the sandwich generation. And I laughed out loud!"

"Marcia's wit, wisdom and way with words is showcased in *Stressed in Scottsdale*. The characters are hysterically realistic and represent what we all strive to do...lead a more peaceful and less stressful life despite our family and friends."
—*E. Lynn Lanoue, CEO, BWI Coaching and Consulting*

"Marcia Fine does it again! From the first paragraph I couldn't put it down until there were no more words to read! Loved the style! Loved the sass!
—*Janita Cooper, CEO, Master Video Disc and Design*

"Jean Rubin's observant eye of the modes and mores of an upscale community enhance a fast-paced lifestyle, rife with satirical situations including an Asian nail salon, an expensive gourmet food emporium and mammogram hell. Why, she even takes us to the spa and a writer's conference! Loved the feminist humor!"
—*Bonnie Lewis, artist*

"Jean Rubin is "everywoman" living life at a break-neck pace while she manages work and relationships. A great read!"
—*Mary Manross, former mayor, Scottsdale, Arizona*

Stressed

in

Scottsdale

ALSO BY

MARCIA FINE

Gossip.com
Boomerang — When Life Comes Back to Bite You
Paper Children — An Immigrant's Legacy***
The Blind Eye*

*Award-winning

STRESSED

in

SCOTTSDALE

Marcia Fine

L'Image Press
Scottsdale, Arizona

Stressed in Scottsdale

This is a work of fiction. All of the characters, organizations, places and events portrayed in this novel are either products of the author's imagination or are used fictitiously. Any resemblance to actual events, places or people, living or dead, is entirely coincidental.

Although many local places, people and events are mentioned, this does not implicate any individuals. It is merely my unbridled story-telling and strange sense of humor. There has been no intention to offend, merely entertain. However, that doesn't mitigate the fact that there really are blind bighorn sheep lurking in Arizona!

Although the author and publisher have made every effort to ensure the accuracy and completeness of information contained in this book, we assume no responsibility for errors, inaccuracies, omissions or any inconsistency herein. Any slights of people, places, or organizations are unintentional.

Printed and bound in the United State of America. First printing 2010

Published by L'Image Press in association with the author, Marcia Fine.

Cover design by Kim Appis
Interior design by Julia Baumann

ISBN 13: 978-0-615-31513-3
Library of Congress Control Number: 2009936273

to the multi-tasking mamas sandwiched between generations

ACKNOWLEDGEMENTS

Any book is a group project. Special thanks to my wonderful group of stellar authors, Deborah Ledford, Virginia Nosky, Judy Starbuck and Marty Roselius. They have been exceptional in their patience and wisdom.

A special thank you to Nancy McCurry and her keen editor's eye for sharpening the stakes of our desert lifestyle; Linda de Nazelle for the quiet apartment; readers Hope Schor and Renee Rivers; an anonymous environmentalist who gave me the scoop; all the librarians who assisted with research and as always, Skip, who supports all my endeavors.

1

ENORMOUS ETCHINGS OF PINK STONE GECKOS and mauve snakes artistically wrap around the retaining walls of the 101 Freeway, better known as Death Alley. When my speedometer slides to 75, I brake for the hidden cameras. A throbbing knot between my neck and shoulder expands, its tentacles crawling into the base of my skull. I take one hand off the steering wheel to massage it.

I've left a client's office at the Scottsdale Airpark. After hours of preparation the cretin rejected my proposal, "Guidelines for Equality in the Workplace: Ten Steps to Avoid Litigation." I may sue him. I sigh in frustration. More wasted hours. I beat myself up over what I could have done differently. More hours? Charged less? A better proposal?

Neck tension radiates to my shoulder. I roll them for release. I inhale through my nose and whoosh the air out my mouth. Keep going. Push, push. My energy shifts. I relax a little, cracking my windows for air.

With one hand I attach the Bluetooth to my ear, turn on the radio and search my tote for a zip-lock bag of pistachios. I listen to an NPR story about obscure bluegrass musicians in Appalachia, the twangs of steel strings blending into the freeway noise.

I munch on the sweet salty nuts, musing on my crazy life. Too much to do, too many people, too little time, too many messages. I turn down the radio and speed dial my voicemail with my thumb.

The first message is from Maury reminding me about the political meeting today. The second one's from our daughter, Lara, admonishing me to call her back ASAP, the third's from my friend, Glee, with tales of a new boyfriend and the fourth one's from my mother. She wants to know why Wolf Blitzer on CNN doesn't shave his beard.

I hang up as a few pistachios fall into my lap. It's amazing the havoc I can create with one hand. I turn up the radio, close the windows and punch up my weak air-conditioner.

It's been a rough year. My beloved dad passed away. While I grieve and miss him every day, my mother is having an even harder time moving forward. She expresses her fury to me: Wasn't I supposed to go first? Why did he leave me? I don't care if he's not listening; I'm going to talk to him anyway.

Her litany requires infinite patience. She can't stay in their large two bedroom apartment. Her loneliness and lack of skills mean I need to find her a new place to live. I've delayed for months because she doesn't like change.

When I go to her place the creeping clutter signals she's too tired to hang things up or she can't make up her mind what she wants to wear. Piles of white filmy blouses, black pants, colorful scarves and flowered house dresses upholster the sofa and backs of chairs. Or maybe her knees are bad so she doesn't want to bend to put things away in the drawers. When I arrived yesterday, the dining room table was covered in a rainbow of berets with costume jewelry laid out on top of them.

"Mom, let's get this put away," I said reaching for a poodle pin.

"Don't touch anything. I'm going to wear it tomorrow."

"All of it?" I asked.

The shoes she's worn in the past week crowd under the table. Stacks of newspapers and magazines, dishes, receipts, unpaid bills, reading glasses, cuticle scissors and medicine bottles radiate onto every surface.

Before I call my mother back, I have to shop for dinner and show up at Maury's meeting. I pull into the parking lot of *AJ's Fine Foods*, the most expensive, efficient grocery store in town. I can't bear to go into a regular supermarket when I'm in a hurry and torture through the self-check out line. People like me who are older than forty can't figure out how to scan an item. Someone always has to come over to help.

My Birkenstocks race down the chic aisles, my cart a weapon of mass intention. In the soft Ingmar Bergman lighting a tousled blonde with wrap-around bug-lens sunglasses and a crisp white tennis outfit passes me. She's got smooth tanned legs and a Louis Vuitton backpack, a camel hump for the affluent.

She puzzles over the yogurts lifting each one for an inspection of the ingredients. *Honey, its yogurt, not wine.*

With deft speed I dump in skim milk, free-range eggs, organic chicken breasts and a dill havarti cheese. I'm offered a smelly one to sample and decide Maury will love it. I add organic tomatoes shaped like miniature pumpkins. I stop to purchase an herbal mint tea, surveying the check-out lines for the shortest one.

A woman with grey hair in pigtails, dark glasses and a worn brown canvas purse with LV printed all over it, discusses the weather with the cashier. The Louis Vuittons are spreading through the store like an infectious disease.

What's there to talk about? It's triple digits today. It'll be hot tomorrow. It's August in Arizona. She's in a track suit with *Juicy* written across her backside.

I shift from foot to foot. Maybe my audible sigh will spur them along. I look at my watch. *Why did I promise Maury I'd come to a Green meeting?*

My semi-retired doctor husband hangs around the house four days a week watching the History Channel, asking me what's for lunch, writing leftist letters to the editor and scheduling golf dates. His newest interest includes volunteering for an environmental campaign.

Juicy retreats out the door. Finally. The cashier takes my cart and slides it near the register on her side, swiping my items. "Hot out there today?" she asks me in a cheerful query.

Weather conversations are ubiquitous.

"Very." I realize I have forgotten my re-cycle canvas shopping bags in the car.

"Did you see the monsoon yesterday?"

"Uh, no," I say, hoping she'll hurry.

"Only rained a few minutes but it was enough to get my car dirty. This is the worst season we've had in years."

I conclude by agreeing with her that yes, it is strange to live in a place that rains gook instead of water.

I exit the air-conditioned glory of AJs, toss the two paper grocery bags in the back of the trusty Volvo and pull out. Mentally I click through the proposal that has to be re-written, more errands, a jury duty summons, at least a hundred e-mails, un-paid bills and finally, the precious but sometimes annoying grandkids. We have three: Jacob, the oldest and a smarty-pants, Tangerine, a princess-in-training, called Tangie and Buzz, a two-year-old with spiked hair and a lisp.

We watch Tangie and Buzz many weekends. Last Saturday and Sunday our daughter, Lara, and her husband, Gus, escaped to northern Arizona known as the High Country. It's 108 degrees in our concrete valley and 75 degrees up there.

In the past we instructed our babysitters with, "There's Coke in the fridge, watch TV and let them stay up as late as they want."

Lara and Gus are helicopter parents who hover over their young. When they leave our verbal instructions sound like a military invasion. "... and don't forget the ba-ba before he goes to sleep and then another warm one if he wakes up and she gets Ovaltine with organic milk in a ba-ba. He gets Cheerios in the morning. She can have a banana if her stool was soft from the evening BM. Otherwise, give her almond milk and special oatmeal cookies. They get baths every night, make sure they brush their teeth with the Elmo toothbrushes, read them six stories each and no TV. NO TV! It kills their brain cells. They can only watch *Winnie the Pooh.* You can pick it up at the video store which is only forty minutes from your house. Also, if Tangie gets night terrors then bring her into your bed and tell dad to make soft-boiled eggs. It's the only thing that'll calm her down. Put the Brahms CD on very low and hum. And don't forget to refer to my written directives for details."

She still gets a bottle at almost four years old?

After five hugs, numerous kisses and multiple admonishments to be good for their grandparents, Lara and Gus made their exit. I brought the kids into the living room. Tangie sat on the sofa with a moth-eaten blanket holding a bottle and Buzz, drooling, hugged his patchy teddy bear with the missing ear. He put his thumb in his mouth. Amber, who loves kids because they drop food, sidles up wagging her tail. She sits down, too.

"Okay, kids," I said, lowering my voice to drill sergeant level. "I'm the Grandma-in-Charge and we've got new rules. I say, drop the blankie. Sit up straight. You, get the finger out of your mouth. Wipe your lip. I've had it with the drooling. Enough with *schlepping* a bear everywhere. I'm in charge now."

"Jean, what're you doing? The kids look petrified," said Maury coming in the room.

"I'm just having a little fun. Right, kids?" Wide-eyed, they nodded. Amber smiled.

I'm stuck in traffic. Every bumpy main artery road back to the freeway is torn up. It doesn't matter where you go, construction blankets the city. Somewhere a diabolic engineer relishes the ditches, pipes and backhoes that narrow Indian Bend, McDonald and Chaparral roads into one lane. Finally, I pressure the gas pedal as I maneuver onto the ramp of the 101.

Tempe's only a short ride from Scottsdale but it's a different world inhabited by tattooed university students, pierced professors and anti-fashionistas. I drive down Mill Avenue, Tempe's main road to the Arizona State campus, searching for a parking space. School's back in session. Backpacks here are blue or green canvas.

The knot in my neck pulses. Please. I need a parking space. I circle again. I'm sweating. If my friend, Glee, were with me she'd tell me to call upon my parking angels. That's what's wrong with me. I can't conjure up any angels, parking or otherwise. Glee has a flock of them. Somewhere in the Universe someone hears my plea. A dude in a gold ASU T-shirt flashes me a peace sign as he enters his VW van. He vacates a primo parking space for me. *Thank you, parking angels.*

I head for Green Party headquarters located above a head shop. In the window a mannequin dressed in black with a marijuana leaf emblazoned on her chest wears a red, green and yellow Rastafarian cap on her head. She stares straight ahead.

I huff up the stairs, breathless, my gym visits sporadic. I

bring my two bags of groceries with me. It's too hot to leave them in the car. Everything melts here. Even people. The sweating iced tea balances in the corner of my tote. As I reach the top landing I stumble and burst through the door into the room. Someone snickers at my entrance. Maury smiles and motions to me, pointing to the seat next to him.

A motley group muses around a beat-up conference table. I crash into a metal chair, dropping the grocery bags. I'm starving. Can I pull out the crackers and smelly cheese? I peel my tote off my shoulder, realizing that my phone has to be switched to vibrate so it doesn't interrupt the meeting. I slip the keys into the outside pocket, hang my sunglasses on the front of my shirt and settle the tote on the faded industrial carpeting. I smooth my khaki skirt.

My entry has been a major disruption. A flush travels up my face and distracts me until something wet leaks onto my foot. The iced tea has fallen inside the tote. Maury pats my leg with comfort. I'm too self-conscious to bend over to rearrange my drink. I'll rescue my soggy wallet later.

". . . the issue of air quality remains paramount. We've got more days targeted by the EPA as not acceptable for kids, asthmatics and the elderly than Los Angeles. Also, they've found contaminants in the Phoenix and Paradise Valley water supply. We should be able to make a campaign out of that," says a young guy with a GQ face, granny glasses and fashionable two-day-old stubble. He commands the room in a rumpled white Oxford shirt, speaking while he taps his laptop. Then he squints at us, a rag-tag group of ten around the table.

A few men have come from work, their ties tugged loose. Two women wear fitted dark business suits. The rest are attired in T-shirts with slogans, except for the rotund man at the end with a snarling bear on his chest.

The air-conditioning is not turned up to a peri-menopausal woman's satisfaction. I lift my forehead's curls to swipe the back of my hand across my brow. I can't believe we're all in any clothes. Then I glance at hairy, sweaty Bear Man. Never mind.

The stubble guy continues, "The ADEQ has issued two notices of violation against our opposition's husband that include running afoul of water quality laws by polluting groundwater and destroying Hohokam Indian remains. There's even an allegation he's damaging bighorn sheep herds."

A few people cluck their tongues, others take notes. I lean over and whisper to Maury, "Who's the ADEQ and what do the sheep have to do with it?"

"Arizona Department of Environmental Quality. Shush, I'm listening. I'll explain later."

Neck and shoulder pains radiate down my back. I drop my chin to my chest and roll my head around for relief. It makes crackling sounds. I should be taking a walk instead of ratcheting up anxiety about the ADEQ. Probably stands for Adolescent Department for Exceptional Quacks.

I study the campaign office. It's a dull grey furnished room with unmatched chairs, gun-metal tables covered in graffiti and election bumper stickers, slump block walls and fluorescent lights that cast green shadows on everyone's faces. I smother a giggle. The Green Party looks green.

My phone starts to vibrate. With exaggerated subtlety I reach into my wet bag to see who's trying to call me before the ringing starts. Lara again. Uh-oh. Maybe I traumatized the kids the last time with my military drill. I begin to get up to take the call outside but Maury grabs my arm to keep me in my seat.

A woman with a grey ponytail wearing an ethnic woven vest asks, "Are we going to sling mud first?"

"The other side plays hard ball. We have to." Mr. In-Control Preppy looks up from his laptop. "We need a writer. One with bite."

I don't have a clue. I don't know any writers who bite. The guy in the snarling bear shirt scowls at me. Why am I here?

I tap Maury's foot to get his attention. I give him the how-did-you-get-me-into-this? glare. It's better than the I-have-a-lot-to-do-raised-eyebrow look. He avoids my gaze. His forehead looks huge in this bad lighting. I must appear wrinkly.

I stroke my neck and let my fingers creep around to massage the knot. Maybe I should try April's new suck-face contraption that's supposed to tighten the skin. But it only lasts three hours. After that you revert back to a shar-pei. I can picture myself, face falling, jowls sagging, begging Maury to take me home from an event before I turn into a puddle around my ankles.

"We need a writer with moxie who isn't afraid to go for the jugular."

"Right. Jean can do that," says Maury, pushing a thumb in my direction.

"Huh? Who's Jean?" asks Mr. Preppy, looking around.

"Right here. Jean Rubin, writer extraordinaire and well-versed in ecological causes. She's been green all her life," says Maury, a bit of pride in his voice.

In moments my adorable, laconic, liberal husband has sold me out to the Greens.

"Wait a minute. I don't write political copy," I protest. "I don't know anything about water and air pollution. My area of expertise is gender studies—you know, men, women, their similarities and differences, sexism in the workplace, harassment in the office."

"You can learn anything you set your mind to," Maury says patting me on the back. "Jean's a bright multi-tasker who almost has her doctorate."

"Wait. I wanted to volunteer for the phone bank."

"Excuse me, I'm Brian Depalma," says Mr. Rumpled Preppy, "and this campaign needs you."

Do I think it's strange he has the same name as the movie director known for blood and guts? No, nothing is strange or weird or crazy anymore. I have a surreal life. The consistent throbbing in my neck tells me so.

The sound of Brian Depalma clicking on his laptop hypnotizes me. Speaking and pecking at the same time, he says, "Look, we've got a Green running against a Neanderthal. It shouldn't be that difficult to come up with a piece that defines our candidate."

I sit in silence. This can't be happening to me. I do not need one more thing to do.

"Don't worry, Honey. I'll help you," says Maury.

Brian's hand slaps the metal table. "Okay. That settles it." Our gore-and-guts director clicks his laptop shut. "Jean will do the copy and Fred, you're in charge of art work and layout. We've got stock photos of the candidate so we should be able to churn this out in no time. Nine weeks until election day so let's build the fire."

"Can do," says the man in the nasty bear shirt I assume is Fred.

Brian turns his attention to me. "Jean, stay focused on the Green issues. There may be more registered Republicans and Democrats in the district, but if our third party candidate can make a showing, we'll be happy. Our message is crucial." Brian Depalma stares me down and I blink. "Think you can turn something out by Monday so we can proof it and go to press on Wednesday? The printer has promised a quick turn around even with four-color. We can use them for the walk-a-thon the following week."

I'm furious with Maury. I don't even know who the candidate is, let alone his positions. I push my chair back and make a grimace at him. He gives me an abashed grin. I am not melting.

"Don't even think about making nice to me," I hiss as I bend over to pick up my grocery bags. I wish I had politically incorrect plastic. They'd shun me. Then I wouldn't have to do anything. I fling my damp tote over my shoulder and with extreme dignity, head held high in my best Nefertiti pose, I exit, dripping a trail of lukewarm herbal tea behind me.

2

I LOOK PAST MY MOTHER'S RED STRAW HAT and pearl earrings. Rubber palm trees decorate the corners of the assisted living facility dining room. A large flat screen TV is tuned to BET.

"Jean, these people don't know how to dress for a meal." My mother whispers as she leans toward me, looking over her shoulder. "That woman is in her nightgown."

"Mom, it's not a nightgown. It's a caftan."

"What? A caravan for lunch? Camels are dirty, disgusting animals that smell." She looks at the half-sandwich in her hand, holding it back so the bottom part of her glasses can get it in focus. "What kind of meal is this? I don't eat white bread. Can't you ask if they have pumpernickel? And what's the matter they don't serve a pickle?"

"Mom, it's not a deli. They serve what the majority of people can eat."

I stare at the TV while a rapper wearing baggy pants goes

through jerky motions. A pimply teen-ager in blue hospital scrubs guides an elderly man, pants belted too high, in front of the set. They move very slowly. My mother's speaking in a loud voice although I probably don't have to worry. All hearing aids are off during meal time according to a sign on the wall.

"Well, if that's your attitude," she huffs, getting up and reaching for her walker, "I'm leaving. I've never wanted to be in the majority."

No chance of that. I make hasty excuses to the manager, following my mother out to the Volvo. It takes me time to get her in the car, strap around the seat belt and place her new candy-apple red stainless steel walker with folding seat and extra basket in the car.

The following day we try another place, *La Vista Serena Luxury Condos for Senior Living*. It isn't much better. More upscale to be sure, but too fancy according to her. We sit across from each other, chatting over a gold tablecloth with a brocade runner and fresh gerbera daisies, a display of elegance.

"For God's sakes, Jean, I don't want to be so dressed up to eat a meal. These ladies are wearing Ferragamos. I'm never going to use all these facilities. I don't play bridge or *bocci* ball, I no longer appear in public in a bathing suit and making ceramic bowls in the craft studio is out of the question. Besides, I can tell all these people are snobs."

I survey the room of grey-blue heads with a few blondes and one bold redhead. Most are slouched in mauve upholstered chairs eating quietly.

"How do you know? No one's even spoken to us yet."

"See? What did I tell you? They're all snobs."

After we finish our chicken cordon bleu, which is only satisfactory according to my mother's culinary tastes, and complete our exit survey with: Yes, the food was good; no, we're not interested in future calls, we wait under the *porte coche* for the valet to bring our car. My mother stands next to me, a purse over her arm, a thin-lipped grimace on her face. She abandoned the walker for this visit. It's a sometime thing. She complains it makes her look old.

A crick has cemented itself in my neck. I massage it a bit and then roll my shoulders back a few times in an effort to loosen it up.

"Why are you always twitching?" asks my mother. "When you were a girl you never did that."

Maury peers at me over his reading glasses as I enter the kitchen. He's eating leftovers and reading a *National Geographic*. "Jean, you look great. Where're you going?"

"I don't know. Wherever Glee and April take me. It's supposed to help me relax. April's picking me up in five minutes. They just told me to dress "Scottsdale.""

"What does that mean?" Maury places his hand in the magazine to hold his spot.

"I'm not sure but it has something to do with jewelry and designers." I've rushed to get ready and pray my perfume and deodorant don't fail me. I should've asked where we're going. It doesn't matter. The crick in my neck has been replaced by ceaseless throbbing. I frown, shifting my head from side to side. Small popping sounds erupt that only I can hear.

He nods his head and takes another bite of beef stroganoff, an emergency purchase from *Smart & Final* last night. The Maury-inspired deadline Brian Depalma set for me to write copy is half done. I worked on it until 2 a.m. Then I couldn't fall asleep ruminating and counting blind sheep.

I sailed through my tasks, relationships and errands like a spit ball aiming for a whiteboard. Don't ask questions. Push.

"Jean, Brian Depalma . . ." I think Maury likes saying his name just to conger up gooey blood and streaming guts. ". . . emailed me to see if the copy's ready. He needs the research for a policy paper. It's important ammunition for the campaign."

"Some of it's ready. I'm a little busy," I say with sarcasm. Then I soften my tone. "But I found out about the guy and the sheep, Charles Dunn. He's the developer of *Los Robles Golf, Tennis and Spa Resort*, a brilliant jewel conveniently located in the Arizona foothills," I add, quoting from the brochure. "He's a bad guy."

"Big time." Maury nods.

I'm on firm ground. "The resort borders the Los Robles Archeological District. He's single-handedly destroyed all the Indian archeological remains in that area by bulldozing 264 acres of state land in the Ironwood Forest National Monument."

"Wow. He's evil. What's the story behind the blind sheep?" Maury removes his glasses, closes the magazine and stops eating.

My husband hasn't been this interested in me all week.

Information turns him on. I lick my lips and continue.

"Desert bighorn sheep known as *Ovis canadensis nelsoni* live in the Silver Bell Mountains near the development. They're known for head-to-head combat with their curled horns. He wanted it to look rural for the big shots he brings in on junkets from the Midwest. Most buy multiple lots."

I can tell he's hooked because he's shifted his chair toward me. He gives me his bedroom eyes look, kinda half-mast with a smirky smile.

"What happened?"

"He shipped in sheep to graze. No idea who ships sheep but..."

"Jean, stick to the story. The blind sheep." I step out of my pointed Italian leather mules with three-inch heels to relieve my toes on the cool tile.

"The sheep got infected because of the goats he imported. Disease spread through scabby sores on the noses and mouths of the animals. The sheep went blind and passed the infection to their young when nursing. What's really sad is the sheep hang out in caves during the day to rest because it's hot but go to rocky cliffs at night. They're falling off."

In my mind I mull over a close-up of sightless sheep, tears rolling down their furry faces, the poor animals stumbling around with eye patches, sunglasses and canes, falling off mountains. "But that's not all."

Maury shakes his head, murmuring, "That SOB."

"It's just not allegations anymore. Did you know the state is suing this guy for violations?" I ask.

"No. That's great. We can use that."

Maury gets up and meanders, glass in hand, into the family room and turns on our TV to watch the History Channel. He becomes engrossed in a program about Battle Creek, Michigan and the cereal industry, dipping his hand into a bag of spicy popcorn that's tucked into his chair.

"Maury, before you get involved in your program I need to find out more about the opponent. I've been so busy with the research about the developer I haven't asked. Who's our guy, Craig Burton, running against?" I pace when I'm concentrating, tracking a short path around the sofa in my bare feet.

"Fluerboohoe," Maury mumbles with the popcorn rolling in his mouth.

My racing brain misses what he's saying. I stand in front of the TV with hands on hips. Sometimes understanding him is as bad as interpreting his mangled handwriting.

"Jean, you're blocking my view." Maury motions me out of the way with his arm. "This is the best part. I love this documentary. Kellogg beats all the competitors. They name cereals crazy names and—"

"Maury." I want to stamp my foot in frustration like little Tangie. "Who is our great green guy running against? You've never given me her name, but I know she's married to Charles Dunn. He's done all kinds of illegal activities. A real doozy."

Maury swallows, takes a sip of his merlot and looks at me. "Well, so is the candidate."

"What does that mean?" I hold out my palm and squint at him with suspicion.

He swallows his popcorn and takes a sip of wine. "The opposition is Flora Boudreaux..."

"Maury!" Blood rushes to my face and I feel hot all over. "Are you out of your mind?" I have an instant trumpet-blowing, saxophone-squealing powerhouse of a headache over my left eye.

"...who is married to Charles Dunn. But it's okay. Just calm down."

I stomp around and put my hand over my palpitating heart. I feel sweat pool under my arms. Might have to change my clothes.

"That woman and her buffed-up daughter almost ruined my life! How could you put me in this position? What were you thinking?"

Maury puts his glass on the end table and stands up.

"Now, Jean."

"She'll freak if she finds out I'm working on the campaign of her opponent. God knows what she'll do. She tried to kill me."

"Now, now. Let's not exaggerate." Maury comes toward me and reaches his arms out to comfort me, but I'm not having any sweet stuff right now. I push him away, swallowing bile at the back of my throat.

"Sweetheart, tell me more about the sheep. Did you know the horns weigh up to thirty pounds?"

I fold my arms across my chest and turn away from him.

"Don't try to distract me, Maury Rubin."

"But, Jean, who better than you? You're ideal because you

know what a wing nut she is. And now we have this scoop on her husband. Don't you see? If I can get you to put your passion—"

"I can't believe you involved me in such a convoluted campaign. Especially with someone you know hates me. Don't you remember the trouble I had with her lying, cheating daughter, Tiffany?"

"We need someone who can push through the crap and show the public what Flora Beaudreux really represents. You're perfect."

"Perfect?" I send daggers in Maury's direction. Just the name of my nemesis who got me fired from my job at the community college and intended to do physical harm, sets me on fire. I feel my body temperature erupt and more sweat breaks out on my forehead. I am not getting involved in this. My resolve hardens.

"I absolutely won't do it. This is going to ratchet my stress up to at least a ten."

"A ten?" He shrinks back.

"It's the worst on the anxiety test I took in *Psychology Today* magazine. It's—it's where you go berserk and throw things and scream obscenities at nice, well-meaning people. People have heart attacks at the ten level."

Maury takes another step back.

"Aaaaah," I scream, pressing my palms to my temples in an attempt to erase the headache.

Maury looks concerned but keeps his distance. "Now, now. It won't be so bad. I'll help you."

"Help me? You got me into this mess. Don't you dare try to placate me. I will not have anything to do with that monkey-haired woman. Or her atrocious family. They're all crooks, especially the kid who wanted me to change her grade."

"Jean, honey, you've got the skills. Now you know who we're dealing with. She's won every election in her district. I admit she's got different views than ours and she's used some spurious tactics, but this time it's different. We have ammunition."

"I'm furious with you. And I've only been furious with you three times in all our years of marriage."

"What were the other two?" he asks, his brows knitting in a frown. "I don't remember."

I throw my head back and scuttle into the killer shoes so I look taller. "I'm not going to tell you if you don't *already* know. I'm thoroughly disgusted and fed up with you and your Green Party campaign and I am not going to do it."

"You're going to combust if you don't calm down."

And, indeed, my heart is thumping like a crazed jumping bean. This level of aggravation can kill someone.

"Aaaaargh!"

I hear April's Mercedes honk, a kind of refined I'm here but not rushing beep. I grab my now dry, tea-stained black tote which I carry everywhere, no matter what because I don't care if it matches my shoes. I march out the door that slams with dramatic punctuation.

3

WHERE ARE WE GOING?" I ASK, slipping my already cramping feet out of my shoes. Maybe I should have changed purses instead of carrying my battered tote.

April and I have been friends since our kids entered pre-school together. We lived near each other and car pooled. If you looked at us you'd wonder how we know each other, let alone share the same space. Her curves are encased in a turquoise St. John knit and I'm in bohemian chic. She has an eleven carat diamond wedding set on her hand; I wear a plain gold one. She's made up and coiffed to perfection; I'm a bit messy.

April slides her black *CL-Class Mercedes* past a bronze statue of three rearing horses at the entry of a fancy hotel that has changed its names so many times I can't remember if it's the *Lowe's Paradise Spa* or the *Doubletree Paradise Valley Resort.* Maybe it's a *Marriott or* a *W.*

"You'll see. Glee and I think you need a respite from all the pressure you've put on yourself. This is going to be fun."

A starched, uniformed young man opens April's door. She makes a dramatic exit from the car, reaching for the valet's extended hand, her knees together in her very short skirt and very high heels. He scans her head to toe, eyes hazy, doing his best to keep his tremulous voice steady.

"Welcome. I hope you have a good evening."

He has fallen in love.

She lowers her aquamarine eyes in acknowledgement.

The valet's all over the car, which Maury said cost in excess of $95,000. "Sweet ride," I hear him say. I get out unattended.

"We're going to a networking dinner," says April, reaching into her silver metallic-studded Chanel purse for a mirror. She checks for lipstick on her teeth, her tongue wetting her lips. She pouts, searches for her lip gloss and applies the wand to her bottom lip. Her profile and face are flawless—long eyelashes, turned-up nose, full lips and a lion's mane of hair.

"What are we networking for?"

"Not sure, but Glee says we can't miss it." I stand up straighter and clip along on the marble floors beside April in her killer heels. My toes, scrunched into the pointed, fashionable shoes, miss their Birkenstocks.

The lobby, well-appointed with contemporary furniture and subtle lighting has a necessities shop and piano bar to the right and meeting rooms to the left.

Before I can ask more questions Glee peeks out from a door, motioning us into a ballroom. She's a symphony of purple—silk blouse, amethyst choker, culottes and ankle-wrapped wedgies. A purple snakeskin purse the size of a feedbag hangs from her shoulder.

"Hurry, I've saved you seats," she says holding the door open.

April whispers to Glee, "You look artsy tonight."

"Thanks," says Glee, touching my cheek to hers for an air kiss.

"What am I doing here?" I ask, sucking in my belly and lifting my head. I swagger in behind my friends, a mini-pageant of over-dressed contestants.

The ballroom with seductive lighting is set with pink tablecloths and fake pink cactus centerpieces in terra cotta dishes.

"You'll love it. Just be open," says Glee as she guides us to a table at the side of the ballroom close to the front.

Some women mill around to greet others. There are squeals of recognition and lots of air kissing.

Every city in our Valley has a personality—Tempe, the university town, is known for originality, Mesa's got retirees, Maryvale has bikers and Scottsdale trumps everyone with trophy wives, social climbers and gigolos. Where do I fit in?

I settle into a chair, place a napkin on my lap and introduce myself to the woman next to me.

"Hello, I'm Jean Rubin," I say extending a hand. If my mother taught me anything, it's manners. I don't feel out of place, but I'm in strange territory.

She turns toward me in slow motion like a creaky door in a

scary movie. "Dr. Roxy Culbert," she says with a clenched jaw. Her pillow lips, larger than Angelina Jolie's and painted bright coral, don't move. Her concrete face remains devoid of any expression at all—no forehead wrinkles, no smile lines, no crinkles or dimples anywhere. And she's shiny, with new skin that's been stretched and painted with heavy make-up. I recognize the Scottsdale ears, the kind that have hairline scars in front of them.

Someone has pulled her face too tight because her eyes, small and tilted, give her an Asian look without the refinement. I surmise she's had a brow lift. Her forehead starts way back on the top of her head with tattooed, arched brows drawn high. Maybe she's had cheek implants, too. One's a little higher than the other, giving her the off-center appearance of a Cubist portrait. In fact, with all the plastic surgery and theatrical make-up she looks a bit like a drag queen.

I'm fascinated with her perpetual surprised look. Nothing on her face seems to be in its original form—not the nose, not the chin, certainly not the lips. She could star in a show called *"Women Gone Wild with Plastics."* Glee and April are busy catching up. I'm sitting next to a woman who could scream and no one would know she's terrified.

"What kind of doctor are you?" I ask.

"A psychotherapist," she says without a twitch.

"Oh." I take a sip of water. I glance at Glee. Did she set me up? My friends sometimes do things "for my benefit." I know I've been a little high-strung lately but do I need a shrink? Maybe. Especially after Maury's news about the opposition candidate.

A waiter approaches and Glee orders wine for the table. I take a breath, let it out and count to five slowly. A tympani in my head reaches a crescendo. Waiters serve our salads.

In the front of the room a woman with a 1970s teased hair in a flip approaches the stage and introduces herself as Winnie Smart. With a twang she says, "Thank y'all for coming tonight. Welcome to the Scottsdale Babes Society. We meet monthly for fun and fighting frump."

The crowd of two hundred applauds wildly. A few women stand up, writhing their bodies, whooping and thrusting their fists in circles. One tosses a cowboy hat with a rhinestone band that glimmers.

"We're a gun-totin', rip-snortin', horse-ridin' bunch of babes, aren't we?"

More enthusiasm from the crowd. I look around at the handbags at their feet. Do these women really have guns?

"We're here to make a difference. As part of the Babe's mission we've got monthly speakers, special desert rides, shootin' exercises, and, the most fun, ladies, field trips to see the best buckaroos in the Southwest! So enjoy your meal and we'll be back with a real treat for ya."

What have my friends gotten me into this time? I feel a panic enveloping me, the kind where I can't concentrate on anything except worrying about my lists of things that are undone or errands I've forgotten or items I've misplaced.

Did she say horses? Do they have naked men in chaps preparing barbecue at their events?

I've got to get out of here. The kids are coming for dinner tomorrow night and the refrigerator is empty; the campaign policy paper isn't ready, although I want to quit now; I have another client deadline; Amber, our darling golden retriever is smelly; my clothes have been abandoned at the cleaners for weeks; someone's got to buy a new microwave since ours exploded; Maury's leaving a moat of food cartons around the TV; my mother's been whining about a painful hip. I shake my head no. I have to get out of here.

Except I'm hungry. I've only eaten protein bars and an apple all day. I touch my face. I feel warm. That's when I remember I missed my dermatology appointment. No! It took me six months to get into this doctor because she's not taking new patients. I sink into my chair. My moles will probably metastasize and I'll be dead in weeks. What will Maury do without me? I begin to catastrophize about my husband and focus on the fact that it's my friends' fault.

If April and Glee hadn't insisted I have my skin tags removed and all my moles checked, I wouldn't be in this position. "Don't you know Arizona is second for skin cancer world-wide?" Glee asked me. Strange how when you get past forty, alien appendages sprout on your body. Now I blew the special of eight removals for $400.

How will I get another appointment into my schedule? Why did I miss it? I carry my planner with me everywhere and check the pages all day long. My hands feel clammy. What else did I blow off today? I can't remember anything. Maybe I can sneak a look at the book I call "my brains" under the table. God only knows what would happen to me if I ever lost my planner.

My hands scramble through my tote. I gasp. My book's not there. I drag the tote onto my lap, remove my water bottle, a folder with my latest client's proposal, a manila envelope with a one hundred word biography with my mission statement at the top, an 8x10 re-touched photo of myself and a press release, a bulging red wallet filled with credit cards and no cash, my mobile phone, a boar's hair brush, keys for the house, car, storage unit, kid's houses and a file cabinet I can no longer find, fabric samples for dining room chairs that need recovering, a binkie, a make-up bag with two old lipsticks, one of Maury's golf score cards with a shopping list scribbled on the back and morning and evening vitamins in gold foil packets. Some of the items are tea stained.

My hand searches the corners for my planner. Not here. I don't recall seeing it on my kitchen desk. What if I have no idea where I'm supposed to be or do—ever?

Being here is a waste of time.

I lean over to April. "I have to go." My foot shakes beneath the table. The waiter puts baskets of bread on the table.

She blinks at me. "What? We just got here." She cuts up lettuce and places a miniscule amount on her fork. She guides it into her mouth without it touching her lips.

"April, listen. I can't find my planner and . . ."

After she finishes chewing she says, "Jean, Glee and I have been telling you for ages to relax a little. Drink some wine," she says pushing a glass of chardonnay closer to me. "Take a deep breath. You're having a panic attack. Your planner's at home."

She sets her lips firm and lifts her chin a little. "My rule is I have to spend as much time at the event as I did getting dressed for it." She takes another baby bite.

Uh-oh. I could be here for hours. I look at my friend who's absent of any wrinkles on her face or clothes. It took me ten minutes to get ready. I glance at my watch. Warm waves ripple up my body.

I finish my salad. The waiter removes the plates. April glances to check on me and removes a hair from my shoulder. Southwestern food is served—a shredded beef taco nestled next to a chicken enchilada drowned in whipped potatoes and smothered in cheese, sour cream and guacamole.

I can't eat. My stomach turns over. I should get up and call a cab. I feel woozy. What if I faint? What if I can't find my planner? What if I don't have all my appointments and numbers and projects? What if I miss another appointment?

Glee's voice interrupts my escalating hysteria. She addresses our table, bending forward so everyone can hear her.

"Hi there. Let's introduce ourselves and say what we do for business or fun." Her well-manicured hand with plum-colored nails and multiple rings presses her chest. "I'm Glee Barstow, soon-to-be Glee Carson because I'm taking back my maiden name. I'm an erotic artist, yoga instructor and personal life and intuitive coach. I can assist you in creating the perfect balance for your universe."

I take a deep breath and let it out slowly. My right foot starts tapping with vigor under the table. I stuff the items back in my tote repeating, *my planner is exactly where I left it.*

The women at the table acknowledge Glee with nods, nibbling at their plates of food. One of them gets her potatoes into a Dairy Queen twirl.

April's next and she speaks in a whispery voice. "Hi, I'm April Lefkowitz. I'm busy being busy." Everyone laughs. She *is* occupied with herself most days. She adds, "I spend time checking my investments and watching my broker's covered calls. Kinda like the hawk that stalks the desert rabbits in my back yard." A few giggle at her last statement; the others give positive murmurs. Women with money earn respect.

A suntanned blonde with cleavage and a pink rhinestone cross hanging between her two melons goes next. "Hi, I'm Bernice Diamond-Crasher-Sparks. I'm an interior stager. I set up your home to make it attractive to buyers. I also play tennis and golf. Oh, and I love the ambiance of Scottsdale, the classy resorts, the great restaurants. If I could only find someone to share it with." She sounds wistful.

The group nods and takes mental notes on whether they know a man. Someone asks if he has to play tennis. Bernice isn't fussy. Upright and breathing will fill the bill. And he has to have money. Lots of money.

I try not to be judgmental but why does she need a man? Maybe I think that because I earn my own money and have one. Women can be capable, strong and independent.

I complain about Maury from time to time but he's *my* Maury. Even if he did get me involved in a campaign with my nemesis. I'm still angry, but I love him, even when he recites detailed explanations of his golf score while I'm checking phone messages, unloading the dishwasher, emptying the grocery bags and making dinner. Although if I didn't have a man, I wouldn't be looking. One is enough.

Soon we're around the table and it's Dr. Roxy's turn.

"I'm Dr. Roxy Culbert. I'm a psychotherapist and MD specializing in sex therapy. I help couples and individuals put the yin back in their yang. So, ladies, if your man isn't getting it up as good as he once could, then maybe Roxy should."

An MD with a jingle? Does that mean she has sex with them?

"What if you're looking for a man?" asks Glee. A knowing glance goes back and forth across the table. Except for me and April I think they're all on the prowl.

I cringe, uncomfortable because Glee is so out there.

"Available?" the doctor wants to know.

"Of course. I'm creating a wonderful guy who adores me," says Glee in coach-speak.

"Can you create one for me too?" asks Bernice of the multiple last names.

"How are you manifesting it?" asks Dr. Roxy.

"I've had liposuction and I'm taking the 'Course in Miracles.' I've converted to Buddhism, so I chant. Courtney Love's a Buddhist. Also, I do the shots for women." Glee appears proud of her progress.

I shoot April a quizzical look. Shots?

The doctor nods. "Oh, you've got it all in alignment, especially the bioidentical hormone cocktail injections to enhance your sexuality."

Tapping on the microphone interrupts the noise in the room. I'm relieved I didn't have to introduce myself. I sound boring compared to this group of feisty-tennis-playing, hormone-dipping, man-hunting women.

In a whisper I ask my new found MD-friend, "What's a hormone cocktail?"

People clink on glasses with their knives. Dr. Roxy gets confidential and says, "You might want to consider it. It rejuvenates your skin and lubricates other areas. Many women are doing it to keep their man. They try that before vaginal tightening."

My eyebrows shoot up, a reflex I know is not possible for her to perform. Now I have to worry about keeping my man? Something else to add to my stress? One of the Scottsdale Babes with a revolver in her Louis Vuitton wants Maury? And she's wet? OhmiGod.

A vision rises in my mind of a six-foot blonde with big hair wearing a miniscule fringed western outfit, a squash-blossom necklace planted between her artificial breasts, kicking her heels up in silver-tipped dyed red ostrich boots. Amazon Cowgirl aims a rifle at me.

The tootsie in the front booms, "Isn't this exhilaratin' to meet all these incredible women?" Applause scatters throughout the room. "Y'all are so willing to share with others and the Babes appreciate it. We're here tonight to show the world we can fight frump and be fabulous."

A cheer goes up and it takes a few minutes to get everyone

calm again.

"But women need to exercise their power to vote. We can run the world. Whoo-eee!" And with that she sticks her fist into the air. Encouraging yelps emanate from the crowd down front. "It's with great pleasure I introduce a woman who's a true cowgirl in spirit, an Arizona pioneer, a woman who speaks from the heart and uses her head, our very own district seven representative, Mrs. Flora Beaudreaux."

No! It can't be.

My heart flutters, a frantic sparrow flapping in my chest. I have to walk out in protest. This diabolical woman has caused me untold grief. I start to push my chair back and April stops me, a French-manicured hand on my sleeve.

"Where are you going?" she asks.

"April, we have to leave. This woman's my worst nightmare," I say in a harsh whisper. "How could you and Glee do this to me?" My anger rises with a throbbing band playing an all-out military march in my head.

"I didn't know there was a speaker, let alone that it would be her. Calm down."

I lean back in my chair, depleted. She's right. Maybe she'll say something stupid. Besides, I didn't drive here. The waiter whisks away my uneaten meal. He places a large wedge of chocolate cake in front of me, guaranteed to keep me up tonight and guilty tomorrow. I put down my head and dig in. I'm going to finish every last bite.

"I just started a glass of pinot. Drink your wine. Relax," says April.

"You don't understand. I can't be in the same room with her without a visceral reaction," I hiss. A few women at our table look in our direction with curiosity.

Glee leans over. "Shush."

I turn my attention to the stage which isn't far away. Flora Beaudreaux wearing a black dress with white cuffs and collar approaches the podium and peers at the audience. Tall and wiry with a pinched look on her face, her black unmanageable hair is piled on top of her head like road-kill skunk.

I shuffle my feet. A shoe drops off. Flora Beaudreaux made accusations after I failed her daughter, Tiffany. She never turned in the assignments and then lied about it. My department head sided with them and I got fired for insubordination. Now that I know about Flora's husband who blinds sheep, I don't want anything to do with any of them.

Later, I saw my leaving as an opportunity to pursue other options like consulting. But how could Maury involve me with her again?

I glance around the table. They're all enraptured.

". . . with the trend in this country to seize land for conservation purposes, we'll have no place for animals to graze or places for people to live. Developers have to meet the needs of Arizona's growing population. Over 100,000 new residents move to our Valley every month. Why, we're way ahead of those trashy people up in Vegas." She gives us a condescending smile. A few people in the audience laugh at the Las Vegas comment, our competitor for state growth.

"Her husband's blinding sheep, for God's sake."

"Jean, shush," says Glee.

How could Flora say that? It's an outrageous slur. She's tossed them off before and no one ever challenges her. This woman infuriates me. Should we really fill up every square inch of Arizona? Where do the Babes think they'll ride their thoroughbred horses if there's no open space?

I tune back in to hear: "And I don't mean illegals either. Those people need to be shipped home."

No surprise. The woman's a Fascist. You can't round-up people. She'd be the first to complain there wouldn't be anyone to prepare her food or clean her carpets. My sweaty palm grabs April's hand. I'm shaking. She does her best to soothe me by stroking my arm.

"The citizens we need here are from the Mid-west, California and other places who want to come and build our economy. And I do mean citizens."

I take a gulp of wine, surveying the room. Women are listening to what Flora's saying. I close my eyes and breathe. I tune her out to go over the five steps I read in the magazine after I failed the stress test: write in my journal, pamper myself with baths, meditate twice a day, exercise at least three times a week and repeat deep breathing often. Who am I kidding? I don't have time for any of those things. Especially breathing.

"So, to conclude, I ask you to consider casting your vote for me in the upcoming election. Don't let the spendthrift Democrats or the crazy environmentalists sell you a bill of goods. Green means mean. Let's keep things the same. Return a known, experienced woman to the legislature!"

Flora the Destroyer receives lots of applause. A few supporters in the front stand up.

Maybe there's a reason I'm here. I have work to do.

Dr. Roxy leans over to hand me a card, her face frozen in a perpetual fright. "The shots would really help you."

4

STRESS RELIEF TIP: Meditating thirty minutes a day contributes to over-all well being.

—*Meditation for a Frantic Soul*

I FOUND MY PLANNER ON THE BATHROOM FLOOR next to the toilet. I kissed the cover with a sigh of relief, contemplating whether I should handcuff it to my wrist like a briefcase of money or sleep with it under my pillow every night.

This morning I sit on a patio chair with my eyes closed, Amber at my heels. Meditation is supposed to be the answer for calm and relaxation. I took a Maharishi-inspired course a long time ago that taught me to repeat the same mantra over and over. It settled my mind. I can't seem to get back into that space. Glee says that method isn't as good as the Easwaren method that teaches people not to hurry. Others are able to train their brain to eliminate chatter. Why can't I? I try again.

Om. Omm. Ommm. It's hopeless. My brain clicks on what I have to do, what I should have said, what I forgot.

I'm still hunting for an acceptable assisted living place for my mother, my client hated my revised proposal, Amber, our ancient golden retriever, needs a sebaceous cyst removed, Maury has lost his third set of keys so all the locks have to be changed, Gus, whose married to our daughter, wants to borrow fifty thousand to open a donut franchise in Israel and our son, Michael and his wife, Rivka, have announced they're trying to get pregnant again.

Regular methods are not working so they want to try in vitro fertilization to the tune of $12,000 a pop. At this rate we'll be bankrupt living at Smelly Arms with my mother.

Om. Omm. Ommm.

No go. I give up on meditation. Back in the kitchen I rush to gather my belongings. When I leave for the day it looks as though I'm moving out: different shoes in case I have to meet a client, hat, sunglasses, planner, shopping bags with things for my mother. I swear we've transferred the same photo album and crocheted sweater back and forth so many times I have no idea who it belongs to. I glance at the clock on the new microwave. I grab my tote and add bars, water, phone, keys, a snack of cheese and cut-up apple that I balance on a paper plate. I'm supposed to be at a Green Party meeting. I check at my watch. Now!

I push Amber's big *tush* into the car. Her sweet face that has graduated from soft red to white, stares at me with sad eyes because she's hungry. She hasn't eaten. Her surgery is scheduled for later this afternoon. We love her despite the unsightly growth and constant gas.

She hangs her head out the window in the passenger seat, her tongue a pink tie in the breeze. She's my companion with few demands. At a red light between apple chomps I pat the large misshapen lump. It doesn't bother me but it grosses out other people. I say it's a pod puppy embedded beneath her skin. The vet says it has to be removed and biopsied.

I slide into a parking space off Mill Avenue, search for coins to push into the parking dummie, hold Amber's leash and hustle up the stairs to Green campaign headquarters.

I turned in the copy for the brochure they asked me to write a week ago. I did a bullet-point list of why Flora shouldn't be elected in contrast to why Craig Burton was the best candidate.

It went like this:

• implicated with her husband in the Los Robles scandal that destroyed Hohokam Indian archeological remains.

• investigated and being sued by the state.

• linked to violations of state land leases.

• supported dredging of the Los Robles Wash that destroyed the water quality of surrounding areas.

• favored her daughter, Tiffany Beaudreaux, with a $100,000 stipend to run her political campaign.

And I didn't even bring up the blind bighorn sheep.

The room is not as full as the last meeting. Only a few loyal volunteers and two staff members are available in the morning. It takes me a minute to spot Maury because he's whispering to the person next to him.

Without an empty chair near him at the conference table, I sit on the opposite side. Amber wags her tail in anticipation that someone will feed her some junk food.

My favorite blood-thirsty preppy, Brian Depalma, addresses me. "Oh good, Jean, you're here. I need you to micro-target likely voters who are sympathetic to green causes."

Micro-target? Does he think I'm Karl Rove? He goes around the table giving people assignments.

"Fred, you're in charge of volunteers and door-to-door canvassing. We don't have budget for signs at $150 a pop so the personal contact with voters is crucial." Fred, who's wearing the same snarling bear shirt as before, nods.

"Maury, we need stats on how many no-burn days we've had in the last year, fine and coarse particulate counts for the last six months and EPA policy on how their new rules have affected everything. Phoenix received a failing grade for ozone pollution yesterday from the American Lung Association. We're in the top ten for most polluted cities. Ruth, you're fundraising. So far we've brought in enough donations to last two more weeks. This office is gratis but campaigns cost money. Start hitting up your friends, acquaintances. Anybody know the Campbell soup guy here in town? Maybe his kids have asthma."

People look around and shrug their shoulders. It's not exactly the Heart Ball crowd.

"And, Starr, get our candidate booked at luncheons, rubber chicken dinners, service clubs, anywhere we can get an open forum."

Starr, who's sitting next to Maury, whispers something back to him. She's attractive in a granola way, auburn hair pulled back in a braid, a black sleeveless turtleneck and hip rimless glasses. My husband smiles at her and nods. Wait a minute. Is she flirting? I may be busy but I'm not dumb.

Coffee and a nibbled jelly donut sit in front of Maury. I wake up Amber who's snoring at my feet, sending her around the table to nudge his leg. I mouth to my husband not to feed her.

A dog can distract any man. Amber rambles toward him and puts her chin on the table between him and Starr.

"She's adorable," says Starr, patting her head. Amber wags her tail.

She hasn't noticed the repulsive tumor the size of a mouse on her back. I've never wished for Amber to let one go like old dogs are prone to do, but now would be great.

"Hey," says Brian, rapping a letter opener on the table. He glares at Amber whose tail is whipping back and forth. "We're having a meeting here." The group refocuses. "It's six weeks until election day and we have work to do. Any questions about your assignments?" Silence. "Okay. Get to work. We may not win this campaign but we're damn well going to get noticed. Our platform is pertinent to local issues." He slaps his hands on the table and pushes his chair back.

"Uh, I'm not clear about what I'm supposed to do," I say, looking around a bit embarrassed.

Brian snorts a bit. "Your job is to find out what people who support green causes buy, use and have."

I'm sure my expression registers surprise. Maury got me into this. He's going to get me out of it.

"Uh, what about the copy I turned in for the brochure? Was

that what you wanted?"

"Stellar. Absolutely stellar," says Brian as he picks up his laptop, balancing a giant soft drink and a pile of folders against his chest.

Gheez. I sweated over that after hours of research online, gave it to Maury to bring in and never heard a word. I admit I looked up the data while talking on the phone to Michael who was haranguing me I need to Twitter and get a Facebook page, but I thought it was a good job.

The meeting breaks up. I head for Maury. I'm not insecure enough to hang onto his arm, but I have to let Ms. Turtleneck know he's mine. He's got his furrowed brow look, glasses slipping a bit from the bridge of his nose.

"The new Environmental Protection Agency rules don't change the daily standard for coarse particles from construction, roadway dust and agriculture. That gives us more high-pollution days than anything else," says Starr.

She doesn't notice I'm there because her large gray eyes are beamed on Maury's coffee brown ones.

He says, "They've raised the acceptable particulate count since 1997."

Why didn't I ever teach Amber to attack? If she can't fart on demand the least she could do is bite. Starr takes a step closer. She's tall with long legs and faded worn jeans that stick to her skinny thighs like an oil slick on asphalt.

"True, but if you examine the statistics of rural versus urban areas and the dust levels where they grow food—" says Starr.

Okay, that's it, honey. He may be a big overgrown kid with ADD but he's *my* big overgrown kid and I'll fight to the death to keep him.

"Excuse me. I'm Jean," I interrupt.

Starr turns to me with a gleaming smile. "I'm so glad to meet you. Maury's told me so much about you."

What? He's been discussing me with this twelve-year- old? I ignore her comment and employ my best interview technique. "How are you involved with the campaign?"

"I'm an associate professor in environmental studies at Northern Arizona University. I'm on sabbatical this semester."

Great. So she has nothing to do? I feign interest.

"Working on post-doctoral research. I know Brian from the brown haze issue we worked on a few years ago." Her voice trails off. I know what that means. It's the "we used to be a couple" voice.

I nod. I am not impressed by young women with tight *tushies* and science degrees. It's not that I feel a need to explain anything to Starr. It's just that I'm feeling like I stormed into something.

I touch Maury's arm. "Honey, Amber's got the appointment with the vet. You're supposed to wait with her. Rivka wants a referral for a good IVF doctor." And, for my clincher, I add beaming at Starr, "And his granddaughter wants him to stop by and read her a story."

I slip my arm through his.

Starr calls after us, "I'll get back to you on the particulates."

I resist an interrogation but put Starr in the keep-your-eye-on-her part of my brain. Information turns this man on. If she's got the right particulates, I smell trouble. *Om. Omm. Ommm.*

The phone is twisted into my neck because I stepped on my headset getting dressed earlier. I need both hands as I pull out plates and silverware to set the table for later. I brush a few stray hairs off a salad bowl.

"Hi Mom, how you feelin'?"

"Don't ask."

"I thought your feet we're better."

"Jean, how can my feet feel good if your father's not with me? I need to go shoe shopping. Nothing fits. My hip hurts too."

"Okay, I can probably take you next week." I fold napkins into triangles.

"Next week? For an emergency like this?"

The rest of the conversation is in the same vein. I make a salad and cover it with plastic wrap, chop vegetables and wash fruit.

"Lara, hi, it's mommy. You all right?"

"No, I never will be. I don't feel like talking now."

"Okay, call me later."

"Rivka, how are things going? Michael home? I haven't spoken to my son in days."

"Oh, we're in tip-top shape. Our little guy refuses to be

potty trained, which means he can't start pre-school, I'm still not pregnant and we've been trying twice a day which is a real chore, the mortgage is due and Michael was fired yesterday for searching online for donut franchise funding."

After those conversations I need a break. I remind myself it's Sunday and most of our country's citizens are doing what they enjoy. I make a glass of iced tea, turn on the classical music station, pick up a pile of magazines and stretch out on the sofa. Maury's in a golf tournament.

I read an article about greening my kitchen which would involve pulling out all the cabinets. Not an option. The next one advises me on how to do a face lift at home with egg whites. Sounds too messy. The third sanctions children's reading skills by having them read to a pet because they're non-judgmental. I envision Tangie with a book on her lap and Amber in front of her with a quizzical look. The magazine falls forward onto my chest and then slides to the floor. I drift into a well-deserved nap.

When I awake my mind is foggy. It slowly clicks through The List: client deadline for new proposal; find a place for my mother; prepare organic, non-fat dinners because Maury and I are both gaining weight; soothe Rivka about her desire to get pregnant; tell Michael we are not buying fast food franchises in foreign countries; beg off baby sitting for next weekend and deal with my upcoming jury duty. It doesn't take long for me to get revved up again.

In moments I'm anguishing about being picked for a

murder trial where I might have to sleep in a derelict hotel sequestered for months, unable to communicate with my family or clients. Or maybe that's a blessing. But . . . what if I'm tortured with one indecisive hold-out juror who thinks the perpetrator might be innocent despite the evidence, four witnesses and a taped confession? What if it's a hung jury after months of deliberation? What if I'm thrust into a never-ending jury pool that goes into infinity? I check the date. Yikes! I have to be there tomorrow.

Amber's recovering nicely but the next morning before I leave for the courthouse, she's sick. I take her to Lara's so she can keep an eye on her, begging Tangie and Gus not to sit on her. She's wearing a huge plastic stand-up collar to keep her from licking her wound.

I drive to downtown Phoenix, find a parking space, wait all day with an assortment of characters, okay, dutiful citizens, from varied backgrounds. Men sit on either side of me. One dozes while the other reads the side of my newspaper I'm holding up. I hate wasting time. I give the front section of the paper to the guy who's awake. He acknowledges me with a nod.

I glance through magazines I brought. Nothing interests me when I'm anxious. I want to segue way into my moving fast mode, getting things done, crossing off my list. I'm anxious about what I'm not doing. I could have accomplished a lot today.

My phone buzzes with calls. Every member of my family as well as April and Glee call or text me to check on my stress level. Just let me out of here. I'm pleading with the Universe for help. Don't pick me. Don't pick me.

A fan in the corner whirrs. The entire day passes with names called, people peeled off into different rooms. The men on either side of me are summoned. I'm sure I'm next.

When the navy-suited, black pump-wearing official woman with a slight mustache and a badge says we can all go, I move with haste toward the door, dumping my load of old magazines and newspapers in the large trash can in the corridor. I trek to my car parked blocks away that's been baking under an unrelenting sun. I am so glad this time-suck is over.

Karl Rove, the election genius and king of junk mail, figured out how to micro-target people by mixing their buying habits, personal history and credit scores into a formula. He researched and discovered that Republicans were more likely to drink bourbon, drive snowmobiles, buy guns, shop at Wal-Mart, attend a mega-church and own a dog. On the other hand, Democrats shop at Target, join Planned Parenthood, drink wine or lattes and have cats *and* dogs at their feet.

I'm no Karl Rove but I log onto my computer in my home office, a kid's converted bedroom filled with toys for the grandkids and a desk covered with our bills as well as my mother's, a $200 receipt from the locksmith who mentioned they have accounts for regulars like us, and a letter from multiple insurance companies marked Urgent Correspondence, OPEN NOW. I could use more space for this important research. I squint at the screen.

The campaign has squeezed up a few notches since our local newspaper wrote a story about Flora, her husband and their special interests. The population of our city are gradually becoming informed that they are not being well-represented by her. I wonder what the lying daughter is up to. Never mind, I don't want to know.

I stop to reflect by kicking off my shoes and putting my feet up on my desk. I've written a few press releases about our man, Craig Burton. He's a hard-working guy with an important environmental message but there's not much sizzle to him. Glee and April say he needs to lose the comb-over and update his eyeglasses. Women love making over men. Especially if they dress funny. Maury wore a Madras jacket when I met him and I married him anyway.

At least I'm not in charge of image. I'm not sure how much I can spin about polluted air and global warming. I have to make the Greens look good and take them away from the fringe. That means no lesbian Eskimos, tree hugging bears or tear-dripping Indians for testimonials. The issue isn't the repetitive 110-degree days. It's the unprecedented 100-degree nights in our pizza-oven city.

Recovering Amber snores at my feet. I turn back to my computer and dig up lots of facts about how we've plowed the desert to replace open space with beige buildings, treeless parking lots which hold the heat and our need for alternative materials and solar energy. I can't wrap my head around all of it. We're destroying our environment to build more shopping centers so people can buy more clothes? Where are they going?

Unless Glee and April invite me some place I never need to get dressed up. I have enough clothes in my closet so I won't be naked until 2025.

I haven't paid too much attention to the Democratic candidate because Flora is such a scene-stealer, but Emanuel Funt's running a good campaign on their ticket. He's a distant cousin of the "Candid Camera" guy. Mostly he talks about the immigration problems facing our border state. "Let 'em in. Forget the fence. We need workers. Just let 'em all flood in."

That philosophy drives Maury crazy. He thinks terrorists might swarm into Arizona and . . . target shopping centers and strip malls? If we joined his campaign and ours together we still wouldn't win. Flora's got money and power.

I peck away for a few hours. Finally, I come up with a viable statement of our pollution problems and feasible alternatives that sound sensible for the urban heat island we call home.

I leave the "Policy for Innovations on Environmental Quality" on Maury's desk. It's an impressive title with minimal substance. But then again, it's for a political campaign. My cynical side says they're all the same anyway. I decide to take another stab at meditating and stretch out on my bed.

Om. Omm. Ommm.

5

STRESS RELIEF TIP: Repetition of calming phrases slows the heart rate and releases tension.

—*Medical Advice for Baby Boomers*

MAURY'S GAINING WEIGHT. He's not fat yet but he's a non-stop eating machine. The man never saw a piece of pizza he didn't like. Worse, he's a sneak eater.

Not too long after I've cleaned up from dinner and announced the kitchen is closed, I hear rustling—cabinets slamming, the whirr of a can opener, the refrigerator door opening. It's like having mice with privileges.

And that's only his snack. An hour after that he says he's looking for something sweet, a hunt for chocolate equal to a hormonal woman's rampage for Godiva. I'm not even around for the 11 p.m. carb raid of a bagel with butter and a thick slice of cheese. He leaves a trail behind him—cellophane wrappers, balled up tin foil, peanut shells on the floor, crumbs on the counter, spilt cream from his coffee.

His clothes look a little snug. He claims the manufacturers are making waistbands smaller.

If I can't button my pants it's time to reign in The Appetite, a tsunami force of desire for cookies, the good home-made kind from a specialty store, gourmet *boursin* or blueberry goat cheese, and pasta, maybe a tasty linguini with cream sauce.

That's when I put myself on the no-white food regimen: no cake, no rice, no bread, no noodles, no twice-baked potatoes, no sour cream, no Havarti cheese. Okay, that's light yellow but it's still cheese.

The pounds don't exactly melt away but when I can get a finger back inside my waistband, I ease up. A little. Maury checks the scale. It gives him encouragement to order the buttermilk pancake stack at our favorite diner.

It doesn't matter what I say, he won't cut back on calories. Glee would try to figure out why he's orally fixated, but I don't have the time. I just know when I hug him our pubes can't find each other anymore. Next stop: shopping for my husband's wardrobe at Phoenix Tent and Awning.

Even Amber's gaining weight. Maury can't refuse her pitiful begging.

"Jean," Maury calls me from the family room. "C'mere. Listen to this."

"Just a minute." I'm loading the dishwasher with the pads of my fingers, careful not to smudge the coat of clear polish I've just applied. I'm also talking to Michael on the phone.

"Have you looked for another job?" I ask.

My new headset wire keeps catching on the dishwasher handle. I look like a 1940s telephone operator.

"Mom, I'm on jobbing.com every day. My friend says there

might be an opening at his place. But, listen. I've got to talk to you about something else. Something important."

Uh-oh. Any conversation that starts with that means it's going to cost money.

"You know we've been trying to get pregnant again."

"Yes?"

"And you know Rivka's biological clock is ticking?"

"Yes?"

"Well . . ."

"Michael, spit it out."

"We want to go on a fertility vacation."

"I've never heard of such a thing." Why not get a job first? Why isn't one child enough?

Michael begins a desperate appeal similar to a telethon's final hour. He insinuates his willingness to forego any imagined inheritance to invest in his future now.

I consider my vacation options—the pool at my mother's senior apartment enveloped by women's fleshy arms, the zoo for an overnight in vile sleeping bags with the grandkids and a Tucson weekend watching Maury chop at golf balls.

"Mom, we don't want Jacob to be an only. He deserves a sibling. Besides, we might not need IVF if we relax and try some of the newer methods."

"What newer methods? We just went to our room, locked the door and shut off the lights."

Michael hesitates. "The old way isn't working. Couples go on these vacations to get pregnant. There's an infinity pool, massages with reflexology and fertility concoctions."

"Fertility concoctions?" The world's technology may be passing me by, but I had no idea I was missing out on special concoctions. I line up soup bowls, turning the chipped ones to the inside.

"They've got sea-moss elixirs you drink three times a day."

"What's sea moss?"

"It's the Caribbean version of Viagra."

"Michael, this place is in the Caribbean?"

"Uh-huh. At the Westin at Lucaya Grand Bahama. They have a 'Birds and Bees' three-day package with oysters, wine and a Barry White CD."

I can tell by his recitation he's reading the last part. "How much?" My head starts a slow throb.

"And they include heart-print boxers, lingerie and a session with a sex expert."

"Michael, how much?" I bend over to put a casserole dish on the bottom rack. I feel a twinge in my back.

It sounds so good for a moment I consider what it would be like to try and get pregnant. The reality of the situation jars me back, reminding me to practice a stress tip: Close your eyes and breathe deeply repeating *I am calm, I am calm, I am calm.*

I take another breath and ask again, "How much?"

"Mom, it's really a bargain compared to IVF. It's only five thousand." He waits a heartbeat before he says the next part. "Per person."

I am rendered speechless.

"It's less than the Procreation Vacation Special that lasts a week," he says with enthusiasm.

"Plus airfare," I add.

Maury calls me again.

"Just a minute, honey. I'm on the phone with Michael."

I put away two frying pans underneath the stove top. They clatter.

"What's that?"

"Nothing." The kids hate it when I do two things at once.

"There's one in Aruba that's only thirty-five hundred."

"Jean! Come in here. Wait 'til you hear this! You won't believe it." Maury is excited about something on TV, which usually means a repeat of his favorite WWII bombing of Dresden or the Allies defeat of the Nazis.

"Michael, your father's calling me. I'm sure this can't be as cost-effective as you think. What about hotels, meals?"

"If you and Dad front us the money, we'll pay you back."

Without a job?

Maury calls, "Jean, you'll flip when you hear this. C'mere."

"Michael, I have to go. Can we discuss this later?"

I hang up with a rumble of bile creeping up my esophagus. I search the shelf of medicines we keep in the kitchen. Where's the Pepcid AC? What does Maury want?

"Okay, I'm coming. What is it?" I ask popping the Pepcids in my mouth and putting away two wine glasses.

The family room's a mess—throw pillows on the floor, plastic containers from leftovers on the end tables, a few cups, an empty bag of popcorn and a huge pile of laundry that's waiting to be folded. Maury's favorite baseball jacket drapes over the back of the sofa. His hat, the Diamondbacks one with a

Green party button, sits next to him. His car keys, wallet, receipts and sunglasses are scattered around the room.

No wonder he can't find anything. I have half-a-mind to take all of his stuff, place it in the center of the room and let him search through the mess every day.

"You won't believe this. Emanuel Funt is dead."

"Who's Emanuel Funt?"

Let's face it. I have a lot on my mind. My unemployed kid has me hostage to get another grandbaby, my mother still needs a place to live, my exceptional proposal on alleviating gender bias has been rejected again and a young granola is flirting with my husband. Never mind the losing campaign.

"He died suddenly of a brain aneurysm. Tragic," says Maury, crunching on a handful of spicy peanuts.

Then it hits me. He's the Democratic candidate running against Craig and Flora. "That's terrible." I step over the laundry to peer at the screen.

Maury leans back smiling and laces his hands behind his head. "This changes everything."

My mother sits next to me in the Volvo with a glum expression on her face. She's dressed in a beige silk shantung pant suit that still fits her, which, she informs me, she used to wear to the symphony. Her pearlized leather bag and shoes match a natural straw hat pushed back on her head.

She surveys me in my paisley peasant skirt and long-sleeved red T-shirt, a scarf casually tied around my neck. My major primping effort to visit my mother includes lipstick and my newest navy Birkenstocks.

"Jean, can't you fix yourself up a little? It's nice to be *fapitzed* once in a while. It only took me two hours without doing my hair." She reaches over and fingers mine. "If I had all those curls I'd do something with them." She brushes my shoulder of stray hairs, real or imagined.

"Mom, we're going to look at places for you. What I look like is of no importance."

She *tsks* at me. "Jean, don't you care what people think? It's important to make a good first impression."

I sigh. There's no use getting into this endless loop. My mother has no concept of how hectic my life is. If I try to tell her, she responds with, "You shouldn't do so much. That's why you're frazzled. Stress makes wrinkles. Look how nice my skin looks."

I spot the *Vista Shadows* sign and pull into a circular driveway. "Okay, here we are. Let me drop you off so you don't have to walk far." I peer into a lobby without too many vistas and lots of shadows.

I get out and assist my mother, setting up her speedy red walker. "I'm going to park. I'll be right back." She looks frail standing there holding onto her contraption.

We enter a well-appointed lobby with fall decorations placed strategically on the fake fireplace. Orange, red and yellow paper maple leaves tumble from the mantle. It must be chilly autumn somewhere instead of 107 degrees in late September. Let me take on those people who say there's no global warming.

A woman in her 40's with glasses hanging from a chain around her neck and chopsticks in her blonde bun greets us. She's wearing a beige cardigan sweater over a blouse and wool skirt. She must not go outside.

"Welcome, you must be Jean and this is your lovely mother, Florence." She folds my mother's hand into hers. "I'm Henrietta Baker. Where are you from, dear lady?"

My mother answers with caution. She never likes to reveal personal information about herself. "Florida. I'd like to move back."

"Mom," I whisper, "Try to be positive."

"What's there to be cheerful about? Your father's gone. I wish I were too."

This is going to be a long day.

Henrietta ignores my mother's comments and continues.

"I'd like to have you fill out a brief survey before we begin the tour of our beautiful facility."

She hands my mother a clipboard with a pen attached to a string. My mother examines it, squints and hands it off to me with a look of "you do it". She stares straight ahead.

I want this facility to work considering she's already rejected eight others. I answer all the questions, including my mother's social security number that I've memorized, waiting for Henrietta to come back.

A silver-haired couple holding hands passes with small measured steps. Workers in scrubs push a few people in wheel chairs. Elderly twins with short curly grey hair and bright blue eyes steer aluminum walkers, both decorated with plastic flowers on their baskets. A woman with carrot colored hair piled on top of her head makes a beeline for us.

"Are you a new resident?" she asks.

My mother doesn't respond. I reach over and pat her knee. "We're thinking about it."

"Oh, honey, you'll love it here," she says addressing my mother. "I'm Marjorie but my friends call me Marge. I've been here seven years since my Ernest died. Do you play *mahj*? We have a Tuesday afternoon group."

My mother rolls her eyes at me. She's made a point of not playing the popular Chinese tile game, *mahj jong*, which most Jewish women play.

"No, I play Scrabble," says my mother.

"That's great. We have a group that does that on Fridays."

My mother remains stoic. She is not joining any groups no matter what they're doing.

Marge is nonplussed. "Well, have to get ready for the pageant. Hope to see you again." She struts away with her head held high and a straight spine.

"A pageant?" my mother asks me.

"I have no idea," I respond glancing at my watch. Still have to pick up the cleaning, food shop, stop by Lara's to see Tangie and Buzz, drop off some extra blueberry soup I made at midnight for Rivka and kiss Jacob, meet my client with a proposal for a gender-equitable workplace he did like, pick up Amber from the groomer's and hit the gym.

Henrietta appears for our tour. We begin with the library and its donated books from the '60s and '70s; we pass the hair salon, vinyl turquoise chairs filled with women waiting; we stroll through a courtyard with parrots in giant cages, and finally turn into the dining room. I pull the chair out for my mother. Henrietta leaves us to have our lunch.

The dining room smells of antiseptic, old ladies' perfume and the aroma of lingering asparagus. We are served overcooked roast beef choked with gravy, canned green beans and apple sauce.

The servers, all high school kids, have been trained to be very polite. Our server smiles with shiny metal braces as she pours iced tea and says, "Hope you're having a nice day." Do they know they're serving mush?

"So mom, what do you think? Nice, huh?"

It would be such a blessing if she liked this place and the search could be over. Even Maury is losing patience with this project. He told me to pick a place and move her.

"I don't know, Jean. If your father hadn't up and left me, I wouldn't be in this situation."

"Mom, he didn't leave you. He passed away."

"He didn't have to," she says with stubbornness, folding her arms across her chest.

"We've been over this a hundred times. He's gone and you can't live alone anymore."

"I don't see why I can't live with you. You've got extra bedrooms since the kids moved out."

A fluttery panic races from my chest to my brain. A very bad direction for this conversation.

"And I never know when they might be coming back either.

Michael moved home once already. Mom, it won't work. Maury's messy and I'm busy and you're not crazy about Amber and the phone rings all the time. You need your own space." I hope I'm convincing.

She gives me an insulted look, puts her head down and eats.

We hear tapping on the microphone. Henrietta appears in the front of the dining hall. "Ladies and gentlemen and honored guests," she acknowledges us with a nod, "we have to get ready for our competition. Please bear with us as we move some tables and chairs. There might be a little confusion for a few minutes. Finish your lunch and we'll begin shortly."

A band of helpers in leopard scrubs push twenty of the elderly sitting in wheelchairs toward the apron of the stage. Other residents drag folding chairs behind that row. From the sidelines a few well-muscled young orderlies move four armchairs onto the stage with a space left in the middle.

I stare at the set-up while my mother dives into a huge piece of German chocolate cake. I don't touch mine. Something about the coconut and all that sugary icing makes my teeth hurt.

A gentleman with a cane approaches a boom box on a card table off to the side of the room. He presses a button. A tinny Chopin polonaise serenades us.

Henrietta, who now has an autumn corsage pinned to her beige sweater, takes the microphone.

"Welcome again to our residents and guests. This is the annual Miss Vista Shadows Pageant. Let's get started and meet our lovely contestants who will be judged on their inner beauty and outward grace."

In slow motion five contestants are escorted onto the stage, red-haired Marge among them. Their names and ages are announced as they file across to take a seat in an armchair.

"Contestant number one is Enid Scheinbeiner who's a spry eighty-four." Enid enters on the arm of an elegant, tall Black assistant in an African dashiki. He looks like a Masai warrior leading a shriveled shrunken head. She waves to the audience in a purple caftan, her hair rinsed blue. Someone has applied make-up skillfully on her crinkly skin.

"Marge Goldenberger hails from Las Vegas and is ninety-two years young." The microphone emits a squeal of feedback as Marge appears in a red outfit, silver shoes, holding an ivory cane. A group to the right applauds wildly. "Go, great-Grandma," a kid's voice yells.

The next contestant is wheeled out by a smiling pimply teenager into the empty space left for her chair. "Lucy Lawyer from Kansas City is eighty-six and plays a mean game of table tennis."

The final two contestants are the twins we saw in the lobby now gussied up in yellow shirtwaists, Macy and Lacy, who wave to their cheering fans.

I'm in a Salvador Dali twilight zone. I watch my mother's reaction. She's watching with fascination. If they have a bathing suit competition, I'm leaving.

But I am surprised. It's kind of sweet. Henrietta stoops down and asks them questions about where they lived, their children, if they ever worked and what they like most about Vista Shadows.

Marge by far has the best answers. She's a former teacher of handicapped children who married three times and loves to watch soccer with her great-grandsons.

I can only see the back of the judges' heads as they confer. I figure my mother is going to think this is very corny which means this place is off the list.

"Ready to go, mom?" I gather my purse, placing my napkin on the table.

"Jean, wait a minute. I want to see who wins."

I'm suddenly intrigued too. What's the prize? A new walker?

Henrietta is handed an arm full of red roses. She bends down to take a piece of paper from the judges.

"All the contestants are elegant and have interesting, fulfilling lives, but there's only one winner. Let's hear a big round of applause for . . ." She unfolds the paper and claps her hands in surprise. ". . . Marge Goldenberger."

A hair-netted kitchen worker carries a glittery crown on a blue velvet pillow. He places the crown on Marge's red hair and hands her the roses. Someone from the audience rushes forward to take her picture with a digital camera.

"Let's give a round of applause for all the contestants and especially our new, Miss Vista Shadows, Marge."

I get up, moving around the table to assist my mother with her chair.

She puts her arm through mine as we make our exit. She

says, "You know, Jean, I think I can beat her. Next year I'm going to enter."

6

"Jean, ya know if you got better at technology you could triple multi-task."

I look up from my chrysanthemum herbal tea, a morning ritual to help me relax. Maury's reading the paper spread out in front of him, an "everything" bagel and cream cheese in hand, reading glasses perched on his nose.

"Why? Why can't I stay in the 20th century?"

"You're so stressed because you don't have a trēo pro." The pinky on his bagel hand taps an advertisement.

"I have enough to do. Last thing I need is a band playing in the background." Grumbling, I brush the crumbs from his bagel into my other cupped hand.

"No, a trēo. It's a phone with Wi-Fi, GPS, YouTube, email, your schedule and camera all in one."

Maury loves technology. When he's talking about it, his voice goes up a pitch. "You could browse the Web, download data, text message, Twitter and talk on the phone at the same time."

"While I'm driving?"

He gives me The Look, the one that says I love you even if you are sarcastic.

I soften. "Listen honey, I wouldn't know what to do with all that. Besides, if I misplaced this trio thing or it was stolen, I wouldn't be able to go on living."

"You're an intelligent woman. I'll show you how to use it. You'll love it. By the way, I have to download updates and install a new security system on your computer."

"Why?" I hate it when Maury messes with my computer. It never works right afterward. He shifts papers around on my desk. Then I can't find anything on screen or off.

"You could get a virus."

"A virus of invisible aliens?" Sometimes my mother's paranoia makes sense to me.

"Internet scams are coming every hour. We have to protect ourselves."

Technology's threatening me. I feel like an immigrant without language skills lost in America.

His phone rings. He leans back and digs in his pocket.

"Hello? Oh hi. Wow. That's really interesting. Hold on while I check my calendar." He removes the phone from his ear. He pulls out a stylus and taps the miniscule screen.

"Who is it?" I whisper.

"Starr," Maury mouths to me.

I spit out a little tea. Why is this eco-twit calling?

He agrees a few more times, says wow again and hangs up.

"What's up? A candidate debate?" I place my elbow on the table, chin in hand. I am suddenly very interested in everything about Maury.

He continues poking at his device. Distracted, he doesn't hear me. I sit back to sip my tea, clearing my throat.

He looks at me, blinking. "Yeah, we're setting that up but uh no, Starr wants to get together so we can go over the new environmental reports."

"Couldn't she send you an email?" My question is code for: does she have to call you in the morning at home?

He ignores me, picking up speed. "One's a 13-year-study about kids who live near highways who have developed respiratory problems and the other's about women 50-79 who are more likely to develop cardiovascular disease if they live in cities with dirty air."

He's biting his bottom lip, concentrating.

"When's the meeting?"

"Huh? Oh, before the next strategy session."

"And when is that?" I'm already figuring out a way to clear my schedule, no matter what.

"Tuesday. This could be big. If we have solid proof that particulates are harming women and children. . ." He drifts off into a policy paper in his head.

I make a mental note to put the meeting in my very dated, old-fashioned leather-bound planner.

Maury's chair scrapes against the terra cotta tile as he gets up. He pats my shoulder. "Don't look so worried. Everything will be all right with the kids."

He has no clue I'm worried about a tight-*tushed* 30-something professor pursuing my pudgy good-natured hero.

The phone rings again. I check caller ID. April.

"Hey kid, what's up?" I ask, clearing the table.

"We were robbed!" April's voice shrieks.

"What?" I stop in my tracks. April never screams, rushes or panics. She is the epitome of sophisticated relaxation. Kinda like an airbrushed magazine ad but alive.

"All my jewelry is gone. I can't believe it! They took my eleven carat yellow diamond Steve bought me for my birthday, my three tennis bracelets and the heirloom ruby—" She starts to sob.

"Wait a minute. Calm down. Have you called the police?"

"Yes, they're here now. It happened earlier. I left a message at Steve's office, but he's in the middle of a big trial."

"Can't they interrupt him? It's a family emergency."

"They said they'd try, but it's the Napoli case that's been in the headlines."

My brain begins to scramble. Is Napoli the woman dubbed the "Botox Bandit" who scammed all the spas by booking expensive treatments and paying with stolen credit cards *or* the socialite who left her sleeping baby with the Neiman Marcus valet and took her rat-dog inside to buy eye cream? Why are they suing? Never mind.

"Please. Could you come over to help me? I need you. I'm so upset." She sniffs, blowing her nose.

"Okay, stay calm, sweetheart. I'll be right there."

"What happened?" asks Maury.

"April was burglarized." I put the phone back into its cradle.

"She okay?"

"Oh, yeah. But I've got to go over and console her. She lost all her jewelry. The yellow diamond's gone."

Maury thinks that ring is ostentatious with its four types of gold surrounded by pink diamonds and emeralds. It's not something I would wear even if I had it but it's so April.

"She's lucky she wasn't hurt."

I'm a mess. I showered and meditated this morning, although I can't tell because my heart is racing now. I haven't put on any make-up. I'm wearing grey sweat pants and a faded Rosita's Mexican food T-shirt. I take a deep breath to center myself. *Om. Omm. Ommm.* No time. April needs me.

I grab my sunglasses, keys and tote, heading toward the door.

"Ya know, Jean, if you had a trēo you could keep track of all your appointments and your mother's."

"Bye, hon."

I park my Volvo on the street because the Lefkowitz's circular driveway has blue and white police cars stacked one behind the other. Across the street gawking neighbors and Latina nannies in pastel uniforms clutch the hands of small children.

I ring the doorbell while I wait under the portico in front of the massive wooden entry. A hand-blown glass chandelier wrapped in wrought iron hangs over my head. It could decapitate me in a bad monsoon. The door opens with a wide swing.

A buff guy in a blue polyester shirt and tie with a weary look says, "I'm Detective Taggert. Who are you?" He eyes me with suspicion.

"I'm Jean Rubin, April's friend."

"Oh, Jean," April screeches from behind him. He moves aside. I see her, hand over her mouth, clutching a tissue. She's in tight jeans, a Bebe T-shirt, the brand name spelled out in glitter and high-heeled gold sandals. She falls into my arms.

"Don't touch anything," the buff cop growls at me.

"I feel so violated," April sniffs. "They took my best pieces." Tears pour out of her aquamarine eyes to make tracks down her cheeks.

"How did they know where to look?" I ask, hugging my friend while I ponder her question.

"How do any crooks know? The jewelry box, the freezer and my closet!" Her sobs renew.

April's closet, a converted bedroom that she calls her dressing area, is something to behold. Carpeted in leopard it has seats, hooks, mirrors and racks of clothes on every wall. It's even been written up in the newspaper. She's organized by type—skirts, blouse, dresses, ball gowns—and color. She doesn't wear pants. Why should she hide her legs?

With dozens of shelves for two hundred pairs of shoes, cabinets that contain sliding shelves for cashmere sweaters, work out clothes and knits, a commercial steamer so she doesn't have to iron and the *piece de resistance*, a chest with drawers that pull out to reveal jewelry displayed on black velvet under glass. It's spectacular, an organized high boy of rings, bracelets, necklaces and pins to assist in accessorizing every outfit and gown.

I tease her about her closet often. It befits a movie star.

The cop interjects without a hint of empathy, "Ma'am, we'd like to complete our questioning. The team taking the prints has finished this area. We're going to process your bathroom and closet now." Without smiling, metal boxes in hand, the technicians head toward the bathroom.

Detective Taggert's outstretched arm guides us into the Lefkowitz living room with its display of leather loveseats, dark woods and Dupioni draperies, all in taupe, beige and black. Expensive southwestern paintings of pueblos, horses and cowboys decorate the walls, illuminated by appropriate pin lights. A large, original Fritz Scholder abstract oil painting of a Native American in bold colors hangs behind the sofa.

April sits down on an oversized hassock, knees together, hands mangling the soggy tissue. "I must look a mess," she says to me.

I perch and put my arm around her. "No, you're lovely as always." She fluffs her mane of hair, giving me a sad look, eyes ringed in black mascara. She dabs them with the tissue.

"Are you sure I look okay?"

"Only your nose is a little red."

April gives me a horrified look, opening her eyes wide.

"Ma'am, you've told me you left your residence at oh-eight-hundred hours. What was your destination?" Taggart asks rolling his eyes.

"I was going to get my nails done. No pedicure though. My regular gal who does the sea salt scrub is out of town and—"

The detective holds up his hand. "And when did you return?"

"I was back around nine because Viola, that's my housekeeper, was supposed to come. Also the gardener and the guy to adjust the plantation shutters." She whispers to me. "They've never hung right in the family room."

The detective cuts her off again. "Was your alarm system engaged?" He takes a few notes.

April looks down. "No, I forgot. Anyway, a manicure doesn't take that long and—"

"When did you notice something amiss?"

"Well, I came in through the garage door into the kitchen. Then I headed right for the fridge because I'm on a grapefruit juice fast."

I interrupt this time. "You're fasting?" April has the body of a very healthy eighteen-year-old.

The detective gives me a dirty look. I am truly shocked she is worrying about what she eats.

"I have the Heart Ball in November. I want my Hervé Léger gown to drape perfectly so I decided to fast and get an herbal body wrap."

"April, Maury says those gimmicks just suck out your fluids. It comes back when you drink a glass of water." Although I'd like to try it one time just to see if I could get into my killer jeans again.

"Ma'am, can you stay on topic?" The officer looks very annoyed. A double crease stitches between his brows. He addresses me and says, "Please," tapping his ballpoint on the pad.

April wipes her nose. "So then I went into my bathroom and saw that the window surrounding the Jacuzzi was broken. I knew something was wrong."

She grabs my arm, her voice choking. "Jean, I got so scared. I felt as if I wasn't alone. The hairs stood up on the back of my neck. I felt all freaky. I ran back into the kitchen. That's when I noticed the patio door was wide open. I grabbed my purse, ran to the garage, locked myself in the car and called 9-1-1 from my cell."

I can see the fear on her face retelling her scary story.

A uniformed police officer with a camera steps into the living room. His heavy black shoes leave large imprints on the plush cream carpet.

"Detective Taggart, I'd like to see if the lady can identify the weapon used for entry."

April winces. Detective Taggart nods, his mouth twitching a little, maybe with impatience. The officer motions to April. I follow them through the open patio door to the back yard and pool area.

"Ma'am, do you recognize these items?" He snaps on rubber gloves and picks up a few broken ceramic pieces stacked on the counter under the kitchen pass-through window.

"We found them around the corner near your master

bath." April's chin begins to quiver and she starts to cry again.

April nods. "It's the statue that guards my beloved Pookie. I buried him last year. St. Francis protects the animals."

"Where are the dogs?" I ask, thinking about April's mobile mops that run around yipping and peeing.

"OhmiGod. They're still locked up in the laundry room. I'll be right back."

Mr. Professional Policeman as well as the other officers stare as she sways back into the house, her size six ass leaving a visible impression. He shakes his head back and forth.

"Why would you have dogs and lock them up?" he mutters.

I know he's not addressing me, but I answer anyway.

"They piddle a lot."

"And you are?" he asks, snapping off his gloves, flipping to a fresh sheet of paper in his hand-sized pad.

"A friend."

"Name and address?"

Uh-oh. Maury's always telling me not to get involved.

"Uh, listen, I don't even live in this neighborhood."

"So how did you know to show up?" he asks me with an arched eyebrow.

"My friend called me." The air is cool this morning but I'm getting warm. I lean against the outside stucco wall.

"You mean she forgot about her dogs to call you?"

"Yes, well, we're really close. We're there for each other no matter what and . . ."

He levels me with a glare. "Your name and address, ma'am."

Sweat pools at the middle of my back. OmiGod! He's interrogating me! Everything I've been saying floats by me. I sound like a fool. Which sometimes happens when I'm nervous or scared or being silly with my girlfriends. I try to pull myself together but my hands are shaking.

"Uh, listen. We've been best friends since our kids were little, along with Glee and . . ."

I'm an idiot. This guy doesn't understand about girlfriends, how important we are to each other. I'm having a hot flash. A spigot of sweat erupts between my breasts.

"Jean Rubin. 1348 Conchita Drive in Scottsdale."

Suddenly, I hear April's wails and a booming voice. Steve Lefkowitz, Personal Injury Attorney to the most litigious wealthy people in town, has arrived.

"Excuse me," I say to the officer.

I hurry back inside. Steve stands in his entryway as the fingerprint team, metal boxes in hand, file out behind him, footprints of black dust leaving distinct marks on the granite tiled foyer.

Steve's silk tie is pulled down and his top collar button is open. His usually slicked back hair has the forelock hanging over his brow. He surveys the scene. April clings to the front of him, weeping.

He demands, "I want to know who's in charge."

"I am, Sir. Detective Taggart, Paradise Valley Police Department. My assistant, Detective Sanchez."

"What happened here? I'm in the middle of a trial. I had to practically beg the judge to take a recess."

"Sir, it appears your home has been burgled. The suspect entered and appropriated your wife's jewelry."

April raises her head from his shoulder. "They were in my closet! My yellow diamond, the ruby bracelet you got me for Valentine's, the . . ."

He hugs her, patting her back. "It's only jewelry, honey. That's why we pay those big premiums. As long as you weren't harmed." His tone hardens again as he addresses the detective, "Who do you think did this?"

"Sir, it appears that your home was cased with your wife's jewelry targeted. With other valuables left behind and the illegal entry accomplished with finesse, it's hard to draw any conclusions." He pauses. "But I'd say the MO matches the Rock Burglar."

My hand slaps my chest. "The Rock Burglar?" April and I say in unison.

Steve asks, "The guy you haven't been able to catch in seven years?" He hugs April tighter.

"Sir, law enforcement works hard to find perpetrators. We don't have enough evidence to catch this particular offender."

Chills run up my spine. We've been hearing about this brazen robber for ages. He breaks in through a master bedroom or bathroom window with a rock, often while people are home. Some victims are eating dinner or watching TV. He targets only the wealthiest homes in the northeast Valley. Gives me the willies that this creep is so hard to catch. Any residual relaxation from my morning meditation evaporated ages ago.

I see this as my opportunity to leave.

"Hey, guys, you've got a lot to deal with here. I'm going to go." I kiss April's cheek, giving her a sympathetic pat.

The detective speaks to me. "Ma'am, can we reach you for further questioning?"

My heart staggers. "Sure," I nod, heading out the door.

The crowd in front of the Lefkowitz's house on East Los Hermanos Muertos Drive has grown larger. Women in beige yoga clothes and men in tennis whites have joined the curious onlookers.

Nothing this exciting has happened around here since a 65-year-old self-described Annie Oakley shot her neighbor in the groin. According to witnesses she poured buckets of bird seed on his lawn to attract rodents, cackling about it. When he came out to complain, she shot him. Our neighborhoods are getting so dangerous.

From the crowd, a woman with blowfish red lips wearing riding boots, a tight shirt, tighter jeans and a cowboy hat approaches me. She's breathless. "I was just coming from the stables and saw all the cars. I live over there," she says, pointing to a pink-tinged hacienda across the street.

"Oh yes, I met you at one of April's parties." She looks me up and down. "Jean. Jean Rubin." I say, standing taller, extending my hand, which she ignores. Wait. She's the one coming from the stables, her boots caked with horse manure.

"They were robbed," I offer, sounding ominous.

She inhales a gasp, her hands sailing to her cheeks. I'm almost blinded by an emerald-cut diamond the size of an ice skating rink.

"Who would do such a thing?" she asks me.

People who want your stuff. I volunteer my insider information. "The Rock Burglar." I say it like the thief's the size of the hulk and morphs his body to fit through small spaces.

"No!" She takes a step back, her diamond blinking in the morning sun. "What is this world coming to?"

7

STRESS RELIEF TIP: Repeating affirmations daily encourages the subconscious mind to believe a new reality.
— *Change Your Life with Affirmation*

I'VE HAD A RESTLESS NIGHT WITHOUT DEEP SLEEP. When I make my side of the bed, I notice my pillow is covered with hair. I brush them away and grab at my head pulling away a handful more from my curly mop.

"Maury, I'm losing my hair." I feel panicky.

"Don't worry about it. Hair thins out as you age."

"You don't need to remind me I'm aging. My hair is my crowning glory." I smooth my pillow case, whisking away a few more hairs.

"Women lose hair like men. You're under too much stress."

"So that's why my hair is falling out in handfuls?"

Maury stops his search and looks at me with my crestfallen expression. "Stress can make your hair fall out. Hurry up. We'll be late for the debate. Worry about it later."

With dismay I watch Maury in the kitchen searching for his keys, lifting up newspapers, moving mail and grumbling to himself. He opens the junk drawer and pushes the contents to one side. Bills, self-stick address labels and a screw driver fall to the floor.

"Jean, we have to be there early. I'm responsible for the debate judges as the Green Party representative. Where are my keys?"

As he bends over to pick up the debris on the floor, I pull out the keys dangling from his back pocket. He grunts as he stands up, takes them from me and pushes the drawer closed with his rear, labels sticking out.

It's been a week since the burglary and April has agreed to meet us at the Hilton for a political debate sponsored by the Scottsdale Babes. It starts at 7:30 a.m. which is very early for her to be glamorous.

I've made minimal effort with my appearance—no eye shadow, no mascara and no heels. Just blush and new Birkenstocks. It's the middle of the night as far as I'm concerned. And I'm losing my hair. Not such a big deal to some but huge for me. How thin will it get?

"Maury, have you seen my jacket?" I ask searching a shelf of supplements.

Glee insists I take a multi-vitamin, vitamin E, valerian, fish oil Omega-3 fatty acids, a pro-biotic and dong quai. I don't know what half of it's for, but I shake each bottle into the palm of my hand. If I stop taking them I'll probably disintegrate.

"Wear the green one," he tells me with a look of triumph, keys in hand. He loves it when I can't find something. The green jacket I wear to walk the dog is not acceptable and he knows it.

I run upstairs to tear through a pile of clothes that I've worn the last few days. Where's my favorite jacket with the embroidered lapels? I clomp downstairs and look in the laundry room. Aha! It's in the dry cleaning pile. Too wrinkled to wear.

"It doesn't matter." says Maury who has the fashion sense of a snail. I may not be stylish but I can look cool.

With my tote on my shoulder I take the stairs again two at a time and, a bit out of breath, scramble through my closet to pick out a blazer from my teaching days. When I pass the mirror a wild animal with frantic eyes stares back. I pull the scarf from my neck to tie the hair I might be losing away from my face without dropping any of the pills.

Maury is waiting for me in the car revving the engine. I get in, sigh and then open the car door again.

"Now what?"

"My phone. I can't leave without my phone." I race back inside, my hand sweating around the colored vitamins.

I get back in the car and buckle my seat belt. But I remember one more thing that I've forgotten. I check my tote. The car is rolling.

"Maury, stop. My planner. I must have my planner."

"Jean." I can hear the exasperation in his voice.

I've resisted incorporating high-tech into my life because

it'll create more anxiety. But this is worse. I have so many things to remember.

I rush back into the house and find the black leather book sitting on my kitchen desk.

As I re-settle into the car seat, Maury asks, "And do we have everything now?"

I've forgotten my sunglasses but I don't dare say another word. I just squint into the morning fireball and acknowledge that indeed, we have another day in paradise.

Maury screeches to a stop in the back of the hotel where the meeting rooms are located. He hops out while I figure out what to do with the vitamins scrunched in my hand. The red and yellow pills have stained my palm. My water bottle is empty. I slide them into the pocket of my blazer.

I pull down the visor mirror and push my hair around to make it appear fuller, line my lips with a colored pencil, add lipstick and grab my tote. Sighing, I close my eyes to concentrate on today's positive affirmations. *It's good. It's all good. This is as good as it gets.* So much for that.

To my surprise there are many people not only awake at this hour but also dressed for business. Gathered at the back of the room are women and a spattering of men. Some of the women wear suits and heels and look very professional while another group is attired in western shirts, broomstick skirts, jeans, cowboy boots and leather holsters with guns.

Guns.

I spot Maury in the front of the ballroom conferring with Brian Depalma and a few other people. I recognize the angry bear shirt man. Fierce Fred, dressed in a brown shirt and pants, tests the sound system with a few screeches while hotel personnel adjust microphones attached to the two podiums. A judge's table sits in front of the risers with three microphones.

April approaches me, dazzling in a grey fitted suit, her mane of hair shiny, glossy lips gleaming like a model. She appears much taller perched on three-inch heels.

"Jean, I'm so glad you told me about this debate. The robbery's made me a little agoraphobic. I've even skipped going to my personal trainer."

I stare at her shoes. They're pointy with blue and green leather strips of snakeskin criss-crossing the front. They are the most gorgeous shoes I've ever seen.

She responds to my stare. "Manolos."

"Where's Glee?" I'm coveting the shoes even though I know I couldn't stand upright in them let alone walk.

"Oh, she couldn't make it. She's facilitating a Holy Yoga retreat this week."

"Really?" I ask, raising my brows.

"They celebrate God through movement and meditation."

I nod, envisioning people with closed eyes waving filmy scarves.

"You should try one of her workshops."

"Oh. I'm sure it wouldn't help me. I'm too preoccupied to bend into a pretzel and breathe at the same time."

We move toward the coffee stand. April drinks hers cowboy style, black. I add cream and sugar.

April shifts her weight to another hip. The shoes may be

magnificent but they've got to be foot binding-concubine-painful. I wiggle my toes in the roomy Birkenstocks. They're ugly but my feet feel great.

"Are all three candidates showing up?" April asks, sipping. She leaves a half-moon of fuchsia lipstick on her cup.

"Only the Republican and our Green one. The Democrat died."

"Mmmm." She seems interested but her eyes are surveying the room.

I mentally wander with her. *It's good. It's all good. This is as good as it gets* I repeat to myself until I spot an auburn head toward the front of the room.

I want to check out Starr but April guides me to peruse the table of goodies. I choose a raisin bagel with cream cheese. She takes a small plate and dots it with fruit.

"Aren't you hungry in the morning?" I ask before my first chomp.

"Of course." April tries to cut a melon ball and it slides. She catches it and mashes it into tiny bits.

"Have something else. Those Danish look great."

"Jean, I don't want a muffin top when I wear jeans." She motions with her chin. "Like that woman over there."

Sure enough there's a leather belt with *AZ Cowgirl* emblazoned on the back wrapped around some portly hips and a roll of fat hanging over the top.

Is she referring to me? I depend on my friends and gay hairstylist to guide me. If it wasn't for them I'd be dressed like my mother. "Uh, do I have one?"

April steps back for her evaluation. "No, but honey, buy Spanx or those girdles that come up to the bottom of your bra. It'll cover a multitude of sins."

I mentally add that to my To Do list behind rehearsing my "Gender Equity in the Workplace" seminar but before my mother's dental and eye appointments. I have priorities but not having a muffin top has moved to the top of the list.

April continues, "Women don't understand that undergarments build a foundation."

It's her hint that I need to spend some more time in the lingerie department. With aplomb April spears a tiny piece of melon on the fork, popping it between her lips. Her lipstick remains unchanged and mine is smeared over my bagel. She points to my chin. I wipe it and mouth a thank you.

April switches topics still nibbling at her fruit which now looks like puree. "I'm concerned about the environment. Especially the way the free radicals affect our skin. Did you know pollution causes wrinkles?"

Another worry to add to my plethora of concerns. "How 'bout breathing? That's my priority."

A voice booms from ceiling speakers urging us to find seats for the candidate's forum. Maury motions me to sit in the second row next to him. He's taken the aisle seat. The candidates and their families have taken up the front row on both sides. As we move down the center aisle a few hungry stares watch April, men and women.

She air kisses Maury and settles next to me. We're asked to stand and say the Pledge of Allegiance. I place my hand over my heart to utter the words I learned in elementary school. Out of the corner of my left eye I see a figure lean forward from the row behind us and whisper something to Maury as we sit down.

Starr. I turn to give her a tight, he's still mine so keep your hands off him, smile and she wiggles a few fingers at me.

I am not pleased.

"Who's that?" asks April, leaning toward me.

"I'll tell you later."

"She's cute."

I frown. Oh, and I'll bet dollars to muffins she's wearing the right undergarments too. Like a lacey thong.

Someone taps on the microphone emitting a few screeches from the sound system. It draws our attention to the front of the room. "Welcome y'all, to our candidate's debate and forum. I'm Winnie Smart, President of the Scottsdale Babes. We're the sponsors of today's event."

A big cheer goes up in the room along with a few yelps.

"I must acknowledge Emanuel Funt, our Democratic candidate who up and died on us recently."

Those in the audience who haven't heard the news gasp. A mumble ripples through the crowd. People turn to look at each other and around the room for others' reactions.

"We are so sorry he's not with us today. Our heartfelt condolences go out to his family."

A murmur of agreement buzzes through the group. Winnie brings us back to our purpose by leaning closer to the microphone mounted on the podium.

"Our forum today focuses on population growth, environmental concerns and the welfare of our great state. All questions will address those topics."

The judges are introduced: a columnist from the newspaper, a bipartisan political consultant and a retired author of *Politics, Numerology and You*, and finally, the moderator, a big man in a white shirt wearing a silver bola tie with a hunk of turquoise in the middle. The rules of debate are repeated.

The moderator says in a theatrical voice, "Topics will be introduced, candidates have three minutes to present, a chance for rebuttal and then each receives a three minute conclusion."

I shift in my seat. Formal debates are boring. I hope something exciting happens to shake things up. Otherwise, I could drift off.

"First, however, we have stump speeches from the candidates for districts five, eight and twenty-seven. Would they please ascend the stage?"

These speeches go quickly. It's an opportunity for candidates running for local offices to state their platform. Everyone wants less crime, fewer immigrants and no new taxes.

I check my watch, keeping an eye on my left wing. I check out Starr again—tight jeans tucked into boots, auburn hair tumbled around her shoulders, eyes big, an innocent expression.

"And now the part we've all been waiting for." He waits a drumbeat for dramatic pause. "Will our debating candidates

Flora Beaudreaux and Craig Burton please come forward?"

They both rise and move to the stage to stand behind their podiums. I fidget with a visceral reaction to Flora. She's a mean-spirited, nasty woman who's vengeful. She might win this race too.

Craig looks intellectual with horn-rimmed glasses clutching a sheaf of papers. He's a small man with a big brain, an ill-fitting collar and a black tie.

Flora looks scary as hell, wild-eyed with her dyed black hair pulled off her face with a velvet headband revealing a halo of untouched grey roots. Her blush, exaggerated on her long pale face, looks ghoulish while her mouth, small and puckered, glistens red. Lantern earrings dangle from her lobes. She's wearing a navy knit suit and matching Ferragamos, the kind with a flat bow that spell old money.

A judge leans into his microphone. "Here is the first question: given concerns about the brown haze hanging over our valley and the paucity of water affecting the entire state, what can you do to make Arizona more environmentally responsible? You have three minutes to state your case. Ms. Beaudreaux, you drew the longest straw so you begin."

She smiles at the audience, glancing in my direction. Her eyes narrow. No. She's giving me the evil eye. She recognizes me. Her eyebrow arches a little and she gives me an Elvis-like sneer. A surge of panic waves through my body.

"I don't agree that the state has to be more responsible. We're already spending millions of tax payers' dollars on environmental concerns and to what end? What about the corporations who have to oblige environmental interests with repugnant regulations? It's costing the public a lot of money. Money that could be put to good use..."

I steal a look at Starr. She's engaged in the speaker. Her cowboy boots are the fancy two-toned kind with a worn heel. Probably does line dancing on Saturday nights and picks up the Marlboro man, anachronism that he is.

"... we need less government interference not more. I will stop the legislature's march toward green freedom."

This ticks me off. We need more assistance toward a green economy. Our state legislature disregards the environment. Flora is finishing when I tune back in. She slaps the podium in conclusion.

"Mr. Barton, you have three minutes," says our deep-voiced moderator.

I touch Maury's arm with concern. Will our candidate be strong?

Craig clears his throat, adjusts his glasses, pulls the microphone a few inches lower and points a finger at Flora.

"This woman has single-handedly undermined clean air and water in Arizona. Check the incumbent's voting record. She consistently vetoed legislation to give our state clean air, the most basic of needs. We've had twenty-one days of high pollution advisories with the large dust particles known as PM-10s exceeding federal standards in the last few months alone. This pollution irritates lungs and is especially harmful to children and the elderly."

Through bleary-eyes I gaze at April's shoes. I lean toward

her and whisper, "Those shoes are a work of art."

April doesn't respond. Her eyes are closed and her chin has dropped to her chest.

". . . our high ozone levels reduce photosynthesis which accelerates the aging of plants and stunts leaf growth as well as affects our respiratory system."

"What did he say?" I ask Maury, who's transfixed. Finally, someone is speaking his language.

"Shh. I'll explain later." He pats my hand.

April flutters her eyes.

Our candidate continues. "Atmospheric deposition like airborne sulfur and nitrogen which, by the way, reaches the soil through rain and snow which is abundant in the northern part of our state, affects farming and crop growth."

I glance as April's ankle falls in and the Manolo with its exquisite strips of blue and green lizard falls over. She has a French manicure on her toenails.

"Ms. Beaudreux, your two minute rebuttal."

Flora grips the sides of the podium. "I do not wish to be addressed as Ms. I am a Mrs. and proud of it. This man . . ." she says, pointing at Craig distractedly shuffling through his index cards, ". . . and his cadre of liberals and environmentalists would see our state budget bled dry from spurious legislation that supports a few small special interest groups." Wild applause erupts from the front row on the other side of the aisle. I crane my head to see a honey-blonde with broad shoulders nodding her head.

"Okay," says the moderator. "Question number two: With

our state as the fastest growing in the nation, what do you see as the biggest issue, air, water or food? The lady goes first once again."

"Our population explosion is a good thing," says a beaming Flora. "There's plenty of air and water. These progressives, as they like to call themselves, will send decent tax paying citizens into the poor house. They raise taxes willy-nilly without any regard for the hard-working business people who put in long hours to create jobs for the masses. The biggest issue is liberals who want to steal our money and take away our guns."

A cheer erupts from the front row as the blonde gives a thumbs-up. Others join her. Maury, April and I sit very still. Flora has noticed me again and glares. It gives me the creeps to be one riser away from this maniacal nut.

The moderator stands: "Order, order. We cannot have any partisan support during the debate."

Flora steps back a little from her podium. She has won a victory; the audience supports her.

"Mr. Barton?" asks the moderator. Craig peers over the top of his glasses, his eye twitching a bit. His hand reaches up to stop it. It continues to twitch. He stares into the audience as though he's curious as to why we're there. He reminds me of a nervous Pee-Wee Herman.

"The biggest issue—ahem. The biggest issue facing us is insuring we have clean air and water for generations to come. We are poisoning our population. Now, my opponent with her perverted ideas thinks breathing air and drinking water without pollutants is radical. Her husband has been cited by the Department of Environmental Quality for a fraudulent development of land in the Las Robles area where. . ."

Flora takes three long steps across the stage and shakes a finger in Craig's face. She towers over him.

"How dare you call me a pervert? You anti-life, tax-raising, tree-hugging creep. My husband has created jobs for this state at great personal and financial risk and . . ."

Craig, papers still in hand, blinks a few times, like a kid hit with a water gun. This is totally unexpected and not in his notes.

The moderator stands up from the end of the judge's table. His deep voice breaks into Flora's shrill one. "Ma'am, you have to stay at your podium. Displays of temper will not be allowed. You can be disqualified if it happens again."

Flora is still shaking her finger at our diminutive candidate. With rage she says, "This man and his so-called Green Party, which stands for how to take our green money, have conspired against me and my husband for years . . ."

The broad-shouldered blonde in the front cups her hands around her mouth and in a stage whisper says, "Mom. Calm down."

We can all hear her admonishment.

Then I recognize her.

It's Tiffany, her daughter. The athletic runner Tiffany. The Tiffany whose grade I wouldn't change. The lying Tiffany I failed. The Tiffany whose mother had me fired from my teaching job. The Tiffany on her mother's payroll. *That* Tiffany.

The girl stands up and motions with her arm. "Mom, go

back to your podium." Flora slumps a bit and goes back to her side of the stage.

Without warning Flora lifts her head, razors her eyes into my shocked ones and says, "Your kind are wreaking havoc on our state."

And then she reaches out her arms, moves in a few swift steps to the front of the stage and starts down the steps in an attempt to reach me. She is so close I see the flare of her nostrils and smell her sickly perfume.

I am frozen. April, now awake, sits tall and grabs her purse to her bosom. Maury, slow to react, realizes his wife is the focal point of an angry monkey-haired harridan with red talons. He lumbers up and leans toward the advancing madwoman. For once I'm glad he's a little chubby and has some stubble. He folds his arms over his chest, an imposing figure in a powder blue golf shirt. My protector, my hero, is going to save me from being attacked by this wing-nut in front of the prestigious Scottsdale Babes. Hopefully none of them will shoot me. I hold my neck with one hand. I feel so vulnerable. That's what she went for the last time.

Tiffany jumps up to intercede and guides Flora back to the podium. The audience has erupted in cheers. Flora drops her arms, re-groups and sighs. She pats the front of herself, as if to make sure she's still there. She clutches the microphone and says, "Sorry about that. The unjust and unfair accusations of my opponent have infuriated me."

Maury sits down.

Tiffany glares at me as though I'm the weirdo here and

takes her seat. The room buzzes. I'm stunned. Flora tried to physically attack me when we had a confrontation over Tiffany's failing grade. My department head was a witness. I never dreamed she'd try it again. Maury puts his arm around me, "You okay, babe?"

I nod. My life has spun out of control. My heart's beating so fast I think I'm going to collapse, the kind where I might fall on the floor sobbing. I was almost strangled by a Banshee woman and my day's hardly started.

Our moderator's voice booms through the chaos. With slumped shoulders he says, "The debate is now concluded and the winner is . . ."

One of the judges leaves the table to whisper in the moderator's ear.

". . . undecided."

April says, "This is the most interesting political meeting I've ever attended."

8

WITH THE DEBATE OVER I'M STILL A LITTLE SHAKEN by Flora's verbal and almost physical attack, but new technology distracts me. Maury comes home with a surprise.

"Guess what?" he asks while I go through a stack of mail at my kitchen desk.

This can't be good. He's too enthusiastic.

"I figured out how to help with your anxiety overload."

"Really? You're going to food shop, pick up your socks and not eat pretzels in the family room?" I use my letter opener with particular violence. He ignores my sarcasm.

"I got you a trēo!" he says with triumph.

I know he means well, but learning a new device will *not* make my life easier.

"Look, its simple. You can text, check email, look up files. It requires an open mind and concentration."

He's oblivious that I am not pleased.

"Remember I said I didn't want one?"

"Honey, this will make your life more efficient. You won't have to *schlep* that big book of yours everywhere. I'm dragging you into the 21st century."

I take it from him with a promise to try.

The trēo, which Maury has set up with assorted ring tones for those nearest and dearest to me, displays a picture of the person calling. I don't know whether to look or listen.

How do I enter and retrieve future events, edit tasks or delete a contact? Maury tries to demonstrate but I forget.

The handy quick reference guide in two languages the size of a large dictionary does not provide easy-to-find, useful information. My insecurities won't allow me to abandon my planner so I run a dual system bringing everything with me everywhere. Maury insists the trēo will make me more productive. I have my doubts when I lift my tote onto my shoulder.

My mother waits for me outside her apartment building, purse over her arm, wearing a white blouse, black skirt and black-and-white strappy heels with a bow. Fully coiffed and made-up she moves toward the car slowly. After our greeting I help her get in, close her seat belt and check my watch. Nine a.m.

"Mom, you know there's a shuttle that will take you to your appointments," I say, squeezing the steering wheel.

"You don't want to drive me anymore? *Yentas* might ask

me about my personal business. Why should they know which doctor I'm going to? Besides, what do you do with yourself all day?"

I don't respond. I re-grip the steering wheel until my knuckles turn white.

When we arrive at the podiatrist a snippy woman behind the desk informs us the appointment is for ten.

"When I called to schedule you said nine-thirty," says my mother, insisting she's wrong.

"Mom, there's no point arguing." I guide her to turquoise chairs in the desert-decorated waiting area.

A dust-catching display of small, rectangular Native American red and black blankets, fake *kachina* dolls with white chicken feathers and broken orange pottery decorate the walls. They are attached to an amateurish hand-painted mural of green and brown cactus. Bad art wounds my soul.

My mother grimaces and stews while I read a tattered, dog-eared two-year-old copy of *Good Housekeeping*.

Finally, we see the doctor. She examines her misshapen toes. "Most people's feet hurt at your age. Try to stay off them. And get some sensible shoes," she says with unrealistic abandon.

After the five minute assessment, which killed my entire morning, I drive her back to her apartment. She'd like me to join her and the few friends she's made for a fall luncheon.

I can't deal with autumn leaves and orange pumpkins when it's 106 degrees outside. I beg off to start a round of errands. I have to be at Lara's by three. And my mother still hasn't agreed on a new place to live.

I stop for gas at the station located on the Pima Indian reservation where it costs less. Bargain gasoline lures people to the casino causing traffic jams. I lean next to my tank, trēo in hand, squinting at the invisible screen in the sunlight while my car fills up. I pull up the list for today:

mother-podiatrist

gas

vitamins

proposal to client

return organic SleepSack kid birthday gift for bigger size

dog food-large

pet luncheon invitations with April

pick up chlorine-free wipes for Lara

Trader Joe's-wine

return calls to vet, cousin in Atlanta, Green Party HQ

book appointments for insurance, dentist, hair

Krishna-O'Halloran-dinner seven p.m.

I try to check email and text message Lara that I might be late. The Blue Tooth's stuck in my ear like a shiny black grasshopper. I manipulate the miniscule keys. Nothing goes through so I start over.

A honk interrupts me. I drop the stylus. The person waiting in the car behind mine leans out and says, "Lady, your tank's full. Let's go."

I search for the pencil-like device on the filthy ground under my car. The guy honks again.

"I'm looking," I yell.

Indeed, gas has stopped gurgling into my tank. After I find the stylus I place it in its tiny hole at the top of the trēo, drop it between my breasts so I don't have to search for it while driving, replace the hose and handle and move into my rolling office.

I stop at the health food store, Petsmart and kid clothing store for the return. I mentally check off my list. Next, my client's office.

He glances through the new proposal pleased with my suggestions. While he urges me to implement a flextime program for his employees immediately, the trēo rings between my breasts.

I forgot to switch to vibrate. Ravel's "Bolero" announces Maury, a piece of classical music that's supposed to drive people to heightened sexual awareness.

"Uh, do you mind if I take this?"

He signals that it's fine.

I excuse myself to turn around and dig into my brassiere.

"Maury, I can't talk now. I'm with a client."

"Hi hon. Don't forget chili peppers for tonight. You okay? You seemed frazzled this morning."

"I'll be home later. I can't talk now."

"Do you want me to start the dishwasher and clean up around the front door? The bougainvilleas hemorrhaged fuchsia petals everywhere. Maybe get the house cooled down for company?"

When has Maury ever called me to volunteer to do housekeeping chores?

"Sure. Anything. I can't talk now." I click him off.

"Sorry about that. I should've turned it off. New device." I say.

"No problem. Happens to everyone."

I exit with promises of a speedy response to his needs.

Back in the car I stretch to look in the rearview mirror. No lipstick. I glance at my watch. If I move fast I can be finished with the ingredients I need for dinner in six-to-seven minutes.

I choose AJ's over Trader Joe's, located near each other, because it'll be faster, although AJ's is pricier.

The doors of "AJ's—Purveyor of Fine Foods" slide open. I charge down the aisles adding organic tomato-basil tortillas, a chocolate *ganache* dessert from the bakery and imported cheese to my basket.

At the produce display I toss in a mixture of fresh spring lettuce, an avocado, heritage tomatoes and scallions. Cracks of rolling thunder followed by sprinklers startle me. Only rich people have sound effects for their romaine and radicchio. My nerves are shot.

I check out, proud that I've remembered to bring canvas bags so I don't have to choose between paper or plastic. I check my watch again.

Yikes! Lara's waiting for me. She's going to the gynecologist for an IUD. One kid wants another one and the other wants no more.

I hustle to the Volvo, put the bags in the back, take a sip of water and put the key in the ignition. The car sputters. I turn off the engine, wait a heartbeat and try again. It hesitates but ignites. I back out. The person waiting for my spot shakes his fist at me. As I make my way past pedestrians I remember chilies, a must for the southwestern feast. I slam my hands on the steering wheel. Damn.

While I'm circling around to find another parking spot, Enya's "Orinoco," a New Age instrumental, envelopes the car. Glee's calling me. I scramble with one hand in my tote for the trēo. The repetitious lyric of "Sail away, sail away" intensifies. I find it, pushing buttons franticly. Nothing happens. Ach. I throw it on the seat next to me. The Blue Tooth! Oh dear. It was there during my client's presentation. I am such a dork. I find the device in my hair, which is still falling out, attached to my ear.

"Hi Hon. I'm really busy right now. Can I call you back?" I ask, driving with one hand.

A woman in a straw hat yakking on her cell phone, grocery bags over her arm, walks in front of my car. I slam on the brakes.

"OhmiGod. I almost hit her." I drop my head to my chest and pant.

"Jean, get a grip. You have to slow down. You okay?" asks Glee.

"I'm fine." I brush my hand across my sweaty forehead.

"I'm having a Day of the Dead party. I want you and Maury to come. You'll meet Stavros."

"Sure."

"It's in November. I want you to calendar it."

"Right. Listen, Glee, I'd better get both hands on the wheel or I'll be there as a corpse. Talk to you soon."

I drive around AJ's parking lot again, scanning for something under the awning constructed to keep their clientele cool. A car backs out. I wait, watching in anticipation, my fingers drumming on the wheel. I space out. What if I hit that woman? I wasn't going fast but still . . .

A black Hummer with intense chrome and dark tinted windows turns left in front of me snuggling into my spot.

"Hey, that was mine," I call out.

A muscular figure in a navy jogging suit, large wrap-around sunglasses, hair hidden beneath a baseball cap, jumps down from the vehicle. I get the finger with a few jiggles for emphasis.

When did Scottsdalians get so rude? "Your Hummer's melting the planet," I say to myself.

I circle again. The woman I almost wiped out is still talking on her phone while loading her trunk. When she turns around and sees it's me, she gives me the finger too.

"S-ssshit," I sputter to myself. I close my eyes. *Calm. Think calm cool waters. Breathe in. And out.*

I accidentally honk my horn which scares her. I wave my hands in apology. She gives me a nasty look. I give up, find a place in the baking sun between a Porsche and an Escalade to rush back inside for my forgotten item.

An attractive display under subdued lights offers orange, yellow, black and green chili peppers. I need red.

The produce manager in a crisp apron announces himself as a chili expert, guiding me to a line of dark green ones. "You shouldn't substitute *habeneros* in a recipe. Way too spicy. Take the *poblanos* instead of the *jalapenos*," he says rolling his r's. I defer to his superior knowledge, bagging a few.

As I check out again, avoiding conversation with the cheerful cashier, the Hummer Hogger stands at the next station. Under the baseball cap I see a light-colored ponytail. Reminds me of someone, but I can't see the face.

Should I tell them how I feel about rude behavior? That this is still a civilized society. I'm under a lot of pressure, too, but I believe being polite is an important part of our culture.

I puff up my chest a bit. My left hand balls into a fist. I bang it on the credit card machine. The cashier gives me a wide-eyed stare. I have embarrassed myself. I stretch out my fingers, squiggling them around, glancing behind me. An elderly woman counts her apples.

I'd better go. There's road rage nuts lurking out there. I don't know who has a weapon, especially with the Scottsdale Babes running around. I watch the object of my anger jog through the sliding doors.

Chili bag in hand I exit, tossing them into the back seat. I realize I'd better drop off the groceries and start the salad for tonight. Loud rock 'n roll envelopes me. Lara. I'm sure she's wondering where I am. I press the Blue Tooth on my ear.

"Lara, I'm on my way."

"No problem. Mom, Gus wants to talk to you. Say hello to Mimi, baby. Yes, that's Mimi in the phone."

"I don't have time for this right now," I say, putting the key in. My car doesn't turn over. A dead battery?

"Lara?" Unfortunately, the baby's sucking the phone.

I check my watch. My six minute AJ's visit turned into thirty. *Calm. I am calm.*

I hang up on a slurping child to dial Maury.

"I have a problem," explaining why I need his help.

"It'll be faster to get jumper cables from Bridwell's. I'm in the middle of a project."

Bridwell's gas station with its sign for "Domestic and Foreign Repairs" is the only one around with uniformed attendants. They actually pump gas, check oil and clean windows. Yes, the gas costs more, but service rules.

I hot foot across the parking lot to a handsome young man with Seth embroidered above his pocket. I point to my car explaining how it's usually so reliable.

Seth gets into his truck to follow me to the parking lot where a black Mercedes faces my Volvo with cars on either side. He can't position his vehicle close enough to attach the jumper cables.

Should I wait until a socialite finishes shopping for *foie gras* and caviar? I call Maury again. "You've got to come and get me."

He protests but shows up ten minutes later in a baseball cap, shorts and a Craig Burton campaign T-shirt.

"Jean, you need a new car."

"Now? I don't want a new car. I just want the old one to work."

"I've been thinking while I was on the ladder. We should get you a hybrid. It'll save on gas and make a political statement." He gets in the Volvo. It doesn't turn over.

"Wait a minute. Why were you up on a ladder?" I ask leaning in the window.

He pushes his cap back to rub his forehead. "I changed all our light bulbs to compact fluorescents so we reduce our carbon footprint."

"Today? Maury, we have company coming for dinner."

He looks at me with crinkled eyebrows. "Don't worry. I only broke three of the old ones getting them out. The new ones use seventy-five percent less energy and pay for themselves in three years."

"Don't the new ones have toxins in them when they break?" I ask, trying not to sound irritated.

"Lot of dust came down from the fixtures."

"Maury!"

"It's not a problem. I'll get it all cleaned up after I watch the city council meeting on C-Span. The mayor's talking about pollutants and dust control measures."

The good and bad of men: they try to do the right thing and create chaos. I'm sure there are miniscule pieces of broken bulbs everywhere. Hope the Krishna-O'Halloran's don't take off their shoes.

Maury says, "I'll wait here to get a new battery installed." He gets out, handing me his key.

I'm frustrated with my car, broken light bulbs, the need to rush to Lara's. But I peck him on the lips anyway. He did show up to help.

I remind him to unload the perishables as soon as he gets

home, seize my weight-training tote and maneuver into his semi-retired-doctor Lexus. Maury walks over to Bridwell's.

I don't like to drive his car because it's complicated. I get in, adjust the seat, put on the belt and search. The key is in my hand but there's no place to put it. Yes! I'm supposed to push a button. I find it. Nothing happens.

Hyperventilating, I call out the window to Maury, "How does it start?"

"Put your foot on the brake."

"No, nothing." I'm panting like Amber on a hike.

"Jean, it's engaged. It's just quiet."

And, indeed, it is a silent engine. A distracting screen shows me there are cars pulling behind me.

I drive a few blocks with my arms fully extended because I don't know which knob adjusts the steering wheel. I take a breath. It's luxurious inside with a burled wood curved console between the seats. I'm in a space ship. My left hand scrambles along the door for buttons to roll down the windows.

A loud ringing echoes around me. I pat my breasts for the trēo. It's not coming from my cleavage. I search the tote. I press the Blue Tooth. Ringing persists.

"Hello? Hello?" I ask swiveling my head. I press buttons on the steering wheel and the dashboard with frantic abandon. A dial tone buzzes. The music of Ravel starts. It's coming from someplace else. But where? Ravel intensifies to a measured higher pitch, the part where some people scream in sexual ecstasy and others commit suicide.

"Hello?" I gasp.

Maury's voice announces itself out of a speaker above the rearview mirror. "Jean, it's me. Look on the steering wheel. Click the black switch."

Thank goodness I'm stopped at a light. My panicky palm palpates the steering wheel like a blind person reading the floors in an elevator. I find it. Ravel starts again with ferocity. I'm in the middle of a violent symphony without an instrument. Maury's voice fills the car. He has surround-sounded me into oblivion.

"Can you hear me?"

I glance at the people in the next car who turn in my direction. "Hear you? Everyone can hear you."

I listen to frantic clicking.

". . . called," I hear him say.

"Who called?" I ask, shouting at the speaker. "Have the Krishna-O'Halloran's cancelled?"

"Lara. She's upset. You hung up on the baby."

9

STRESS RELIEF TIP: Make quick decisions. Let your intuition guide you. Agonizing wastes time.

—A Primer to Spiritual Guidance

THE POST-ANALYSIS DINNER PARTY DISCUSSION GOES LIKE THIS:

"Maury, what made you think the Krishna-O'Hallorans would make interesting dinner companions?"

"He's a psychiatrist. Very bright. She's a radiologist from India. I thought they'd be scintillating."

"He barely said a word the entire night. And she was beyond boring."

"I know, I know. I'm sorry. You're better at picking friends."

"Even one of Glee's crazy parties is better than two silent, glum doctors."

And so it goes.

Meaningful communication happens every day in our comfortable but messy bedroom. With my croaky morning voice interspersed with Maury's deep one, we engage in intimate conversations about what's happening that day, the kids, their problems, our work. Later we often chuckle about people and their strange behaviors. Sometimes it's even family members.

There's a stack of political, historical, and environmental books on the floor. The last four weeks of *The New York Times Book Review*, *Ms.* and *Newsweek* sit on my nightstand and a travel-size Scrabble set for a hot midnight game graces Maury's side.

A flat screen TV with extra speakers hangs opposite our king-size bed that's covered with beige pillows. A silky spread turned to the wrong side covers it. Maury wants to know why we don't use the "good" side. Women get it. We have towels in the bathroom just for show, too.

Our robes drape across the bench at the end of the bed. Under the bed another world exists—a few pair of sneakers, plastic slip-on shoes, his inside-out socks, discarded magazines and two suitcases. A lounge chair with a chenille throw nestles an unfolded basket of laundry. A humidifier and air filter stand at each end of a room, *de riguer* for mid-life baby boomers with a host of allergies.

I'm drying myself after a quick shower while Maury goes through an assortment of treasures on his dresser: old golf tees, unused money clips, receipts, five different remotes for the TV, CD and DVD players, single socks, plastic name tags, lots of change, an assortment of spare batteries for all his electronic devices plus a giant set of earphones so he can watch the invasion of Normandy *ad nauseum* on the History Channel while I read. He picks up each item as though it has infinite meaning and puts it back in the same spot.

He's told me not to touch his stuff so I wait until it gets really bad and issue ultimatums like, "I'm cleaning up your dresser today, like it or not" or "I read an article about mental illness. People who hoard junk are borderline schizophrenics." Then I attack with a vengeance leaving everything in neat piles. He usually doesn't notice it's been straightened up.

Maury continues to examine each item as though he's never seen it before as he recites his golf game to me. He holds up a black sock to a brown one, sniffs a T-shirt, dropping it to the floor and smiles with pleasure. The dresser looks the same as when he started.

"I shot a forty-five on the front nine and a fifty-two on the back. My best drive was on the eleventh. I'm thinking birdie, but the second shot looked perfect when it left my club. But it took a bad bounce at the edge of the green."

"I feel kinda funny."

Maury doesn't hear me.

"I wound up in a trap. Took three strokes to get out 'cause it was a fried egg. Anyway, I finally, got the ball on the green. I was convinced it was going to break left, but it broke right so I three-putted for a snowman."

Fried eggs? Snowmen? It's sweet that he shares, but I'm lost.

I hang up my towel and retreat inside my closet to spar with a feisty pair of Spanx I bought. I still feel a little weird. No matter. I pull and tug elastic over my thighs and hips, biting my bottom lip. If only they had this for upper arms. I suck in my stomach. Time to eliminate baked potatoes, linguini and bread pudding.

Maury has no idea of the battle raging behind my closet door. I wiggle, jump and squeeze to get my squashed body positioned. With a few more wrenches I'm in a contraption that smoothes me. I feel dizzy from the effort.

I'm being strangled from my thighs to my crotch to the bottom of my brassiere. I'm svelte but I can't breathe. My arm feels numb. My breasts are pushed so high I look like a pre-menstrual Dolly Parton.

Maury's transported himself back to the golf course.

What is he talking about? He continues as I step with caution out of my well of a closet. Hanging onto the door jamb I may look slimmer, but I can barely move. If someone placed me in a mannequin pose, I could stand breathing in a shallow fashion for about fifteen minutes. Otherwise, I don't think this is going to work for me. A sudden headache plows into my frontal lobe.

Maury turns around. He eyes me up and down.

"What?" I ask, heaving a bit.

"Wow."

"Maury, it's a girdle." I lean with my back into the doorway, a bad imitation of a young Lauren Bacall luring Bogie.

He squints at me. "A girdle? I thought no one wore those anymore."

I explain about muffin tops and muffins in general. "Trans-fats are ruining our bodies." Suddenly, I double over with the excruciating pain in my head.

"Jean, what's the matter?" Maury rushes to my side.

"I dunno. Really bad headache all of a sudden. My arm's numb."

"Look at me." Maury tilts my chin toward him.

"Huh? I'm okay. Just a little dizzy. Have to get to my mom's and . . ." The words feel funny coming out.

Maury stares at my face. "I'm calling 9-1-1. Don't move."

I collapse where I'm standing. "Waz happening? I don't feel very well."

I hear Maury but he sounds far away. He's calling an ambulance?

When I open my eyes at Scottsdale Healthcare my family is surrounding the bed. It seems as though they're all asking me questions at once: How do you feel? Did you black out? What does this mean? Can you still babysit?

Maury says, "Shush. Your mom had a TIA, a transient ischematic attack. It's a mini-stroke. She had all the symptoms but there's no damage."

Lara gets weepy. "But is mommy going to be all right?"

"Honey, don't cry," I mumble, reaching for her hand.

"Your mother is getting excellent care. I checked my watch when it happened. When I saw one side of her face was droopy and she had a sudden headache, I called nine-one-one."

"Why didn't you just pick her up and drive her to the hospital?" asks Michael with an edge in his voice.

"Because patients who don't arrive by ambulance wait an hour longer in the ER. She needed a clot-busting drug ASAP."

"Oh," says Michael, sheepish.

I sense the tension in the room. "That's enough. I feel fine," I say, still wondering how I got here and why I'm wearing a hospital gown. I put my hand under the covers and touch my midriff. "Where's my Spanx?"

"They cut that nonsense off you," says Maury.

"Maury! Do you have any idea how long it took me to get into them?"

"Yeah, forget about wearing them ever again. You probably had a stroke because of it. And no more stressing out over too many things to do. I'm going to be your doctor and nurse."

"Do me a favor," I say. "Don't tell my mother."

10

A FEW DAYS AFTER MY SCARE I'm getting back to my routine, although it's at a slower pace. The mini-stroke has shaken me to my core. I felt so vulnerable lying in the hospital bed. Maury says it was a warning and I'd better heed it. We start our day at the kitchen table.

"I was watching the Discovery Channel last night. Did you know the ice shelf at the poles is melting so fast polar bears and grizzlies are mating?" he asks me.

"Really?" I say with a touch of fake surprise, taking a sip of tea. I don't have any physical residual from my "episode" as I refer to it but mentally I'm on high alert.

"Yup. Scientists found a specimen they're calling a *prizzlie*." He looks at me with interest. "Hey, you look great. Where are you going? You may not have to go to therapy but you've got to take it easy."

My dress, a summery affair with flowers, is hippyish with

some style. "I am. I'm picking up my mother to take her over to visit the kids. They have temper tantrums because she won't let them touch anything at her place. After that I'm helping April with her pet luncheon."

"Are you sure you're not doing too much?" he asks me.

I peck him on the cheek as he stares at the newspaper, which has shrunken to two sections and ten pages.

"I can handle it," I say, making an exit with my loaded tote.

The kids play in Lara's empty living room with wall-to-wall plastic Playskool toys and Big Wheels. They shriek and throw empty containers of Tastybabys, an organic frozen food that's essential for caring, eco-friendly mommies.

"Children were seen and not heard in my day," says my mother. Lara and I look at each other. Our visit is almost over. GG, short for great-grandmother, has left little impact on the child rearing capabilities of my daughter.

I drop my mother off and drive to April's to assist with Pets on Parade, a major fundraiser for a no-kill shelter on the outskirts of Phoenix.

April answers the door glammed-up in a low-cut yellow top, a wide snakeskin belt with studs, jeans and yellow stilettos. She jingles an animal charm bracelet at me. "It's all I have left except for a few pieces in the bank vault. Police still don't have a clue. No fingerprints. No witnesses. Not even a vehicle sighting."

She hugs me. "How are you feeling?"

"I feel great. Good as new. How is he casing the homes?" I

ask, avoiding more discussions about my health.

"I don't know. That's the mystery. I'm using my insurance money to replace it with fakes."

She guides me to her dining room table, a contemporary glass slab with a metallic art base surrounded by zebra fabric chairs. It's the staging area for addressing and sorting invitations into zip codes.

"Where's Glee?" I ask.

"She had an appointment with her nutritional coach. He has her on a diet of no meat, no chicken, no fish, no dairy and no fruit."

"What's she eating?"

"I don't know, but she looks great."

"Sorry I missed her. Would've been fun for us to do this together. I couldn't come earlier. Took my mom over to see the kids."

"Honey, you've got to slow down. I'm busy, too, but look how relaxed I am. If it wasn't for the little bit of stress I have getting ready for events, I'd have no heartbeat at all. People die rushing. Stress kills."

"I know, I know." If that's true I'm almost dead.

"I read in *Vogue* that there's a link between emotional stress and health. Heart attacks and strokes strike type-A personalities. You've already had a neon-light warning." April leans back in her chair, crossing her arms.

Everyone thinks they're a doctor. "I'm not going to keel over from doing errands. I'm just a little maxxed out, that's all. It was a fluke." I pick up a handful of envelopes addressed in gold ink with paw prints scattered across the outside.

"Jean, I worry about you. Glee and I are putting together a relaxation plan for you."

"April, I don't have time for any more activities."

April shakes her head in frustration as she snaps rubber bands around envelopes and stacks them in a Louboutin shoe box. A photograph of the shoes is still pasted on the end—pumps with periwinkle netting, black heels and trademark red soles.

I slide out an invitation printed on heavy card stock with gold lettering. A table near the runway goes for $25,000, the AKC Standard Poodle level. Individual seats in the back are $150, the Dog Catcher section.

My phone interrupts with a serenade of *Hava Nagilah*. Rivka. I bend over to search my tote. April touches my arm. "Like that. Don't answer it. You can't be everything to everybody."

"But . . ." I sink backward.

"Nothing will happen if you don't answer the phone." April sticks on a stamp with precision.

"What about checking emails? Should I blow those off too?"

Hava Nagilah has accelerated to the part where, when we're dancing the *hora* at an event we've all gathered hands, crowding into the middle, crushed by revelers.

"Emails are time-consuming with all those jokes and forwarded slide shows of cute animals. Want to know what I'm doing?"

"What?"

The musical ringing has stopped.

"I'm shutting down. Email's been cutting into my personal time."

"April, all your time is personal."

"I know. And I want to keep it that way. Listen to me." She bends toward me with her dark-fringed aquamarine eyes blinking. "Dump the email. Get a Swedish massage. It's for your own good." She picks up my hands that have been busy sorting zip codes. "Get a manicure." She looks through the glass table. "At least a pedicure."

I curl my toes, pressing my lips together. "I'm taking care of it later."

When I leave I consider her suggestions. Maybe she's right. Do I have to respond to everything? What would happen if I never checked email again? The thought gives me chills. Worse, am I going to be at the Dog Catcher's table?

The good news is I've already scheduled a pedicure that will smooth my sandpaper heels and give me pretty feet. Best of all, it's time to relax.

The salon, located in an upscale strip mall in Scottsdale, is operated by Vietnamese women who exude an air of slight hostility. No one ever says hello or smiles but it's packed. It's inexpensive and convenient. Glee and April, accustomed to being fawned over, go to one of the fancy spas where they lean against red and purple tasseled silk pillows sipping mint refreshers. I'm a few minutes late for the appointment.

Mai, a petite Asian with diminutive features, stands at the

counter berating a well-coiffed woman. Her high-pitched nasal voice sounds accusatory. "What you mean no appointment? You sink we fit you in? You see we busy."

"But I called earlier and you said to come in."

"Oh no. You no talk to me. You must call different salon." Mai peers at her appointment book.

"But I have a wedding. I need Kabucki Crème. Look," she says, thrusting out a diamond encrusted hand with chipped polish. "A broken nail."

Mai stands her ground. "You no in my book. No one can take you now."

"But that lady's not busy," says the potential customer, pointing to an eighty-pound doll with a dark bob.

"No. No appointment, no nails. You come tomorrow."

The woman leaves, dejected.

Tinny elevator music emits from an overhead speaker while a silent television tuned to a local show displays lawn mowers. Besides the standard pictures of manicured nails with charms glued to them, there's an altar on a red-foiled shelf with a Buddha, incense sticks and a vase of green bamboo.

"Ah, Jeanie, how you been? Why you so late? You pick polish," says Mai, shaking a finger at me.

I grab a pearl beige color and follow her pin-sized ass to the middle of the room.

The scolding continues until I sit perched high in a vibrating Barclalounger, the rolling fumes of Clorox wafting around me.

"Why you pick this color? No good against your skin. You

let Mai pick for you." She hops up, returning from the front of the shop with a purplish-brown prune color. She pulls my feet out of the disinfectant, towels them off and starts her routine of clipping, filing, massaging and deriding.

"How come you wait so long? Mai have to cut so much. You come more often." The top of her small head shakes back and forth in disgust.

I say nothing as she spews out what sounds like Vietnamese curses to the woman next to her. They both giggle.

Mai's in a long line of other straight-haired Asian women filing, pumicing and painting. They wear glittery T-shirts and miniscule jeans on Barbie bodies. Most have little flowers painted on their toes with jeweled accents, their feet pushed into rhinestone flip-flops.

Above them perch plump blondes on cell phones. I'm one of them disguised as a curly-haired brunette. We're all making our feet beautiful. High-heeled expensive sandals sit next to each vibrating black chair, except for my well-worn navy Birkenstocks that I changed into after I left April's.

Mai bends over my feet clucking. The woman next to me speaks into her red mobile with a megaphone voice, reviewing her entire stock portfolio. The social engineer on the other side chatters about a society event she attended, her fingers splayed to dry her nails.

I overhear her say, "Did you know the Rock Burglar struck again? Maureen Devoro lost her heirloom emerald necklace. Been in her family for ages."

I am eavesdropping. Mai squeezes psychedelic rubber

separators between my toes so they stick out like a fan.

The busybody continues with pauses. "Yes, she's heart-sick about it . . . about seven carats . . . through the laundry room window . . . they were out at the pool having sunset cocktails . . . no one saw a thing . . . very brazen."

The Rock Burglar again? This is so scary. Is someone looking at the Rubin household? The idea that a robber could be so bold shocks me. I hyperventilate as I go through my "what if" litany.

What if he broke in while I was at home? What if he threatened me? What if I had to defend myself? What if he finds out I don't have anything valuable? Maury says if I'm ever in danger I should make loud noises and start kicking. Instead of spinning and spewing I'd be frozen with fear.

Mai nods at me. "Okay, you finished but you need to bake," she says, tapping my leg. With precision she folds thin pink rubber thongs between my toes.

I shuffle over to a table with ultraviolet light and position my feet. Mai drops my tote bag, keys and water bottle next to me. "You pay now."

As I scramble through my purse *Hava Nagilah* begins to play in earnest.

I put the phone to my ear, "Rivka?" I hear crying. "Are you all right?" More sobbing. We haven't had much contact since I nixed the fertility vacation plan. "Honey, stop crying. I can't understand you." With the phone in the crook of my neck I hand Mai money plus a tip. "Whatever you're so upset about can't be that bad." Rivka continues to blubber incoherently.

I glance at my toes in the incandescent light. They look like ten spoiled grapes. Not that Maury will notice, but if he does, he'll hate the color. I can hear him now. "Jean, it looks like something died on top of your feet."

"Sweetheart, I can't understand you. Is Michael there? Put him on."

A blowsy blonde with fly-away hair and plumped red lips sits down across from me. Her clothes are too tight for her body. She puts her spread-out fingers under the purple light at waist level, her feet across from mine. She glances at my toes and makes a face.

I listen while Rivka continues to whimper in the background. Michael talks. It takes him a few minutes to register his plea. I furrow my brow forgetting where I am.

"We've been to three specialists. I feel guilty asking you and dad about money for IVF, but Rivka's family can't afford it. Her mother's a devout Catholic and it's against the church's teachings."

"What's wrong with IVF if a couple can't conceive? April's daughter is pregnant with $40,000 twins. Why's it the Pope's business?"

"Mom, I don't know. Rivka wants a big family. We're stalled. We want Jacob to have siblings. She got pregnant so easily the first time."

He doesn't have to remind me of the year we all lived together. "I'm aware."

He continues, "Don't think we haven't been trying either. It's not even fun anymore."

This is way too much information.

"It's just so expensive. She was scared to call you so I'm asking."

Do we have a choice? "I want you to be parents again so we have another grandchild. What can I do? We'll cash in dad's IRA and raid his pension plan."

"Oh, mom. I don't want you to do that."

"Darling, where do you think money comes from? We're not ATM machines. All I can say is, when we're old and drooling, pick a modest but clean place and don't make me go to craft classes to make pine-cone turkeys."

"Mom. You know Rivka and I will take good care of you. Lara and Gus too."

Oy. If these four are in charge, we'd better make plans to start our seniors-for-peace commune now.

"Mom, there is another solution."

"Let's have it."

I lean back in my chair.

"Rivka thinks you'll say no."

I pull my feet out of the light.

"Shit."

The blonde's mouth makes an "O" and her eyes get wide.

"Mom?"

I've *shmushed* the polish on my olive-looking big toe. I lick my finger and bend down to mash the hideous color back in place. It doesn't work.

"Rivka and I found a place that does IVF for $3000."

"Michael, this is not the time to look for bargains. Your dad and I will do what's necessary so you can expand your family." *Even if it bankrupts us.* I examine my toe.

Should I ask Mai to repair it? She'll yell at me. "Jean, you no sit still. What's matter with you?"

"The Czech Republic does IVF for $3000!"

A serious medical procedure in another country? "Do you speak Czech?" I pull out the rubber thongs. With extreme dexterity I unwind the *separators* between my toes. *I am calm, I am calm*, I repeat to myself.

"Well, no."

"Honey, listen to me. Are you paying attention?"

"Uh-huh," says Michael without enthusiasm, knowing he probably hasn't sold me on the idea. He's not one to give up. A vision of him as a five-year-old who wouldn't stay in bed flashes in front of me, the original *Let's Make A Deal* kid. I slip into my Birkenstocks without doing any more damage.

In a soft measured voice I say, "Listen carefully. I want you and Rivka to go into your bedroom, turn out the lights, put on a Barry White CD and screw your brains out."

My blonde nail buddy stands up and gives a grunt of displeasure, staring me down.

"It is highly inappropriate to use that kind of language in Scottsdale," she says, grabbing her Gucci bag and shuffling away in green rubber.

"Michael, are you there?"

"Yes," he sighs.

"It's free."

My nail-buddy speaks to Mai, pointing at me. Mai shakes

her head.

Michael has hung up. I gather my belongings. It's hard to move with ease or dignity—keys in one hand, a water bottle in the other and my tote on my shoulder.

Mai's voice screeches above the din of the salon.

"You upset my customer."

I shrink.

"You no come back to my salon."

I feel eyes boring into me as I hustle toward the door. *Hava Nagilah* begins again. I juggle my belongings to find my pesky trēo.

"Hello? Hello?" I change position holding the instrument closer to my ear.

"Mom? We got cut off. Hold on. Rivka wants to say something."

"Momma Jean, I want to thank you for helping us have another baby."

"Uh—stop sniffling. Of course we'd love for you to have more babies. I think it's a wonderful idea."

I've committed. Wait until I tell Maury he's not retiring 'til 2022 and that I'm banned from *Sassy Nails* forever.

11

STRESS RELIEF TIP: Evidence shows that regular deep breathing reduces food cravings, improves sleep and boosts energy.
—*Breathing for Beginners*

MAURY'S ON A DIET.

I wouldn't say the pounds are melting away, but he appears slimmer. Sandwiches on toasted rye slathered with mayonnaise, Dijon mustard, stacked with salami, turkey and cheese have disappeared. There's no evidence of bread crumbs or tomato seeds down the front of the cabinets. I can't find Diet-Coke rings or spilled smelly pickle juice on the counters either. He's been eating low fat yogurt for a week.

This morning he plunges into the day early, zipping past me after a shower, a waft of fresh soap in his wake. No tightie-whities either. Instead, he's wearing dark black-watch plaid boxers.

"Maury?" I pause, my brush hovering mid-air as I try to wrangle through my hair.

"Hmmm?" He's searching his closet which is unusual. He usually grabs whatever his hand touches. Color, not important, texture, superfluous. As long as it's solid on the bottom he wears it.

"You bought your own underwear?"

"Huh? Oh these? Yeah, a few of the other pairs had a coupla holes so I tossed them."

I narrow my eyes. Maury hasn't bought his own underwear and socks in . . . years. More like never. "Where did you get them?"

"Stopped into Dillards. Three in a package. You like them?" He turns around for me. He's definitely looking slimmer.

"You bought underwear retail?"

"Jeez, Jean, where else do you go?"

Before I start a lecture on discount shopping I bite my lip. This is unusual. If he signs up for Hair Club for Men next week . . .

I mull over his new behavior. I've checked out magazine surveys to find out whether your husband is faithful. Has there been a change in his diet? Yes. Exercise? Yes. New interests? Who knows? Has he bought new underwear? Yes. Three in a package.

I turn around to study him. I'm slathering moisturizer on my face and neck. I'm religious about my skin care. I don't want to shrivel up in the desert sun like an overcooked quesadilla.

He stops in front of the full length mirror and turns sideways, stroking his belly with a smile. Then he curls his arm, flexing his bicep.

"Okay, hon, I'm off to the gym. Then I have office hours. Love you. See ya later." Maury's index finger holds a hanger with a shirt, tie and pair of pants over his shoulder. He exits clutching a gym bag in his other hand.

I check my watch. Today I need to stop at Trader Joe's to stock up on wine and gourmet goodies, check-in with my mother, which she hates because no matter how long I stay she says, "You're leaving already?", fill in for a professor on a panel, attend a client's staff meeting to educate them on the new gender equality procedures and oversee a stump removal from the olive tree in our front yard that activates my allergies into a dripping faucet. I also want to see Jacob and mend fences with Rivka.

My whirling mind spins past the Green Party, Pets on Parade and the kid's infertility worries to Maury's changes. In a moment of insecurity I call Glee.

I stretch out on my bed, pillows propped up behind me. It's a luxury to talk on the phone without multi-tasking.

I love hearing about Glee's boyfriends. I've been with the same man so long that we communicate in sign language and grunts. Glee has the experience of exploration—new ideas, new customs, new sex.

I hunker down, holding the phone close to my ear. We chat for a few minutes about her new European boyfriend, Stavros, who sounds like an improvement over the last guy, a half-Apache, half-Jewish guy with a long ponytail and rage issues.

"Glee, can I ask you a question and you promise to tell me the truth?"

"Jean, I'm a certified professional intuitive life coach."

"Well, I've never considered this before, but . . ." I throw my head back to gulp for air, inhaling and exhaling a long breath.

"Get it out, honey."

"Do you think Maury would ever cheat on me?" The words tumble out like tragic clowns in a toy car at the circus.

"Why are you asking?"

I spit out my story of the sexy environmentalist and diets and new underwear in bursts of I know this is ridiculous, but.. . and I can't believe my Maury would and clichés such as the wife is the last to know.

Glee doesn't say anything for a while.

I take a few more deep breaths with my eyes closed, brushing my hand across my neck. Damp. A stickiness has invaded my pits, cleavage, the back of my knees.

"I would never say a man can't be tempted, but from what I know of you and Maury and your relationship, I'd say it's highly unlikely."

I let out a sigh of relief. "How do you know?"

"Because Maury is a no-nonsense guy who's bright and uncomplicated and devoted to you. No way is he going to jeopardize his family. Besides, he adores you."

"But how do you know?" I nibble the cuticle on my thumb.

"Because you're still having wild sex."

Suddenly I'm embarrassed at how much I've shared with my friend. I look around at my bed. "I am?" Have I exaggerated?

"That's what you said. Remember the time you dressed up as a French maid? What about the time you practically fell off the bed after my biker party? Men love black leather. They don't stray if they're satisfied."

"It was *pleather*, not leather." I grab a tissue from my night stand to pat my neck. "I'll relax." I breathe in through my nose and expel the air slowly through my mouth. My heart stops the struggle to get out of my chest.

"Doesn't mean you shouldn't keep your eyes and ears open, but you've got a winner. It would help if you took a walk. Smell the flowers. Are you taking St. John's Wort to alleviate stress?"

"It's hard for me with so much to do."

"You have to do something for relief. Take the supplements and go outside if you're not going to incorporate yoga and meditation into your life. Join a self-help group. You'll expire at this rate. The level of stress you're under is corrosive. You've already had a health warning."

"I know. April tells me to slow down too. It's amazing the burglary hasn't made her more nervous. I'd be a wreck if someone had been in my space. She's still peaceful, doing her routine, working on the pet luncheon."

"April's a very evolved soul."

"What does that mean?"

"I'm an intuitive so I can tell which souls have been through the life cycle many times. She's an old soul who's learned a lot."

"What about me? Am I an old soul?"

"Well, let's just say you're in the learning process."

I change the subject. "How do you think the burglar knew April had that much jewelry at home?"

"I think the Rock Burglar targets victims when they know there's a big event coming up like the Heart Ball," says Glee, her bangle bracelets tinkling. "Burglars know women go to their safe deposit boxes to take out cocktail rings, his and hers Rolexes and diamond earrings. Since the events are on the weekend no one gets back to the bank until Monday."

"Oh. But that wasn't the Heart ball weekend." My hand settles on my chest. Sympathetic anxiety.

"Yes, but they probably knew she didn't wear that yellow diamond to the salon. They watch people for weeks. Maybe months."

"But how do they know who to target?" Would anyone want my three wood bead necklaces from Chico's?

Glee loves to be an authority. "First of all, there are free magazines with socialite photos of all the charitable events. April's been in those publications dozens of times draped in her jewels. They're want ads for crooks. They read too."

Evil people clipping my friend's pictures for a file labeled Rich Broads? Disturbing.

"Secondly, a crook can follow you home from a luncheon and case your house. Didn't you read the article that the Rock Burglar has committed over two hundred robberies in the last five years?"

"Sort of." Sometimes I just skim. "But how'd they know where to find April's treasures?"

"Women usually have them near the bathroom sink or tucked away in their closet until they can return them. April has that highboy with all her jewelry displayed. If they're like me they usually try on a few different pieces to see what looks best with their outfit. The best decision is a personal safe. I've had one built in to every house I've owned."

"I don't know what I'd put in it. My mother hid her jewlery in the freezer. I almost ate a pearl earring with the defrosted string beans one time."

"Only you. Oh, have to run. Stavros is picking me up for tantric yoga. You should try it. It sustains orgasms. Later. And don't worry about Maury."

I finish up early at my client's so I stop at Rivka's and Michael's to see my grandson, Jacob, on the way home.

"Hi baby. Mimi's here." He hugs my legs as I stroke back his hair.

Rivka bursts into tears.

"You don't want me to have another baby," she says bawling.

"What? I never said that. I said we'd help."

"You implied it." With a runny nose she looks awful—uncombed hair, wrinkled clothes, sloppy. When Michael met her she was a Jennifer Lopez look-alike in a pencil skirt, stilettos and talon nails. A lot has happened since then. The voluptuous Latina, Rosa, who has evolved into a modern Orthodox maven, Rivka, observes the Judaic laws of modesty. She wears full length skirts, long-sleeves and reveals none of the Mexican bosom that drove my son wild.

However, she doesn't cover her hair. The truly observant only let their husband see their tresses. She told me she doesn't wear a wig or scarf because it's too hot.

"C'mere," I say, gathering her up for a hug, stroking her

thick mahogany hair. "Everything's going to be all right. You have to be relaxed to get pregnant. Tell you what—Maury and I will babysit this weekend for your anniversary. Go out on date."

Ugh. What did I just do? Another Saturday night of Disney videos, making peanut butter and gooey jelly sandwiches, playing Lincoln Logs and chasing their yippie dog around the living room?

I play Fish with Jacob, read him a book and get out of there. I head for home without stopping at my mother's.

Maury's home watching the local, if it bleeds it leads, news with a bottle of water, nibbling a rice cake.

I'm bushed after a busy day and presenting on a panel at the community college for an ill professor. Where I once had status, my former department head met me with derision, even though I was doing her a favor. She thinks I'm an insubordinate.

Before I was fired from my job as a Women's Studies professor, which Flora Beaudreaux engineered, I was well-respected in the academic community. I still have the credentials but I'm viewed as a trouble-maker. I've got some satisfaction knowing I forged a new career for myself. And, my client and staff loved the revised proposal today.

"Did the stump removal guys show up?" I ask Maury who's taking small bites, oblivious to an anthill of crumbs on his chest.

"Nope. Guy called. His mother's sick. He'll call you back to re-schedule."

That makes me angry. People make appointments, then don't show up. I dump my things, wash up and start tossing salad greens in a light poppy seed dressing. Maury has instructed me not to use calorie-infused, trans-fat ranch. I heat up left-overs, set the table and let Maury know dinner is ready.

"Honey, you gotta hear this next story. It's about the Rock Burglar."

I sit down on the end of the couch holding glistening salad tongs. The lady news anchor in a neon yellow dress has a fake spray-on orange tan, long black hair extensions with teased bangs and gold hoop earrings.

". . . and tonight, finally, a break in the Rock Burglar case which has stymied detectives. Watch this rare video clip from a security camera of a burglary in progress."

Fuzzy footage of a figure dressed in dark clothing exiting a French door fills the screen. The burglar wears a baseball cap pulled low and carries a small duffle bag. When he turns to the camera his face is covered with a ski mask. The obscure image raises his hand in an obscene gesture which the camera blurs out because he flips everyone off.

Ms. Anchor's male cohort in a matching yellow tie and extreme-whitened teeth chimes in, "If you recognize anything that could give police a clue as to the identity of the person seen on the video, please call Silent Witness." The number flashes across the screen.

The two of them banter back and forth about not having enough valuables to attract the Rock Burglar. Maury despises this kind of frivolous chatter and hits the mute button.

"Wow," I say. "But who can recognize someone in a ski mask? Maybe they'll catch 'em and April'll get her jewelry back."

"Don't count on it. That stuff's been fenced, the stones taken out and sold to the next buyer within hours. Besides, no one can identify someone from that blurry footage."

"But someone must know something. They couldn't be functioning this long unless they had an inside track. I bet if they offered a bigger reward someone would come forward."

"I doubt it. The fact is with all the problems in our Valley like violent crime, immigration issues and environmental pollution, people just don't care about jewelry. Hey babe, only salad for dinner tonight, okay?"

"Well, I heated up some *kung pao* chicken from Costco."

Maury struggles out of his slouched pose in the corner of the sofa and gathers his wine glass, magazine and rice crackers packaging.

"Jean. Don't you know there are more calories in *kung pao* chicken than eight Big Macs?"

"No. Since when have you cared?"

"I don't know. Just staying in shape."

In all the years I've been married my husband has never bought new clothes or counted calories. I eye him with suspicion.

12

I NEED A NANNY. I need someone to check my calendar, make appointments, pick me up, drive, deal with bureaucracy and handle technology. My mother has a nanny. Me.

The trēo isn't cutting it. If I can find it in the bottomless tote, I have to remember to look at it and sync it at night. The miniscule print on the tiny screen makes me want to hunt for a magnifying glass. It's not the same as having two pages laid out in front of me. I miss paper.

Although I've had a stress scare it's my mammography appointment that puts me close to the abyss. Maury insists it's a necessity for women over forty to have their breasts flattened into *latkes*, those potato pancakes we eat at Chanukah. One in seven is diagnosed with breast cancer which freaks me out. Is it the gene pool or the environment or both?

I schedule the appointment weeks before with a twenty-something chomping gum in my ear. I tap the time and day into my trēo. Her voice uses an up-tick at the end of each sentence so all her communication sounds like a question.

"Like bring your insurance card? And don't wear cream or deodorant or perfume? Park in front if you can find a space? Like if it's crowded? Park across the street?" Chomp, chomp.

Anxiety ridden, I show up early with my water, magazines, insurance information and a list of doctors who need my results—my gynecologist, my internist and of course, Maury.

Two silver-haired volunteers sit behind the information desk at the Scottsdale hospital where I'm scheduled. One of them is hunched over scanning her planner. "No, the sixty minute hot rock gets the kinks out. Not the Swedish." I give the other one my name.

She's hard of hearing so I repeat myself. Then she asks me to spell it. I'm patient. After all, I have an elderly mother.

"R-U-B-I-N."

"Rubine?" she asks.

"No." I spell my name again. She looks at her computer screen and then squints at me.

"You're not here. What's your social security number?"

I lean down to whisper it so the entire lobby can't hear my personal information.

"I'm sorry. Can you speak up? I have a hearing problem."

I repeat. She doesn't get it. I write it on the corner of my magazine and show it to her.

She nods, pecks at some keys, puts her glasses on and announces, "Nope. I'm sorry. You're not in here."

"But I have to be. It's a good thing I came early. This is very unsettling." My throat feels dry. I swallow a few times.

"What are you here for?"

I'm forced to announce, "A mammo." I wish the other one would get off the phone. She's up to, ". . .forty-five minutes is fine, the sixty minute one will bother my sciatica."

Veronica, whose plastic nametag lets me know she's a volunteer from Minnesota, blinks at me. "We don't do mammos here anymore."

"What? That's impossible. I spoke to a young woman weeks ago when I made the appointment. She told me to come to this location."

A wave of nervousness slides over me. I search in my tote and check my trēo. I peck a few keys. The appointment is there.

She squints at the electronic contraption and shrugs.

"Wait a minute. Let me call radiology. I've been out with a surgery myself. Bad gall bladder."

She checks with the radiology department. No go.

"We haven't done mammograms here for the last two years. You need our other facility on Second and Cattletrack."

"What?"

"We have a number of clinics now. Scottsdale's growing."

I appreciate the update on my city, but I was early and now I'm late, especially if I have to drive someplace else to re-park. A nanny would be helpful right now.

"Please call and tell them I'm on my way." I speed-walk out of there, my pits damp without deodorant.

At the new place a lady in pink scrubs with tinted eyeglasses and teased hair addresses me. "Welcome to Girls

Best Friend Breast Center." She's sitting in a line of desks with plexiglass partitions, a computer at each station.

I collapse on a chair in front of Beverly C. and give her my name. I also spell it two more times, give her my birth date and social security number.

"I'm sorry. I can't find you in our system."

Bile seeps up the back of my throat. "What? The other facility sent me here. I have an appointment for ten a.m." I look at my watch. 10:15.

"Maybe you're supposed to be at our Shea facility."

"No, I made an appointment for downtown Scottsdale."

Shea, many miles north of here, sits in the part of Scottsdale that's been overrun with red tiled roofs on mini-mansions, fancy golf courses and hip restaurants.

I must look pale because she asks if I'd like water. I take a deep breath and close my eyes for a moment.

Glee says to envision a place in nature that gives me peace. I focus on daisies even though I've never actually seen a field of daisies.

"No, thanks. I have water." Maybe I should join a self-help group. This kind of pressure damages me. I don't want to be a patient in a hospital. Again.

"Let me call and see if you're scheduled there."

As Beverly C. talks on the phone a droplet leaks from my hairline. I wipe it away.

"You were due there fifteen minutes ago."

"Can't I just do it here? Please?"

"I'm sorry. We don't have doctor's orders for you at this

facility."

"Can't they fax them to you from the Shea office?"

"We have to get a special order to receive paperwork from a different facility. Besides, we're booked today. I'll call Brooke in scheduling for you." She reaches for the phone.

"NO! I mean no. Please don't call Brooke. She created this mess. I'll figure it out another time." I'm losing my grip.

I gather my belongings to leave, dejected that my mission wasn't accomplished, that I've wasted half the morning. I exit though their glass door with Beverly C. shaking her head.

I smell something near my car. I look around. No one's watching. I take a quick whiff of my own armpit. I'm fermenting. I have to go home, shower again and apply deodorant.

Once I get there I tell Maury my boondoggle story.

He hugs me. "Jean, it's not you. We're living in a country with a third world medical system."

"I'm not crazy?"

"No, you just have to know how to work it. Try again," he says, crunching on a celery stick.

I re-schedule my mammogram and go to the correct place the next day because there's a cancellation. I'm uneasy all over again. My most sensitive appendage gets squashed while I wait around half-naked to see if the breast technician says it has to be re-done. I don't look at the other women in their paper robes; they don't look at me.

I feel a loss of individuality without my clothes, wedding band and watch. I have separation anxiety being away from my tote. What if someone breaks into the flimsy locker? What if they take my trēo? What if they steal my identity? Wait a minute. No one could follow my schedule.

I lean my head back, closing my eyes. The wall feels cool. I'm in the woods, Monarch butterflies dancing around my head, wood nymphs prancing around trees, their diaphanous costumes floating in the air. I open my eyes. Daydreaming doesn't help. I'm anxious until I know I can leave.

Finally, I get the nod that I can get dressed. But I can't breathe a sigh of relief yet. This clinic lets you know results within 48 hours. I hope the doctor in Bangladesh reading my x-rays has good news for me.

I feel traumatized managing my life. I go back to the nanny idea. No, that won't work. I decide to take Glee's advice and join a self-help support stress group. She has provided me with the particulars.

A few days later I find myself in the community room of a church sitting in a kindergartner's chair. Participants introduce themselves. I stare at my knees which are almost up to my chest. This group of aberrants, many also addicted to alcohol, gambling, cigarettes, sex or shopping, meets weekly. Maybe they're just addicted to meetings.

I catch on to the *modus operandi* quickly. "My name is Jean and I'm a stress addict." Murmurs acknowledge me.

I take in the environment. With tables pushed to the sides of the non-denominational Sunday school classroom, we perch on tiny chairs in a circle. The room, painted a mint green popular in the '80s, displays a crowded bulletin board of announcements and children's drawings under a large sign of "Jesus Loves You." That's a relief. I need all the help I can get.

Our facilitator, Bob, wimpy but caring, wears a blue polyester striped tie and a short-sleeved white shirt that exposes his very hairy arms. He does his best to make everyone feel involved, nodding with encouragement as each person speaks.

I listen, trying to stay focused on the others and their stories. They're average people you'd see in the mall. Who knew? We pay attention to a woman named Aubrey who's attracted to gardeners, painters and plumbers. If their cracks show, she's turned on. She's hyper-ventilating with excitement.

"Stay on point," admonishes Facilitator Bob.

My mind wanders from Aubrey, her snaky dreadlocks silhouetted in the window, who pleads her case about sweaty men and their hairy butts.

What am I doing here? Is this another waste of time? The left side of my neck and shoulder cramp up. Usually I try to rub it out, but I feel self-conscious, child-like in the miniature chair. The pain penetrates and radiates. Regurgitating my personal life with strangers makes me uncomfortable. Glee says it's therapeutic.

"Let's all welcome Jean." Bob's voice cuts into my thoughts.

Uh-oh. I've been caught checking out. I open my eyes wide and nod with enthusiasm.

"Welcome, Jean," the participants say in unison.

"Would you like to share?" Bob asks me.

I don't know where to begin. Should I start with I'm doing too much? My family is dysfunctional? I'm over committed to fixing everything for everyone?

I look down at my folded hands, twirling my thumbs. I squirm in the plastic seat. A fan in the corner of the room whirrs through the clacking of an air conditioner that rumbles on and off. It's October and very warm. Let them try to convince the population of Arizona there's no global warming. Temperature doesn't matter. I'm in a brain freeze.

"Uh—I do too much."

The group sits, supposedly without judgment. A few grumble with affirmation. "Amen, sister," murmurs Aubrey.

Encouraged to speak out about the absurdity of my world—the over-scheduled, over-achieving life I lead, the adult children with neuroses, my dependent elderly mother, my consulting business, my wonderful but distracted, possibly straying husband—I don't know how to explain my insane life.

I sigh as the group waits. If I start it'll be a train without brakes. Maury says to take things as they come. What does he know? He's semi-retired. "No one can accomplish everything in a day," is his motto. Maybe because it takes him weeks to do most things. I don't have that long. I feel compelled to make life happen now!

"Jean, would you like to offer what drives you?"

"I have a lot to accomplish. I'm a productive person who multi-tasks."

One of the men clucks his tongue, giving me an exasperated look. Our facilitator hushes him. I'm alone in a chasm of appointments, management and problems.

"Is there something that's not a priority?" Bob asks.

They don't get it.

"I can't hang up on my lonely mother or my daughter whose kid just bit another child at preschool, or my client who's waiting for a proposal, or my best friend who's starting to date after twenty years of marriage, or cancel my dentaleyegynecologistmammogramhairmanipedi appointments, or abandon my intelligent but disorganized husband, or give up my dream of writing the great American novel, or never cook, eat healthy food, exercise or. . ."

I'm out of breath and I haven't even mentioned Rivka's fertility issues. I shift my head from side to side to loosen up my neck.

"I need a nanny. Oprah has someone to shop and chop for her."

"Jean, have you thought about what you can leave out?" asks our fearless leader who's in remission from a vitamin addiction. "Let's prioritize your most important activities. I see this more as a time management problem. Even Oprah has a schedule." He pushes back in his seat to sit taller and look more authoritative.

"And three personal assistants," I add.

Suddenly I remember that I forgot my vitamins this morning. What will happen to my body without glucosamine, iron, black cohosh, dong quai, St. John's Wort and fish oil? I could dig them out with my bottle of water, but it'll be distracting. I'll do it while I'm driving to my next appointment. I don't want to tempt Facilitator Bob with his hairy arms.

"Maybe I could leave out taking my mother to her doctor, but I'd have a seventy-five-year-old Yiddish yelling woman to deal with, which is worse than taking her to the podiatrist."

Bob leans forward, his sincerity a hot water bottle of soothing words to quell my angst. "Jean, is your mother controlling your life? Are your best instincts for self-preservation being smothered?"

I chew on a hangnail. A few more people share. My mind buzzes out. It's hard to stay engaged when my list keeps rolling like never-ending credits on a bad movie. It's not that I'm not interested in the others; it's just that I can't focus on anymore problems, no matter whose they are.

Bob glances at his watch. "Well, that's all for today. See you next Tuesday. Make sure you keep your support list and phone numbers with you for life's temptations. If you haven't hooked up with a sponsor, get on it."

He claps his hands and meets everyone's gaze with a laser stare. "And for those of you with shopping issues, I have a pamphlet on why you're being fueled by big box centers."

Chairs scrape the linoleum floor as we make our exit. Daisies. I think about daisies. Not the kind pushing up on my gravesite. Just a field of beautiful yellow daisies waving in the breeze.

13

EVENTUALLY I GET MY MAMMOGRAM RESULTS. I am in excellent breast health. I sigh in relief. It puts my crazy life in perspective. I languish in that good news.

"Glee Barstow's office. Amanda speaking. How may I assist you?"

"Glee?" I adjust my headset.

"I'm sorry she's not available right now. Who's calling please?"

"Who's calling? It's Jean, her best friend. Who are you?"

"Ms. Barstow's personal assistant. How may I be of service?"

I sputter. "I'm RSVPing for her dinner party."

"We're not taking RSVPs over the phone. Only electronically. Please consult your online invite."

"But I got an invitation in the mail. Why can't you check me off on your list?"

"I'm sorry. We're not set up for that."

We're? Glee's a company? "Please tell her she'd better call me back," I say in measured tones.

Although I love and adore my precious munchkins, sometimes grandkids give me a headache. Every weekend involves a school play or carnival, pre-school graduation, dance or theater recital, religious or secular holiday, barbeque, family brunch and endless games of T-ball, soccer and basketball for midgets. It all takes place in hellish weather that requires lawn chairs, hats, portable umbrellas, sunscreen, snacks that don't melt, preferably organic granola bars with the texture of corrugated cardboard, and a cooler with bottles of water and drinks to replenish electrolytes. I feel green guilt using plastic that wastes in the landfills for eons, but the politically correct re-usable one that Lara carries makes the cooler too heavy to lift.

The most tortuous events are the birthday parties, rituals of competition for miniature princes and princesses who are oblivious to the hours of preparation for an extravaganza in their honor. I've been to a Barney party with the living room-cum-playroom decorated in furry purple animals, a Power Rangers cook out, an Oscar the Grouch event with garbage cans and a princess party that included trunks of costumes, a manicurist, wigs and satin shoes with ostrich feathers. What happened to one clown?

There's competition between moms to see who can be the most creative. Stealing an idea constitutes a serious offense. Presents have to be age-appropriate, without too many moveable parts. Moms vigilant about their progeny don't want anything swallowed, put up their nose or lost in the sofa, especially the latter because it could leave a permanent impression on someone's behind. Gifts must also be ecologically-sensitive.

I want to be an A+ grandparent, abiding by their wishes, but they're so much more particular than we were. It's a miracle our kids survived without special car seats, daily sunscreen number fifty and overdosing on red dye number two from all the Jell-o we fed them. The host mom, responsible for the required favor so every child leaves with a gift and feels special, has to reinforce the theme and be politically correct. At Buzz's last birthday with rainbows and unicorns, I wrapped party favors for twenty with three sheets of tri-color tissue paper. I also helped Lara strip buns off hot dogs for kids who were gluten-free, took away snacks from those allergic to peanuts and hid candy from a pint-sized package of neuroses who couldn't eat sugar because of ADHD. One child had all three maladies. I'm not sure what she ate, but at one point I saw her gnawing a stuffed bear.

Small talk drives me wild. The robotic *kvetchy* mommies, all blond and bobbed, talk about nothing. At the last birthday party I got stuck between one worrying about what age her child should be to have a Wii and another making play dates for her two- year-old on her Blackberry.

Did we spend endless hours discussing scheduled C-sections, breast pumps and toilet training? I sent my kids outside to play. Apparently that's unheard of now.

In fact, the ones wearing maternity tops decorated with lace like my grandmother's nightgowns over expensive jeans are *not* with child. If they are, they flaunt their mommy martyrdom by wearing bikinis or a tight top, belly buttons exposed.

Sometimes Maury accompanies me so he can take pictures or video. Then he disappears into the family room with the other men who have shown up to watch a game.

I, of course, am required to assist, especially with the massive clean-up, which includes moving furniture, keeping the gifts straight so the parents can be thanked, and disposing of piles of wrapping paper, plastic decorations, plates, forks and disgusting half-eaten food. Not exactly an ecological example.

I miss empty weekends. I hope Jacob's bowling bash will be uneventful and that no one drops a ball on a tiny foot. Maury's been called for first aid a few times.

It's only three weeks until the election. We've got lots to do including door-to-door canvassing, calling Independents from phone lists and soliciting for funds. I'm responsible for helping Brian with some stats; Maury's in charge of drafting policy and supplying the candidate with accurate information. The latest poll says Craig Burton's twenty-five points behind Flora. It's a huge gap but our team remains positive with a glimmer of hope.

I have a complete inability to sleep. If I take a sleeping pill I'm exhausted the next day. If I don't, I'm a zombie. I get up in the middle of the night to write my feelings in a journal, which creates clarity according to the experts. I'm so clouded.

While Maury saws wood and wrestles mammoths, I wander the house communicating my inner thoughts. Supposedly if I get it all down on paper, I can let it go. I write and write, creating dialogue of what I should have said to my client about the necessity of child-care resources or to Michael about finding a job or to Rivka about having another baby. Finally, I wander back to bed to stare at the ceiling another few hours. Maury says insomnia points to depression.

The trēo, rather than simplifying my life complicates it. I dial the miniscule keypad a few times before I get a number correct. I can't carry a magnifying glass with me a la Sherlock Holmes; the tote's heavy enough. I check my old planner often to make sure I'm still functioning.

The trēo's impossible to use while driving. I have auto-dial but sometimes I don't hold down the key long enough for a connection. I'm supposed to be hands-free but have trouble co-ordinating it with the Blue Tooth. It loses stored numbers; I forget to synchronize and lose data.

Maury tries to assist me but gets frustrated. We spend hours at the kitchen table going through the mini-reference guide, a small square book printed in two languages that doesn't stay open. An improvement would be larger print, spiral bound and not upside-down half-way through. Even if we do get information it doesn't help.

"Sometimes these devices are quirky," he tells me.

"Quirky? Quirky makes me crazy. It has to work all the time."

"Now, Jean . . ."

In desperation I take it back to the big box electronics store located in a giant discount shopping center where it was purchased. I've failed. It's like returning an untrained puppy.

I wait for a very long time at the counter. Only one person runs the check out, an eye-brow pierced, three pony-tailed young woman. An elderly gentleman can't find the right credit card. In turn she can't figure out the return policy because his camera is not in its original packaging. She lisps with her pierced tongue. Eventually he leaves after signing multiple pieces of paper.

Once in front of her, I put the trēo on the counter.

"I need help with this. I get can't it synced to the Blue Tooth and . . ."

She listens, a bored look on her face, and interrupts. "Excusth me but that's noth our department. Let me call a thales rep for you." She reaches behind her to a wall phone and her microphoned voice echoes through the store. "Thervice to the floor, thervice to the floor."

I move down the counter so a couple wearing Bermudas with socks and sandals can make a purchase. I lean back on my elbows to wait, wondering about the skill level of the person in charge of personnel and human resources.

Achmed, whose name is printed in bold white letters on a

blue plastic nametag attached to his white shirt appears through grey swinging doors in the back of the store. He's in the middle of lunch. There's a small stain on his tie, a drop of orange oil sits at the corner of his lip. He has large brown eyes fringed by very long dark lashes.

"I'm having a lot of problems with this."

He nods.

"I can't get my Blue Tooth and phone to synchronize."

He nods.

"It's dangerous for me to drive with one hand. My Blue Tooth is a necessity."

He takes them from me and disappears. Thirty minutes passes. I can't even make phone calls because he has my lifeline. I wander the DVD section. Who buys movies? Isn't it enough to watch a bad one once? Why watch it again? Unless they're children. Tangie's watched *Shrek* two dozen times, fascinated with the big ugly green guy.

Finally, Achmed appears. The orange spot is gone from his mouth. "It is working now," he says, handing me both devices.

I don't ask what the problem was because I won't understand it anyway.

"Great. Thank you so much. You have saved humanity from a reckless driver."

I slip the Blue Tooth around my ear, dialing my mother. I don't really want to talk to her right now, but she doesn't get up until after the fourth ring anyway. I hang up. It works.

Achmed punches information into his computer while asking me a few questions. He's probably tagging me as a nutcase who shouldn't be allowed to have an electronic device.

I leave, get in my car, snap on the seat belt with its hot metal clasps and dial Maury. The dial tone burps from the phone. I pick it up and press it against my other ear.

"Maury? Can you hear me?"

"Sort of."

I explain my dilemma. He suggests I go back inside. I click off the scorching seatbelt, get out of the car, return to Achmed and demonstrate my problem.

I look him in the eye. "You absolutely don't want a maniacal woman on the road."

He agrees, eyes wide, and disappears into the back again.

I wait, this time exploring the phone accessories aisle. The complicated technology is encased in hard plastic. However, I'm delighted to know that I can purchase a carrying case for my trēo in pink camouflage.

Achmed returns, expressionless except for his large liquid eyes that say, 'Please let this work and make this insane lady go away.'

"It is fixed," he says with satisfaction. A wet spot gleams on his tie where he must have attacked the stain.

I slip the Blue Tooth around my ear again, pressing Maury's number with my thumb. Achmed watches me with anticipation. The call does not go through.

"The numbers on my auto-dialer are my lifeline. I have to reach my friends and family anytime, anywhere."

He nods. I take off the Blue Tooth, handing him the trēo. He fools with it a few minutes, putting it up to his ear, looking at it, even shaking it a bit.

"I will ask my manager," he says, heading toward the grey swinging doors.

Who has he been asking until now? I envision tables of employees drinking Cokes, eating sub sandwiches, laughing at incompetent, technically-challenged women.

He reappears. "We cannot fix this."

"What? But my husband bought it here."

"I am sorry. You need to go to a free-standing mobile store. We are not technicians." He hands the phone to me.

I don't want it.

Achmed views me through his long dark lashes. "Your Blue Tooth has died. You have to purchase a different one."

I'm not sure it's broken and can't be repaired, but what choice do I have? He shows me shelves lined with electronic ear buds in every size and color. While I'm looking at the critter-like devices, a fast-paced Arabic tune with a strong tambourine rhythm fills the air. It echoes around us. Achmed's hands search his pants pockets.

"Excuse me. Hello? No, I'm with a customer. I'll call you later."

I purchase a new Blue Tooth that's guaranteed to give me four hours of talk time. As I check out with a myriad of instructions, Achmed says, "Don't forget to plug it in for three hours to charge it." He grins.

I've wasted half a day and he's telling me it has to sync as long as it takes to cook a small turkey. Four more journal pages at two a.m.

But then I realize he's really been patient aiding me.

"Thanks, Friend," I tell him.

"Mom, you're late," says Lara on the other end of the phone.

"What time is it?"

I've been reading the packaging from my herbal tea bag. *When you sip this tea, you are benefiting from the healing power of plants and the wisdom contained within the world's systems of traditional herb formulations.*

I feel relaxed for the first time in days.

"It's nine o'clock. Remember Buzz's allergy appointment? He's got hives. Kept us up all night crying and scratching himself raw."

"Oh no." The trēo beeped at me but I forgot that meant I had an appointment.

"Mom, are you okay? Dad says you're falling apart."

"He did?"

"Yeah, he says you're not sleeping, that you wander around in the middle of the night mumbling things."

Those affirmations. *I am calm. I am so calm. I am really really heart-stopping calm.*

"I'll be right there. Better yet. Take both kids to the doc and I'll meet you there. I'll take the Tangerine for a Starbucks."

"Mom. She's only three. She can't have caffeine."

"I know that. I'll get her a juice. Where's the doctor's office?"

After giving me a series of complicated directions that I try to enter into my trēo poking at the screen with the stylus, Lara hangs up. I write them down on the back of our electric bill.

I slurp my tea, springing into action.

Just when I thought I had my day under control, the trēo plays Ravel. I plunge my arm into the tote. It's driving me crazy, ringing, buzzing, vibrating as a separate entity.

I'm up to my elbow when I find it, a fisherman's catch on a lonely day.

"Maury, you've got to change this ring. Can't you call me on the land line?"

"You okay? You sound harried."

"I am. I'm late for Lara. I'm taking Tangie for coffee."

"Jean, caffeine stunts growth in rats."

"I know. Maury." The man wouldn't hurry if there was a fire on his tail.

"Speaking of rats . . ."

"Yes?"

I take the stairs two at a time, the phone in the crook of my neck. I search my closet for jeans that fit, all stacked on a shelf. I pull out a pair. The rest fall into a heap on the floor.

"Honey, I don't want you to be upset but . . ."

"I'm already upset. I didn't realize the beeping was an appointment."

I sit down at the end of the bed, struggling into the jeans.

Maury says, "Jean, don't look out back. I'll be home soon to clean it up."

"Clean what up?" I ask, sliding my feet into the Birkenstocks, racing down the stairs to the patio doors. I zip my pants on the run.

"Aaargh. Oh no! What is it? Why is it all bloody? OmiGod! It looks like a dead dog." Instinctively, I look behind me for Amber who greets me with a smile, tail wagging.

"Jean, calm down. It's only a dead roof rat."

"A roof rat? Since when do rodents only use upstairs real estate? Where did it come from?"

"They live in citrus trees. I think the neighbor's cat left us a present."

"Rats spread disease," I say packing my tote. I decide to leave the house for the first time without my planner. I'm flying solo with the trēo.

"Just don't go near it."

"Right. Like I'm going to play with it." *Has the bubonic plague invaded Scottsdale?*

"Gotta go. Patients waiting. Bye."

I'm taking Tangie for a tall double espresso mocha unskinny latte. I don't care what anyone says.

14

AFTER DAYS OF SCOURING BEHIND SAFEWAY and Albertson's in 105 degree heat because it's cooled off, I have enough boxes for my mother's stuff. She made a decision.

We spend one day at the bank shifting money from different accounts, requesting cashier checks and checking her safety deposit box. Another day we visit the apartment complex office to sign papers, pending inspection, of course, to get her deposit back. Another afternoon we commit to a new lease at Vista Shadows, paying more deposits. I change over her telephone, electric and cable reassuring her numerous times everything will be glorious. Le Grande Move requires a large green dumpster, tattooed men and infinite patience.

My mother waits in a flowered housedress with a scarf covering her hair. It's not quite as gloomy as the Russian-peasant-babushka look, but it's a strange one for a woman who prides herself on being *fapitzed* at all hours of the day and night.

I could wake her up as a kid, and even though her skin was shiny from Pond's, she'd be outfitted in an elegant embroidered satin nightgown, every hair in place with the help of a few clips and a hairnet. She's convinced herself these remnants of cultivated ways descended from her royal European heritage.

When my mother sees me she gets up to drag a box across the living room.

"Mom, what're you doing?" I lean over and kiss her hello. "That's too heavy for you. Leave it. I'll get it."

"If I put all my accessories in the kitchen then I can start to pack the nightgowns and matching robes. An outfit's never complete without a belt, scarf and jewelry," she reminds me eyeing my T-shirt and Capri pants.

"Remember we don't pack drawers? We'll tape them shut. The dressers go intact."

She collapses on the only available spot on the sofa, slumping from exhaustion. My mother, the original re-cycler, never throws anything away. We pass a crocheted shawl in a fancy shopping bag back and forth with each visit.

"Here," she says holding out a bag. "It's still good. Give it to Lara."

I survey the living room, a chaotic mess of everything my parent's ever owned. I appealed to them many times to purge their belongings. They survived the Depression and WWII. "We had boarders, for God's sake," she's told me, the epitome of disgrace. Her experiences make her queen of the pack rats.

Worse, I think I inherited the gene. Statistics say we own fifty percent more than previous generations. My share is going to go up to one hundred percent when I take over my mother's possessions. Her stuff won't fit into her new compact living space. I have to eliminate unnecessary items *now*.

When my dad passed away I had to fight with my mother to get rid of his clothes, shoes, toiletries. "Mom, he's not coming back. He's never going to wear these again."

She just stared at me. "We bought that sports coat on sale at Saks. Such a shame. It was a real bargain."

Grief manifests itself in different ways. I think she wanted to keep his belongings in the closet and bathroom so she could pretend he went out for a walk and would be back at any moment. It's not healthy to save everything.

A few weeks later when I showed up for a visit, she was napping. I took three armloads of stuff to my car, including shoes and toiletries, found a small Mexican gardener who was resting with a blower next to him, motioned him with my hand to the trunk of my vehicle and unloaded an entire wardrobe.

Somewhere in Guadalupe there's a male attired as a well-dressed Miami Beach gentleman, spiffed up in a lemon-colored shirt, palm tree tie and fancy jacket, smelling of Old Spice.

Of course when she noticed his mostly empty closet a few days later, she called to bawl me out. I explained that there was no way to get them back, that it had all been re-cycled into the Universe and someone was enjoying the benefits of her excellent, stylish taste. It mollified her.

It's the dismantling of a life she shared with my dad that

makes me sad. I feel empty, missing the parents I knew from my childhood.

I think about my brother, David, and the great times we had as a family, especially on vacations. He's living in Baltimore with his wife and kids and offered to help, but I couldn't see the point pulling him away from his business and family. He wouldn't have a clue what to do.

Besides, if he brought my opinionated, pseudo-intellectual, always dressed in black, sister-in-law, there would be trouble. Daughters get stuck with family obligations.

With a consulting deadline, a bone density test and a gift for Jacob's fourth birthday bowling bash on my to-do list, I don't have a minute to waste.

I snap open two large black trash bags, one for Goodwill and one for the dumpster. I begin the sifting and sorting in her bedroom.

"Mom, let's clean out your closet. I'm sure you have a few things that don't fit anymore."

"Absolutely not. I've kept my figure." She sits down on the bed to watch me.

Her shoes, stacked in clear plastic boxes, some of which I've never seen her wear, are a good place to start.

"Do you still want these? They're kinda outdated." I hold up red patent leather shoes with thick barrel heels.

"They're still good. That style might come back."

Only if the designers are looking to make ladies with fat ankles club-footed too.

"But we have to get rid of some things. Your new place is

smaller."

"If my feet stop swelling I'll be able to wear them again."

This is going to be a long day. I ignore the rolling clothing rack she has against wall with her evening clothes and coats she hasn't worn in forty years, and won't need in Arizona unless there's an Ice Age. I cull twenty white blouses down to five. It's obvious we buy the same articles of clothing over and over, just like the women who pick spouses with the same bad habits again and again.

I put on the classical music station, assign my mother to sort a pile of black pants and skirts and rev into motion. If only they'd play *Flight of the Bumblebee.* I spin with activity. She won't realize it for a few weeks, but anything with stains or repairs or is out-of-date disappears into a black garbage bag.

I tackle the living room.

On chrome and glass shelves she refers to as her *étagère*, she has numerous glass figurines, ornate ash trays and vases. I pick up an old flower vase. My father used to joke they could start their own funeral parlor.

"Don't touch that," I hear behind me.

"Mom, I can't pack it if I don't touch it. I thought you were working in the bedroom."

From the doorway she explains, "I bought that in 1959 on a road trip with your father in Maggie Valley, North Carolina. You were just a baby and we stopped at a roadside stand. I know the man gave me a better price because you were so cute."

I handle it gingerly, wrap it in newspaper and place it inside a box I've labeled *tsotchkes.*

"We don't have time for a story about each piece. How 'bout I put everything valuable in this box and we look through it another time? Take a rest."

"No, I know you. You'll throw away something good."

"What constitutes *good*?" I ask, wrapping three Japanese ashtrays together.

"It still has use in it."

Now I could start a discussion about the purpose ash trays have for non-smokers, but I'd never win.

"What about this?" I hold up a china figurine of a woman with dust collected in the crevices of her neck and folds of her skirt. I can't imagine anyone ever wanting it. It's been painted with poor technique, sporting one caterpillar eyebrow.

"Save it," she tells me. "Rivka will love it."

My Orthodox/Mexican daughter-in-law will *not* love it. Besides being on a tight budget, when she and Michael do purchase something for their home, if it's not toys or child equipment, they buy religious art. They have a room with menorahs, Israeli statues and a few paintings of sad rabbis with beards. I feel guilty going in there.

At this rate we'll be here until the end of the year.

"Mom, sometimes you have to let go of things."

"I already did. Your father."

"I'm talking about material possessions. You can't take all of this with you."

"Who says? I want it to look nice at my new place."

"At your age people can't see or hear very well. It won't make any difference."

"I want them to know I come from good breeding."

What are we, cows? Who cares? I work around her, humming along to Vivaldi's *Four Seasons* which helps me pick up the pace.

Every item she thinks is precious has a story meant to inspire me to carry it through life. At this rate I'll be the only elderly person with enough possessions to decorate the entire lobby of a large hotel.

She tells me, "That was your grandmother's. She brought it from Poland." Or "Your great aunt Goldie on your father's side carried it from Russia. The Cossacks were chasing her. She escaped with it in her bosom."

"I'll strip the bed so the movers can get to the box springs and mattress." One has to be donated. I feel desolate that she only needs one bed.

I enter the bedroom, another wreck, and take off the four pillows she sleeps with, her purse hidden underneath them.

"Don't touch my purse."

"The movers will find it. What's in it anyway?"

"My good jewelry."

I open the clasp to look inside. It holds a tangled bunch of chains, earrings in a plastic bag, a change purse, eyeglasses she told me she lost weeks ago and three bottles of medications—heart, blood pressure and stool softener.

"Why don't I put it on the top shelf of your closet?"

In my reach for the top shelf of the closet, I trip over an enormous gold velvet brocade chair, twisting my knee. I collapse on top of a stack of clothes encased in clear plastic dry cleaning bags to examine my wound.

No blood but it hurts. I moan, rubbing my throbbing knee. Limping a bit I tackle the kitchen.

My mother's not going to need nut crackers, meat thermometers, tongs, colanders, pots for boiling pasta, faded dishtowels, rolling pins, plastic ice buckets and casseroles without tops. I stack them into a box to smuggle into my car for Goodwill.

My mother sits glassy-eyed on the sofa.

I clear the credenza of thirty picture frames. Inside the ancient piece of furniture, plastic bags, discards from rainy Florida days, are filled with photographs. I drop them into a box labeled "photos." I sift through linens, lace tablecloths, plastic placemats and napkins. Nothing matches.

I've got to pick up the pace. The movers will be here for the furniture in two hours.

I remove art from the walls, stacking the pieces next to the monster sofa. They include numbered lithographs bought at charity auctions to raise money for Israel, two Chagall prints, a staple in every middle-class Jewish home and six large oil paintings. The latter are originals executed by my mother's sister, an abstract artist who rebelled, ran away with a musician and took up residence in Coconut Grove, an artist's colony near Miami.

I reminisce about Aunt Beryl with her wacky ways for a moment. She's the reason my parents moved to Florida. She also gave me my first cigarette and glass of vodka. Unfortunately, the big "C" claimed her.

A sharp rap pounds the door. When I open it, three guys in sweaty T-shirts with dirty bandannas tied around their foreheads are ready to move my mother. A sour aroma greets my nostrils. I empathize because it's so damn hot. Hard way to make a living.

Two men with dollies hang back while one steps forward with a clip board. "Ma'am, I'm Tony." He points his thumb, grime under the nail, over his shoulder. "This here's Miguel and Bruno. We're here to move you."

"Not me. My mother." *Does he think I'll be living at a senior center? Maybe I do need a little fixing up.*

I nod toward her, perched on the edge of the sofa, the purse she retrieved when I wasn't looking, on her lap.

"Ma'am, we need you to sign this and pay up front."

I scramble for my credit card, placing the stack of dishes I'm carrying back in the kitchen.

Tony hands me the clipboard, a pen attached on a string. There are extra clauses and charges, but I don't have time to read it all. I want to finish. I take my copy and stuff it in my pants pocket.

The men begin multiple trips moving my mother's furniture down the hall to the service elevator, through the back entrance to their waiting vehicle. A truck with SOLE SURVIVOR MOVERS—ATTENTIVE SERVICE TO YOUR DOOR painted on the side blocks the driveway. It's stacked high with other people's stuff. We're the last load of the day.

Tony and friends maneuver my mother's bed out of the bedroom around the maze of discarded items, shoe boxes and garbage bags. Endless clutter.

I make a silent vow not to do this to my kids. I'm going to dispose of everything long before Maury and I have to scale down. We can live like Buddhist monks until it's our time. I look good in saffron.

My mother, purse over her arm, follows me downstairs in her housedress. It's the first time in her life she has stepped outside her door in anything less than full regalia. A straw hat sits on the back of her head. She stands next to me as they wedge her white sofa inside.

Bruno, perspiring inside the truck, re-arranges the innards. He holds brass lamps, their shades encased in plastic. A swastika bulges on his arm. Let's hope my mother doesn't see it.

"Why is it so hot?" she asks me.

Should I explain that it's the desert, there's global warming, that it's not air-conditioned outside? I take the easy way out. "I don't know."

A few pieces shift in the truck as an end table falls out, smashing to the ground. Fortunately, it's not hers. The men exchange a few curses.

"Hey, tell them to watch it. I don't want any of my good things broken or scratched," she says.

Bruno, dripping sweat, looks up at me. Maybe he's going to kill her. Our eyes meet. He's met crazy ladies before.

"Let's let them finish their job," I tell her, guiding her into the lobby to wait. "You'll get heat stroke out here. I'll drive you over to the new place and make up your bed with clean sheets."

"But I want to watch to make sure they don't steal anything," she whispers.

I'm praying they do.

"Will you put everything away? I can't do it myself." She feels insecure about this change. I put my arm around her.

"I know you miss Dad."

She nods, her chin quivering a bit. "He was my heart."

"I know it's not easy to be on your own. It's going to take a few weeks to get settled. We'll find you some new friends."

"Okay. But you know I can't sleep if there's disarray. It upsets my equilibrium."

I limp back upstairs to drag and pull boxes down the hall. My knee aches dragging her belongings to my car. I have to leave a spot for the driver and passenger. I'll come back tomorrow for the rest. Maybe Maury will help me.

In my effort to be efficient and move with haste, I trip over the damn gold chair again. It's huge. I don't know how I could miss it. My knee throbs from banging it twice. I rub it. I pull up my pants leg. It's turning black and blue.

On my last trip upstairs I spot Tony, sweating violently, leaning on my nemesis, the gold chair, near the freight elevator.

He motions me over. "Lady, no way will this fit in the elevator. We could stand the sofa on its side but this hunk is so fat I can't even roll it on."

I look at my watch. Two hours until the 7 o'clock dinner seating at the new place. I make an executive decision. "Leave it."

"Where?"

"Right there. Just leave the hideous chair right there in the corner. Let someone else figure out what to do with it."

"Okay, lady, but you'll have to sign the paper again."

"No problem." She'll never miss it.

After I make up my mother's bed with the appropriate number of pillows and smooth the spread, I wait in the living room with all the boxes while my mother adorns herself.

She emerges from the bedroom wearing a white blouse, black skirt, medium heels, the straw hat on her head and all of her jewelry.

When I question this last choice, she responds, "You don't think I'm going to leave it in the room for the maids to take, do you?"

There's no point explaining that the personnel here have been carefully screened or that there's no maid service at night. Purse in one hand and a shopping bag clasped in the other, she's ready for the seven p.m. seating.

My mother appears worried, her lips pursed, as we wait at the dining room entrance. Should I stay to sit with her while she eats her first meal? I'm a dirty mess. I give her a hug and kiss for bravery. This isn't easy.

The hostess comes over, takes my mother's elbow, guiding her to a table. She's introduced to a group of people who lift their heads with interest. They're ready with welcoming smiles for a fresh prospect. Senior centers are revolving doors.

"Wait," my mother says, walking back to me. "You can use

these. It'll spruce your place up."

She passes me a shopping bag, returning to join her new friends, chin held high.

I open the top of the bag to see exactly what I need: two pleated circular throw pillows in gold satin with a strong moth ball scent, a large vase with dusty fake silk flowers and a plastic bag filled with metal and plastic shoe horns.

15

MY MOTHER IS SLEEPING IN HER NEW PLACE TONIGHT. I'm sure I'll hear from her in the morning that something has not met her standards, but now, it's my time.

At eleven p.m. I fill the tub with hot water and light candles. I open a spa basket Glee gave me ages ago with essential bath oils. It's the kind of present I usually save for a special occasion. This is it. I deserve a prize for completing the monster move.

A loofah glove, terry cloth pillow and an elaborate chart for oils falls out. I study the enclosed information: lavender to ease worry or irritability, sage for anxiety, ylang ylang for anger and jasmine for physical exhaustion. I dump it all into the water.

The combination of fragrances envelops the bathroom. It smells like a New Age happening. The only thing missing is patchouli. I sink my exhausted body into the warm, fragrant water.

A few fat candles shimmer, their intoxicating aroma of green tea and cucumber hanging in the air. I position the pillow behind my head, sighing as the tension rolls out of my body.

What a day! Now it's quiet, except for the occasional scratching of a tree branch. Or a roof rat? I can't go there. We haven't solved that problem yet, but for now I breathe deeply and let it go. I send rodents flying into the Universe. With a languid motion I pick up the newspaper that I didn't get to peruse this morning.

I dispose of the news. I've caught up on NPR during my drive time. In the real estate section I focus on a photograph of a familiar mansion. *The Arizona Daily News* lists the most recent transactions. I love to read about the consumption of my neighbors. The caption under the picture says, "Exquisite Homes Top Sales."

$7,100,000

A corporate entity controlled by Esther and Jerold Cohen of La Jolla, California, purchased a five bedroom, seven bathroom, 8000-square foot pueblo home from Theodore and Glee Barstow. Situated in the foothills of Camelback Mountain it has a multi-tiered theater, a master bedroom with juice bar, meditation room and three stone fireplaces. It also features a sports center, flower greenhouse, zen garden and 850 bottle wine room and includes a chipping and putting green. A separate casita on the property has three bedrooms.

Glee's former home has sold for an eye-watering amount of money. A wry smile flashes across my lips. She says everyone needs a starter palace. Glee and Ted's last shared asset extended by a prolonged rabid lawyer fight concludes their divorce. Their Sedona hacienda perched in a red rock cliff sold last year.

I drop the paper outside the tub, close my eyes and think about my loyal friend. We met when our kids were in pre-school and Ted was starting a construction business. I was drawn to her artistic exuberance. Glee created drama with home décor and themed parties on a tight budget. With the growth of our Valley Ted bought Chandler cotton fields and Scottsdale desert when our city was an outpost of tourist shops, stables and a few Italian restaurants. Glee learned how to spend money as a one-woman economic stimulus.

I turn on the spigot and add more hot water. I bend my knees, sinking into the soothing tub. I know I have to get my life under control.

Although I'm Glee's lifetime project, a Pygmalion-in-progress, I contribute to our relationship by feeding her good literature, fostering political awareness and making her laugh. I'm the rock solid one, married forever.

She's weathered the storms of obscene money, bankruptcy—not atypical for developers until they can reinvent new monetary sources—multiple moves, divorce and an evolution of original interests. I hesitate to use the word careers although she has earned income from her wild assortment of pursuits, which included selling ceramic Vag

Badges we wore on our lapels.

She's a new woman now, reinventing herself as a sunny blonde in a contemporary condo with a new boyfriend and a fresh undertaking as a life coach.

When I asked her about guiding people in their life choices, she told me, "The Universal Coaching Network has taught me to be the 'intersection between personal development and a terrific life.' That's a quote from their literature. But I've been doing that for years. This is the perfect culmination of all my skills."

I agree that she's good at giving direction and expressing an original point of view.

"I'm enrolled in the 98-hour Advanced Fast Track Comprehensive Teleclass for certification. Only costs thirty thousand."

I can't believe anyone is certifying Glee to do anything. And that she's paying them that much money for it. Creative, yes. Practical, no.

"Jean, you know I can focus when necessary, especially if it's enhancing my ability and skills. I'm even on speaking terms with Ted, although he's not thrilled about giving me half the money from the sale of the house. But, hey, he traded it for a thirty-two-year-old with plastic boobs."

When I repeated this to Maury over his morning coffee, he looked up from his Sunday *New York Times* that he reads all week and said, "It's BS, Jean."

"What is?"

"The course. The coaching. All of it."

"I don't think so," I responded in my friend's defense.

I let out some tub water and add more hot again. My body is morphing into jelly. Per my bath kit's instructions I begin a self-massage starting with my feet. I knead them, manipulating up to my ankles and Achille's heel, rubbing my calves. My knee is bruised and sore from the hideous chair so I skip it, continuing on to my thighs with long strokes and find aching muscles all the way up to my shoulders.

I close my eyes.

I recall defending Glee's new profession to Maury.

"How can you say that? Look what she's done for her own relationship. She and Ted are speaking in a civil manner. She'll be a benefit to people's personal communication."

"And, pray tell, how is she going to do that?" he asked with an arched eyebrow, lowering the paper.

"She asks clarifying questions about your life's purpose," my voice softer. "So people can address their situation and take effective action."

"How long did she study for this superior knowledge?"

I began to lose confidence in Glee's new career choice, re-arranging my flatware on the placemat.

"She took a course on the internet."

Maury's paper rose to eye level. "Need I say more?"

"Yes, but look how she's managing her transition from being married to single. I'd be a wreck but she's uplifted and consumed with positive energy."

Maury dropped his paper. "Jean, millions of dollars assuages most problems. Glee is no more certified to assist people with their lives than you are to practice medicine. Her life is a mess and her kid is a bundle of neuroses."

"Hey, that's not fair. Lots of people are in therapy and rehab. Well, maybe not their whole lives. Our kids aren't exactly paragons of mental health."

I knew what he was saying about Glee was true, but she seemed so happy while my life languished in a quagmire of complications and stress. I was a bit chagrined.

"Jean, think about it. Why would people need coaches if they were self-actualized individuals in the first place?"

"Well, they have situations that don't require a shrink but could use some insight. Like me. My self-help group shows me how to manage my tension. There are all kinds of coaches—business, life, fitness, corporate and . . ." I realized it sounded ridiculous to him with his scientific mind steeped in empirical thought. I left out intuitive. I think it involves Glee's hunches.

Anyway, we have more serious problems right here at home. A few more roof rats have taken up residence. We found another dead carcass and droppings on our patio.

Maury attended a free clinic sponsored by the city on how to deal with the pesky rodents. This is after he displayed two half-eaten oranges to me in his gloved hands through the glass doors. The meat of the fruit had been scooped out which gave me the willies. I could see ugly rat teeth marks.

"Do not bring those in here," I told him.

"Orange rinds can't hurt you."

"No. They have germs on them." I stick out my top teeth and pretend to munch.

"Then hand me a plastic bag."

I did. He disposed of the rinds in the garbage can in our back alley.

I haven't stepped out on the patio for a week. I can't even let Amber out for a fast pee which means a bonafide walk when she stares at the door. When I reach for her leash she leaps in exhilaration. I grumble because it makes me late for whatever I'm trying to accomplish.

Maury returned with a full rat report, carrying wire mesh cages. "We have to buy some poison for these bait stations I bought."

"Poison?"

"Yeah. We have to trim back the landscaping because they're expanding their territory."

"Wait. You bought them? What happens when we're finished? We have no storage space."

"We keep them. Once they infest a neighborhood they return. Like Zonies going to Coronado Island in California."

I've heard of banks red-lining a neighborhood and not loaning money to home owners for improvements, but rats-in-charge is beyond my comprehension.

"I've also got people coming over to glean the trees. If there's no juicy fruit in them, we can tackle this problem."

Reaching over the edge of the tub, I gather the newspaper to fold in half. I catch a small article at the bottom of the last page. A miniscule headline reads "Maricopa County Gets Failing Grades for Air Pollution."

The American Lung Association has issued a report card and our Valley of the Sun received an F in ozone air pollution and a D in particulates. In fact, Scottsdale is the 19th most polluted city in the country. This makes me furious. Where are our local newspaper's priorities? This should be on the front page.

Maury probably saw the article, but I tear it out anyway with damp fingers. More ammunition. The campaign's been stagnant lately with funds drying up. Flora Beaudreaux's been quiet—no harsh statements, ridiculous accusations or incipient scandals. Craig Burton, a bright guy who lacks charisma, isn't making any headway. Why aren't people questioning their inability to breathe or the hazy air?

I grab a big gulp of air and sink myself under the fragrant tub water, holding my breath for as long as I can. My hair snakes out around me. I'll wash it tomorrow. I lie there until I crash through the surface lifting myself out of the tub, an ecological mermaid without a fishtail. I wrap myself in a terry bath sheet, collapsing on top of the covers next to a slumbering Maury and snoring Amber.

16

JEAN? MY GOLD CHAIR IS MISSING."

"Hi Mom. How's the food? Make any friends?"

"The food and company here are acceptable but I'm missing my favorite chair."

What am I going to tell her about the chair? "What did you have for dinner?"

"You are not going to distract me. Those moving men were thieves. Molly Goldfarb warned me. She had her French underwear stolen."

Why does my mother have to notice the monstrous chair is missing? She's been in her new place for five days. At eight a.m. I barely have my eyes open. After daily efforts to get her new apartment in order, I thought I was home free.

She still thinks she owns a hundred pairs of shoes. I pray she won't notice the multi-colored spike heels and metallic go-go boots are gone when she costumes herself for her next appearance in the dining room.

Should I ask why her seventy-five year old obese friend has French underwear? I choose a path down the middle, the placating side of me aiming for a truce. I pull myself into an upright position in the bed with a twinge and a groan. Besides my aching knee my back hurts from the repeated motion of bending into boxes, lifting and putting her *objects d'art* on display while she sits on the sofa and directs.

"Are you listening to me? My good gold chair is gone! The one with the brocade and all the tufting. I've had it for years. Your father and I bought it at Modernage when they opened in 1959 on Miracle Mile."

I slap my hand on my head in an effort to forestall a headache. "Mom. Listen. Maury will call the movers to see what he can do. If they can't find it then we'll get you replacement money." I swing my legs over the side of the bed and rub my back.

"Replacement money? I want the chair. It's a beautiful creation. Money can't replace it."

Maury and I agree that it's the most ghastly pieces of furniture we've ever seen with its barrel shape, multiple buttons, vomit color and awful fringe that drags the floor.

"You don't have room for it anyway. You're squeezed into your apartment like a fat foot in cork wedgies."

"Jean, don't start up with me. I want my chair."

"Okay, mom, I'll talk to you later."

Oh God. What am I going to do? I fall back on the bed and close my eyes. No way to meditate. A litany of how-am- I-going-to-get-the-chair-back, damn chair, what-if-I-lie- and-write-her-a-check-for-three-hundred-dollars, damn chair, but-it-won't-be-from-the movers-so-I'll-get-a-cashier's-check, damn chair. She'll argue three hundred isn't enough. Ugh. Five hundred dollars for the worst, ugliest chair on the planet. Damn chair. It all goes round and round in my head. Just what I don't need: another problem.

I breathe deeply to calm myself. A vision appears of me with my sharpest kitchen knife slicing through gold fabric. Blood leaks out to stain the velvet brocade before the fluffy innards diffuse onto the floor. I'd better call Maury.

I explain the new dilemma. "She thinks the movers took it. I abandoned it there. It wouldn't fit in the elevator or the truck or her new apartment."

"Jean, I'm in the middle of office hours. People are sick. There's a foreign flu epidemic and a shortage of serum. I can't do anything about that disgusting chair."

"Maury, please. You have to."

"Okay, I'll stop at the old place before I come home. Maybe someone knows what happened to it."

April stops by to see me. I would never drop in on her without calling first, but she knows it's okay to do with me. It doesn't matter if I'm not groomed. Her philosophy of everything can be fixed with the right shoes, a stylish haircut and a good lip pencil doesn't apply in my own home.

She has a birthday present for Tangie. We air kiss.

"I've had this for ages," she says, handing me a colorful bag streaming with ribbons, tissue paper bursting from the top. "I couldn't resist."

I don't open it, but I bet it's some indulgent little girl accessory like the sparkly red Mary Janes she got her last year.

"You look fabulous. Where are you going?" I ask. She's in a Diane von Furstenberg wrap dress that emphasizes her *décolletage* and Jimmie Choos that caress her ankles.

"Just meeting with my banker."

"Would you like some coffee?"

"No, I can only stay a few minutes." She pulls out a chair at my kitchen table still messy from our breakfast.

I share my mother update.

She suggests I sketch out the chair. "I have a superb designer and upholsterer who can re-create anything. I'll give you their number."

"Thanks, honey, but I don't have time for another project. How's the pet luncheon coming?"

"Great. I'm in charge of the silent auction. We have weekends at some of the best kennels, a year's supply of imported vegetarian dog food and a two week stay in Paris where you and your dog can dine together at a chic restaurant." She examines her nails looking for a flaw.

The store owners who see April will give her anything.

"The French are crazy about their dogs. They treat them like people. I'd love to take my babies to lunch." She crosses her smooth, shapely tan legs.

"I can't take Amber anywhere. Her butt's too big."

"Guess what? The new upscale dog boutique that sells

doggie beer for $19.95 a six-pack made a donation for the raffle. It's a combination of malt, barley and beef stock. For an extra charge they put your dog's picture on the label. Isn't that cute? I'd serve it with dog pretzels."

"Sounds wonderful. Although I'd worry Amber might start snoring even louder if she was drunk."

I admire April's good-hearted charitable works. She raises thousands of dollars and has donated even more for the no-kill pet shelter with the Lefkowitz name over the door. Her aquamarine eyes tear up just talking about people's cruelty to "God's living creatures who can't speak for themselves" and their expressive little faces that tell tales of neglect.

But, honestly, I'd rather write a check than spend the days in preparation to go to the events. I can barely execute the essentials of my personal no-frills maintenance without shopping and rotating ball gowns, creating up-dos with the hairstylist, waxing everything and consulting with multiple friends about which $900 shoes to wear.

"Any news about the Rock Burglar?"

"Not about our case. But Steve's made friends with the detective and the guy has hit again. Scottsdale and Paradise Valley are such fertile ground. Want to hear my theory?" She becomes animated with enthusiasm.

"Shoot." I cut up fruit for a salad.

"Well, I think he follows women home from hair salons, the Biltmore, the society luncheons. Women wear their best jewelry to impress everyone. Maybe he gets some info from the shampoo people—they make hardly anything so I always tip them extra—or the valets. He sees where they live, learns their habits, tracks their pattern of appointments. Isn't that creepy? The idea that he was watching me gives me chills. I don't even walk the dogs now without putting on the alarm."

"What does Steve say?"

"He says I could be a great detective with my dark wrap-around Ray Bans. I've been examining all the license plates in my neighborhood."

"Have you seen anything unusual?" I'm imagining April as a female Bond spy in a tight gold lame jogging suit with heels, mincing up and down her street.

"Not yet. But I'm very aware. Unfortunately, all my neighbors pull straight into their garages so I never see anyone at all. Once in a while maids bring in the mail, but I recognize their Chevys and Hyundais."

"Do you think they'll ever catch him?" I'm washing red grapes, high in anti-oxidants for Maury.

"Maybe. Steve said the detective told him he executes every job with perfection. It's not random at all. I think there's more than one perp. One of them parks the car nearby while the other one comes in fast and jogs away. If they use a quality car or fancy bike and wear running clothes or walk a fashionable dog, they can move through our streets with ease." April sounds triumphant.

"Honey, anything is possible. Most people here drive expensive vehicles and wear designer yoga clothes with their diamonds. Sometimes I can't tell if I'm in an upscale Olympic village or a Mercedes dealership."

She laughs and says, "You've been having such a hard time lately. Glee and I want to take you for a spa day. Our treat. Check your calendar. We're open. We haven't had a girl's day in a long time. Well, maybe after the Heart Ball, Pets on Parade and Glee's bash. I forgot how booked I am." She stands up and picks up her Chanel purse with the double "C" logo. "I've got to get going. I'm checking my safe deposit box at the bank. I also found a crack in one of my nails. I love the silk wraps but they take time when I'm so busy." She holds out her hand for inspection.

"April, darling, you are *not* busy. Live my life for a few days."

"Oh, I couldn't. I'd be exhausted. I don't do anything myself that I can hire someone for."

We exchange "love you's" as I walk her to the door.

"Don't do too much," she tells me, waving.

Yikes! My day is half gone and I haven't started yet. I'm off to another client who has finally gotten the concept that his company has to embrace diversity, flexibility and innovation in the work place. He's implementing my plan to provide child care and more personal days for his employees. I must ask him about a job he mentioned for Michael.

Then I have a dental appointment. A filling from a childhood of Cokes and Snickers has caught up with me. I need a crown. The best thing about the dentist is I'm immobile and can't talk. It's a good place to practice my relaxation techniques. *I am a calm person, all is well, I am at peace.* I jump up to get dressed, walk Amber and soar out the door, my aching knee a reminder of the gold chair.

Later, I sigh as I pull into our driveway, my jaw numb from Novocain. I pull down my visor to check the mirror. I have a fat lip. I look pale without any color. I want to eat a mushy dinner on one side of my mouth, sip a glass of wine and read a good book. As I put the visor back in place, a strange vehicle catches my eye.

A sheriff's van is parked in front of our house. I move faster. What's wrong? Michael. It must be Michael. That kid is always in trouble. Or maybe it's Gus, my enterprising son-in-law, who gets involved in schemes like last year's Dial-an-Alibi for cheating spouses. I hustle inside.

Maury's stretched out watching a golf tournament drinking a diet soda, Amber's head in his lap.

"You okay?" I ask before I start my interrogation.

Maury hates it that I ask so many questions but it's because he never gives me details. I want the story. I'm not the type of person you can say, "The Rosens are getting a divorce" to and not have me want to know why.

Maury lacks the social inquisitiveness to find out. His intellectual curiosity goes into overload if someone mentions an EPA report or obscure battles from ancient wars but not gossip.

"Sure. Look at this tape from the Masters. Unbelievable how Tiger showed everyone up."

I don't comment on the fact that he's watching a golf tournament that's already happened. He knows who won. I glance outside. "Who are those people in our back yard wearing pink-striped scrubs?!"

"Oh, that's the chain gang. They pick the fruit for free and it goes to the inmates. Saved the county seventy thousand last year. Watch this shot. You've never seen anything like it." Maury motions with his chin toward the screen.

I drop my tote to focus on the men working outside. "Wait a minute. You have incarcerated criminals picking our fruit?"

He doesn't take his eyes from the set. "Wow. Phil Mikkleson made a birdie. The kids from the church groups were all booked. Said I called too late."

"You invited criminals into our home to pick fruit?" There are no bounds of where this man's impracticality will go. I can hear my mother now: "Jean, they could be rapists and murderers. Where's your jewelry? Sonia Ruttenberger was wiped out. They even took beer from the fridge."

"It's only the back yard. They're on work detail. It's either that or pay the landscaping service seven hundred dollars. Or do it myself. You don't want me up on that extension ladder, do you? Roof rats love citrus. The fruit has to be picked. The trees need to be topped. We've let them get too tall."

"Trees are supposed to be tall." My voice is edgy.

"Jean, relax. They're nice guys. Go out and say hello. They're all in for minor stuff or petty theft."

"Theft? What if one of them is the Rock Burglar?" I'm many decibels louder.

"Wow. I can't believe how Tiger is so close to a birdie. He's tearing it up. Watch this shot. They're going to do a replay."

"Maury." I move and stand in front of the screen.

"Oh no, I can't see. Jean, relax. Stinky said he's a deadbeat dad and Jesus' in for pot. A deputy's with them. Now will you move? I can't miss this round."

I walk over to the glass doors to peer out, eyeing the guys on ladders hanging out of my orange and grapefruit trees. Garbage cans sit nearby filled with citrus.

"What's the third guy in for? He's covered with tattoos. There's a big one on his arm. It looks like a swastika. OhmiGod! That's Bruno, the mover!"

"Yeah. Nice guy. Says he crushed something with his head. Maybe he can help you get the chair to your mother's. He should be out by next week."

"Maury! Are you kidding? Get them out of here this minute. I insist."

"But they haven't finished picking all the fruit. They still have to cull and trim the trees so the rats can't make more nests."

"I don't care. Buy rat poison. Lots of it. I don't want criminals in my backyard."

"Aw, Jean."

I feel confrontational. "Get them out of here this minute."

Maury moves Amber's head and struggles out of his comfortable position. He walks over to the glass door and opens it, motioning to the sheriff's deputy.

After a hushed conversation Maury closes the door and sits down, arms crossed in front of him.

I am staring at him.

"What now? They're leaving."

"Did you check on my mother's chair?"

He sighs. "Mario, who works in the kitchen at your mom's old place, has it. Wife loves the chair. He said he understands. He'll bring it back next week. For a price."

"You mean we have to pay him?"

"Yup. Four hundred bucks. Said he 'found' it.

You have to figure out how to get it over there."

"How am I going to do that?" I ask, sitting down feeling overwhelmed.

"Bruno's available," he says with a thumb jabbed toward our back door.

I walk over to make sure everything's locked. The men are packing up. Dejected, I pull the drapes closed, walk back to the sofa, and sit down near Maury to pat Amber's head.

He squints at me. "Hey, your lip looks funny."

"Thanks."

17

TELL ME AGAIN WHY WE'RE PARTYING FOR DAY OF THE DEAD. Will the guests be dead?" asks Maury on a ride up to Glee's penthouse in a plush mirrored elevator. It's the middle of October and I'm warm. We have no autumn here.

"Because Glee felt like having a theme party."

"Will my Uncle Herschel be there? He dropped dead in 1933 at the height of the Depression."

"Maury, behave yourself," I say, exiting the elevator to a spacious foyer. I hear faint music that gets louder as we get closer.

A tall, willowy blonde with tortoise-shell glasses, spiky hair, tight jeans and killer heels, answers the door of Glee's apartment. A lit fountain and its dribbling water accompany her introduction. My bladder twinges.

"Welcome to Glee's Day of the Dead party. I'm Amanda, her *major domo*. Let me know if you have any personal needs throughout the evening. I'm here to be of service. Guests are at the bar on the terrace. Pomegranate margaritas are our signature cocktail for the evening."

She breezes past us to greet the next group of people. Maury whispers, "Who was that? A *major domo* is the top *male* servant in a royal household."

I suck in my stomach and adjust my posture for our stroll to the patio. I can hold this pose for at least three minutes. I want to make a confident entrance.

Maury leans into me, "At a real dead party I could've worn my Jerry Garcia T-shirt."

I smirk and squeeze his arm to behave.

I wonder if this is the same crowd from the botox party where Glee invited a sleazy cosmetic surgeon who had a frozen smile with super-whitened teeth to inject her friends.

At that event I was the only one who refused to put pig/cow urine into my face. Glee said the frown line between my brows was a cavern. I don't care. I'll be the older, wiser friend.

Outside, a small crowd of well-dressed, well-coiffed, supremely tightened people drink margaritas and *mojitos* made with gold rum, mint leaves, lime and pounds of sugar. No extra pounds here. Some are socialites I recognize from the magazines while others are new faces from Glee's people collection.

Most wear black. I'm in a Mexican multi-colored fiesta skirt with a splash of sequins that I bought on impulse while waiting for my mother to find shoes in Nordstroms.

Glee's erotic clay statues have been relegated to the corners. The patio terrace, resplendent with overstuffed, white canvas lounges made from bamboo and decorated with the lush foliage of large Areca palms, looks wonderful. Glee's created a sexy ambiance. She stressed about getting the Holler and Saunders pots from Mexico in time for the party. Supposedly, they're authentic antiques from a hacienda in Nogales. At least that's what they told her. I can tell there's going to be a wonderful sunset behind a panoramic view of Camelback Mountain.

Glee rushes over when she spots us. Our sculpted hostess wears fitted black pants, an off-the-shoulder top and a huge *concho* belt in addition to many pieces of chunky, gleaming silver jewelry. She's stepped out of a decorating magazine.

"Jean, Maury, I'm so glad you're here," she says, greeting us with hugs and kisses, a bit breathless, her perfume overwhelming. "Can't wait for you to meet Stavros."

"You look fabulous. What did you do to yourself?" I ask.

She smiles as she puts her arm through mine as Maury wanders toward the bar. "Orgasms, honey. Ever since I went for the vaginal tightening my juices are flowing again." Then she peels off to greet new guests. I head for April and Steve. He looks bored and she looks spectacular. I tell her.

She strokes her throat. "You think so? I feel so naked without any jewels."

"Your cleavage is the only accessory you need," I whisper.

Maury appears at my side with a margarita tinted a deep pink with a marigold perched in it. He air kisses April, leans over, planting one on my cheek too. "Glee said margarita is Spanish for marigold." He raises an eyebrow.

Maury toasts Steve with a lift of his glass. "How're doing? Heard you had some excitement at your house."

Steve shakes his head. "Can't believe those creeps. Stole all of April's diamonds, my Rolex with the pavé face. Probably the same jerks who hit up my favorite cigar store, too, so they could celebrate."

Maury bends forward to sip his drink before it overflows and drips. His eyebrows pop up over the rim of the glass. "You're kidding."

With a disgusted look on his face Steve says, "Bastards ripped off Buddha Cigar Company for sixty thousand in inventory."

Maury and I speak at the same time. "Cigars are worth that much?"

"Oh yeah. They took Porsche lighters, Ashton humidors, imported stogies. Even the private stash of Cuban Cohibas." He flashes his I'm an annoyed lawyer look. "Hey, ten murders in Scottsdale this year. Crime's on the rise."

The hair goes up on the back of my neck. April's lucky she wasn't home.

"So, any leads in your case? Sure it was the Rock Burglar?" asks Maury, shifting his stance.

"No doubt in my mind it's that scumbag. Cops say Scottsdale and Paradise Valley are tops for property crime. Only twenty percent of the cases are ever solved. Even had a jump of eight percent since last year."

The sun lowers in the sky silhouetting the mountain. It's a soothing time of day when the sky turns inky outlining the strange mountain shapes. This conversation about crime gives me the heebie jeebies.

"Wow. That's scary. I'm locking every door and checking it twice." I say.

"Jean, you're already neurotic about security. What about the times you locked the door when the kids went out to play?" asks Maury.

"What about the criminals in our backyard?" I shoot back.

"You have criminals in your backyard?" April asks, horrified.

Maury makes me look foolish. Fortunately, no one's listening. Roof rats and convicts aren't dinner party talk.

April says, "I heard on the news that $200,000 in circuit breakers and copper wire were stolen from a Scottsdale hospital construction site."

Steve shrugs it off. "Honey, we lost ten times that in jewelry. They're after gold now anyway. Insurance probably won't cover the yellow diamond."

I'm shocked. I knew April had a lot of quality pieces, but I had no idea it was in the millions. That probably doesn't include the safety deposit box treasures and what adorned her body that day.

A gong sounds. Amanda's pushing a small table decorated with yellow, red and orange *papier-mâché* flowers. She strikes the gong again. With a black lace mantilla on her head, she announces, "Let the fiesta begin."

Within minutes we are ushered into Glee's living room where an enormous altar dominates the end of the room. "Oohs" and "aahs" emanate from the group. Glee stands in front of her *ofrenda*. A large banner with small silver mirrors drapes across the wall. It proclaims, *Mi familia, mis amigos.*

"Welcome to my celebration for *Dia de Los Muertos*." The "r" rolls off her tongue like the newscasters who introduce themselves in enunciated English and Latinize their last names. "This is Channel Ten wishing you a special good night with Meredith Juarrrez," her last name whooshing by like a mini-desert storm.

I tune back in to Glee.

"I'm a little early for the actual Day of the Dead which is October 31 through November 2, but I love to celebrate. It's time to honor those who came before us. We all have loved ones who have passed to the other side."

Maury and I stand near the back of the group. Surveying the sleek women with defined jaw lines, I observe one whose eyes keep fluttering closed. Glee's explanations can be verbose.

Maury touches my arm. "What other side? Isn't she an atheist?"

I shush him but he's got a point. I flirted with reincarnation in the past, but now I believe when we make our final exit, it's over. No big parties in the sky for the good guys where you reunite with other languid souls while the partiers hang out in hell. When I leave this earth, I'm finished. No coming back. Not ever.

Glee takes a breath. "This holiday, based on a three

thousand year old tradition, means spirits return from the afterlife to celebrate." The front row of her audience leans in. With her voice escalating, she says, "Some *ofrendas* are communal while others are more personal. As an artist I created this for my dear departed parents who nurtured me." Her hand sweeps in a wide arc.

The three-dimensional altar, constructed on a large table with many levels, has an impressive array of flowers, candles, photos, scarves, mementoes and candy.

The guests, transfixed, sway a little. She picks up speed, speaking with animation. "Traditional altars are always decorated with marigolds because the departed can follow the scent home. I used cockscomb and the favorite foods of those I'm honoring. *Mi madre* and *padre* loved sweets." Glee points to a tower of gold Godiva boxes stacked into a tower, their rich chocolates glued to the outside.

Madre? Padre? Glee's parents weren't Latino. Her mother was an Episcopalian-Jewish-Catholic-multiple-married-country-club-social climber with a legacy of hysterical drama. And her father was an often disappearing Irish Protestant gambler whose fortunes changed with the casino personnel.

I stand back and take in the entire display with its dozens of intricate pieces collaged one on top of another. Lit by prayer candles and covered with glass gemstones, glitter, and charms, she must have drowned in hot glue.

"It's interactive so when we're seated I want you to taste the skulls and *milagros* I've put at your place settings. They're made of spun sugar and meringue that represent death and the sweetness of life. The *milagros* made of tin and ceramics are for you to take home. My gift to you." She smiles with pride.

"What are they?" asks a buxom woman wearing square tinted Prada glasses, the gold logo prominent on the side.

Glee picks up a white chocolate arm and leg. "*Milagro* means miracle in Spanish. They're religious charms the faithful believe have magical powers because they heal, restore and preserve. They're made for different parts of the body." Glee looks in my direction and nods. "They bring balance into the lives of people who carry them or those they pray for."

Ms. Inquisitive asks again, "Is that incense? At my nail salon they burn it in front of a red-lacquered Buddha."

Glee does not miss a sincere beat. "Authenticity is important. I couldn't use copal because the resin's too smoky. This is regular incense. Nowadays everyone's got allergies and asthma." We all collectively take a deep breath. "Incense lures the spirits home."

She claps her hands and announces, "Everyone find your place card and let's feast in honor of the dead!"

Our group, with a few people almost dead from the lengthy explanation, move into Glee's dining area.

No one dresses a table like my friend. This long one, covered with layers of linens in purple, orange and yellow, has an array of fresh and *papier-mâché* flowers, candles and bones propped into centerpieces. *Milagros* of hearts, eyes, heads, arms and legs are scattered around them. Place cards, installed in the forehead of a miniature skull, sit on silver charger plates.

I am seated away from Maury between two men with

shaved heads. There's an empty seat across from me. Glee's new beau, Stavros, who has a full head of salt and pepper hair, wears a powder blue silk shirt with a paisley ascot. Suntanned and too good looking, I surmise he's ten years younger than Glee.

I lean forward to introduce myself while fluttering a beaded purple napkin to my lap. "How do you do? I'm Jean Rubin." I nod to the gentlemen on either side of me.

"Stavros Sistovarospapadoulas." He smiles with sparkling piano-key white teeth, reaching a hand across the table. It's warm and lingers in mine. "Glee has told me of her attractive friends."

I'm flattered but wary. Men with ascots are suspect.

The twin Mr. Cleans on either side of me, both investors, start a conversation about their sport bikes.

"I own about twenty of them. Really set me back," says the one on my right.

"Yeah. I'm into thousands too. Can't ride without the latest padded mesh jackets either. Need armored protection for the knees and elbows," says the one on my left.

Sport bikes equal motorcycles equal death in my mind. I engage Stavros.

"I'm happy to meet you. You're certainly keeping my friend happy. May I ask what do you do?" *Besides meet wealthy women and have a lot of sex.*

"Of course. I'm owner of Acropolis Publishing and a book consultant." His manicured hands twirl the stem of his margarita glass.

I take the marigold from mine and stick it behind my ear. His resonant voice and throaty accent are seductive. "What does that mean?" I narrow my eyes. *Who is this guy who has my friend's affection?*

"Today it is difficult to publish through traditional channels, competitive to get an agent and a publisher. A large German corporation like Bertlesmann owns Bantam, Doubleday, Dell, Random House, Knopf. They want to market books like cars." He shakes his head as though it offends him.

Waitresses in colorful Mexican skirts and white peasant blouses serve us gazpacho, a chilled spicy tomato soup in small hollowed out pumpkins covered with gold-leaf. I bet Glee got the idea from Martha Stewart. She watches her show all the time.

"So if someone came to you who wants to write a book, what do you do first?"

"I find out how viable their idea is, whether they're serious about the process, if they have started their manuscript. I guide the author toward success."

I eye him with caution. "Are you a coach?"

He throws his head back and laughs, his ascot quivering. "No."

Interview Jean has taken over. "Do you believe everyone has a book in them?"

"Of course. People have great stories to tell. Especially women." He leans in and smiles.

"Why is that?" I ask, dipping my spoon into the soup, bringing it to my lips with a crouton balanced on top. His smile seems sincere but it can't win me over.

"Women have pushed to the forefront of the world stage with great odds against them. They have been thwarted along the way by religion, governments, the male patriarchy."

He is speaking my language. I'm impressed that this is being spoken by a man. Especially a European male.

"Have you published any authors I'd recognize?" I finish my gazpacho with gusto.

"Maybe. I have many strong sellers. A whole selection like the Chicken Soup series. *Men Who Eat Too Much and the Women Who Love Them, Men and the Women Who Love Their Pets More, Women Who Do Too Much and the Men Who Love Them.*"

I need to read the last one. I refrain from sharing that I've always wanted to write a book titled, *Men Don't See Dirt.*

"They languished on authors' shelves or editor slush piles until Acropolis. Stavros revises them, puts on a snappy cover and *opa!* It is a hit." He leans back with satisfaction. He hasn't touched his soup.

The woman with the Prada glasses next to Stavros interjects, "You're a publisher? Oh my God! I so want to write a book." Her padlock-sized gold earrings jiggle. The server fills one of our multiple glasses with champagne. There is an empty seat next to her.

Stavros turns his profile to me and evaluates her. "What about, my dear?"

"IMS."

She must mean IBS which is Irritable Bowel Syndrome. I've

had a few bouts myself with all the panic in my life. If I look at it with objectivity, most are triggered by my mother.

Stavros cups his dimpled chin in his hand. "This is an interesting topic. It means?"

"Irritable Man Syndrome. I thought about calling it *Bridging the Gap between Bearded and Cranky* but I think that's taken. By the way, I'm Kelly Hershman, Glee's attorney. I specialize in mediation." She reaches out her hand. She touches the empty seat next to her. "My friend hasn't arrived yet but she's got a book in her for sure." She points to the shaved head guy to my right. "That's my husband."

"There's way too much litigation," I offer, trying to get back into the conversation but feeling a bit woozy. A fresh margarita has appeared at my place setting.

She nods. "Mediators keep doing it until everyone is satisfied."

Glee taps her glass with her knife for attention. "A toast to my lovely friends for welcoming the spirits."

Everyone takes a sip of champagne. The bubbles tickle my nose. I really shouldn't have any more to drink before the main course. I haven't eaten all day. Two drinks is my absolute outside limit. If I get silly it could lead to outrageous and shocking behavior. Sometimes my language deteriorates. I take a few sips of the light gold liquid.

I move back to Mr. Greekfest. The waitress has whipped away his untouched soup, replacing it with our next course. Stavros starts his *cerviche*.

Ms. Hershman keeps talking about herself. "We're selling

our home in Desert Mountain because we can't stand the traffic. Takes an hour and fifteen minutes to get home from the Herberger and Orpheum theaters."

Okay. I buy in. "Are you moving downtown?"

"Oh no. We're selling our seven bedroom, six bath home in the back of Desert Mountain and moving to the front."

"But that's the same area," I say, confused.

"Yes, it will save us twelve minutes. . ."

"Wow. Twelve minutes."

". . . of winding through all those streets. Pitch black out there. And, we need more bathrooms." Her head bobs with satisfaction.

More than six?

"Bertram's at that age where he gets up a few times a night to pee. We need to add a third water closet directly next to his side of the bed so he doesn't have to walk so far."

I nod like I understand but inside I'm appalled at the extravagance.

Our silence doesn't affect her.

I'm positive Kelly has an acute case of Asperger's. She continues to talk about herself without regard to whether any of us are listening. Dishes disappear and new ones appear with grilled steaks and small luscious lobster tails.

I continue my interview of Stavros. "How long have you lived in the States?"

"I came in my twenties with a Greek folk dancing troop to teach Americans how to dance like Zorba."

"Is the Greek culture so different from ours?"

"Ah—yes. Americans have much to learn—our joy in the simple pleasures of sharing our table, our bed, the gift of music."

His nostalgia-tinged voice makes me think about how important the table and bed are in our house, although I don't want to share my bed with anyone except Maury. I feel light-headed.

A variety of *mole* sauces graces the table. I spoon some onto my plate. My mouth bursts with the combustible flavors of dried chili peppers, ground almonds, cinnamon and *cacao*, Mexican chocolate.

"Do you find American women very different from their European counterparts?" I love to eat while someone entertains me.

"Ah, good question. I am encouraging your friend, Glee, to write her book. She has what American women strive for—casual sexiness, earthy creativity, that *joie de vivre* that European women ooze. I want her to express that. In Greece women grow up comfortable, relaxed. Here they try too hard."

I pull myself up from a wine slump. "We don't have great role models today. In fact, they're abysmal. We had Jackie, Gloria and Grace when I was growing up. Now young women have Brittany, Lindsay and Paris. No wonder girls aren't wearing underwear on dates anymore."

Maury has overheard me. He shakes his head no.

"It's true." I'm belligerent because those three twits have set back the cause of feminism fifty years. "It was exciting when women promoted sexual freedom. Who knew they were going to use it all up in rehab?"

"Jean!" Maury is giving me The Look, the one I usually give him.

"And not only that . . ." I point my finger for emphasis. ". . . we still haven't broken the concrete ceiling. Why here in Arizona all the twenty largest corporations are headed by men." I am satisfied with my speech and put my hands on the table to steady the spinning votive candles.

Suddenly the two shaved wonders on either side of me engage. Nothing like a feminist throwing down the gauntlet to get macho guys riled up. Mr. Sports Biker Number 1 on my right asks, "You one of those libbers who complain about equality, driving up my corporate costs with sick leave and maternity pay?"

"Maybe women aren't up to the task of competing in the workplace," offers Sport Biker Number Two on my left.

"Now, Bertram," scolds Mediator Hershman to Biker #1.

No one gets away with that. I have a Masters degree in Women and Gender Studies. I know how to use it. I have endless data in my head about women and their ability to rise to the top given equal circumstances. My blood roils. I take a quick breath and count slowly to ten. Since my health scare I work on being more patient.

"Excuse me. Insecure men create roadblocks to women's success. Women and men deserve to have flexibility in the workplace so they can enjoy family life, too."

"Listen, honey, if women want to play in the big boy arena they have to stop the baby machine or turn the kids over to a nanny." Bertram sits back and crosses his arms across his chest.

Ugh. How can his wife stand him?

Maury anticipates an explosion by furrowing his brow. "Now, Jean . . ."

I'm furious. No one calls me honey without getting a response. "A woman's reproductive system has nothing to do with her ability to think and take action. How many women have you promoted in your company with that sexist attitude?"

"JEAN!" Maury is pushing back his chair and coming to get me.

Stavros, oblivious, makes his point. "Glee is a wonderful soul with such charisma I want to bottle it. I have seen talent before but not like this." He pushes the food around his plate.

Bertram says to Maury who's hovering over my chair, "You need to keep your wife under control."

As if.

Maury leans down and says in a loud whisper. "Jean, let's get some air. You've had too much to drink."

The entire table falls quiet watching us. "I have not. I may be foggy and agitated but I am not drunk." I brush my hands down the front of me for imaginary lint.

I turn my body toward Bertram the Sexist. "Do you have any idea of how women have been taken advantage of? What our struggles have been? How—"

Maury pulls back my chair and lifts me up by my armpits. I am still sputtering as he guides me through the glass doors to the patio.

"Jean, what's the matter with you?"

I take a few deep breaths. "Men like that make me furious."

"Jean, calm down. How much have you had to drink?"

"Two margaritas. And a little champagne. No big-shot investor is going to intimidate me."

Glee sticks her head out the glass doors. "Dessert's in the living room. You guys okay?"

"Absolutely. We're fine," I say. I look up at Maury's big brown eyes. A sympathetic smile crosses his lips. He thinks I'm out of control.

"Jean, Kelly Hershman's friend arrived. Just giving you a heads up," says Glee.

"This is the 21st century. The fact that attitudes like his still exist. . ."

"Jean, get a grip. We're at a party."

"So?" I say shrugging my shoulders.

18

GLEE'S LIVING ROOM FILLS WITH HER SATIATED PARTY GUESTS. I'm feeling more centered as Maury and I admire her over-sized contemporary coffee table covered with burning candles, fresh flowers and an array of buttery pastries. A mountain of fresh fruit surrounds a lit silver fountain dripping chocolate. I don't think he's going to leave my side.

The bar, returned to its rightful place at the end of the room, becomes the next stop. The bartender has transformed into our barista with a new uniform. Standing behind a few complicated machines in an elaborate red jacket with gold braid epaulets reminiscent of my high school band uniform, he asks, "Cappucino? Espresso? Latte? Shots of liqueur?"

If he says *vente* I'll scream.

A few women, chatting, line up to place their orders when the whirr of the machines begins. The barista is consumed with pulling levers, moving small metal pitchers, asking questions about skinny, tall, decaf or not, the lexicon that invaded our language even if we're not in the official coffee den of the world. "Free trade African blend or Jamaican Blue Mountain?" he asks with an anticipatory smile.

The guests place their orders and continue babbling, blasé that Glee has brought an entire Starbucks franchise into her living room; however, I am impressed. When she swirls by I give her arm a small squeeze and whisper, "You are awesome."

She grins at me with an "of course" smile and waves her hand. "It's nothing," she says. I know that it consumed her with weeks of effort and arrangements. Of course she did have Amanda to help.

Maury and I stand at the outskirts to observe what people order, where they position themselves. I'm fuming a bit. Mostly at myself because being tipsy makes me feel out of control. What's happening to me?

After ordering their coffees Bertram and his scary mediator wife—I imagine both sides of a case she mediates losing instead of compromising—sit on a love seat. He pushes his cup and saucer onto the table, throwing an arm around her shoulders. She must be bright because she has a law degree, but how does she live with such a jerk? I'd be arguing with him all the time.

Suddenly, wild black hair appears from around the corner. No! It's Flora with a plate of food. Kelly's missing guest.

Kelly makes room for her next to Bertram. "Glad you made it. See you got something from the kitchen."

Flora, in a black shirtwaist dress, wiggles into the spot

they've made for her. I'm in shock. My nails dig into Maury's arm.

"She's here," I say.

He's oblivious until he sees where I'm staring. "Oh no."

I rush over to Glee who's supervising the coffee. I huddle next to her and whisper in a panic, "What's Flora doing here?"

"Kelly Hershman said she wanted to bring a friend. I had no idea . . ."

I feel sweaty all over. My body gives out distress signals.

My other biker buddy and his wife choose a spot on the semi-circular red sofa, re-arranging some purple silk pillows behind their backs. Others join them including April who crosses her legs discreetly and Steve, who sits and then jumps up to shake Flora's hand. April does a double-take and then searches for me. I give April a worried look. Maybe Flora will behave herself. Maybe I won't.

Maury and I perch on two black-lacquered bar stools placed behind the sofa. Maury has switched to a standard cup of cowboy coffee, no sugar or cream. Coffee doesn't affect his sleep habits. He drinks ten cups a day. I now sip a decaf-café mocha with whipped cream and chocolate sprinkles. I must be drunk.

Stavros molds himself into a butter cream leather lounger, one leg tossed over the arm, taking center stage. He's a European film star, commanding attention, his ascot slightly askew. His suntanned hands hold a demitasse cup.

He clears his throat to announce, "We must acknowledge our exceptional hostess for this evening."

The group applauds while Steve puts two fingers in his mouth and whistles while stomping his feet.

I yell, "Bravo!" and then eye Flora who is bent over eating her food, the plate balanced on her knees.

Glee, sitting on a hassock at the head of the room, tilts her head and blows Stavros a kiss.

He continues. "And, not only is she an extraordinary hostess, she is also a gifted writer with creative ability. Would you agree?" The group responds again with clapping and shouts of encouragement. "She has to write down her ideas about *hara tis zois*, our Greek phrase for the happiness of life. If she will do this, I can get her on the *New York Times* best seller list in two years."

A murmur of approval rolls through the satisfied group. I'm impressed with his confidence in her. Flora's eating without acknowledgement.

Glee says with a nod and smile, "Thank you, darling, for your faith in me." Maybe her intention is to write a book. She's never mentioned it although I've talked about it often.

She leans forward to spear pieces of banana, strawberry and mango from the base of the fountain, dipping it in the flowing chocolate. She places two or three on a hand-painted Mexican plate. With bowls and spoons in front of her she asks, "Would you like blueberries, fresh mint, *crème fraiche* or almonds on top? Or all of the above? All organic, of course."

I keep an eye on Flora while people pick and choose the toppings. Most want to try everything. Glee passes desserts to the guests on the sofa, a small silver fork balanced on the side.

Flora accepts a dessert.

Suddenly, Glee says, "Everyone, I want to introduce one of our state legislators, a guest of Kelly and Bertram, Flora Beauxdreaux."

Flora nods and waves to the group as they acknowledge her with hi's and hello's.

I am frozen. Maury says, "Careful, honey, you've had a few too many." He knows I'm churning inside.

"No, I haven't had enough to drink," I say through clenched lips. Flora's eyes lock in mine.

"April?" asks Glee.

"I'll have one spear. Strawberries only, please."

Glee looks at her expectantly for the toppings, her hand on the *crème fraiche.*

"Only mint."

That's why April looks the way she does and I wrestle Spanx in my spare time.

Some of the plates are returning to Glee for seconds with laments about diets, trainers and the gym. A few of the women moan in ecstasy.

Bertram says, "This is delish, Glee. You're the best." He turns to his wife and asks, "How come you never make this?" She elbows him into silence.

I'm salivating waiting my turn for fruit shish-ka-bobs. Is there anything better than warm chocolate?

Finally, our plates are passed back to us. Maury and I eat them with haste, each exceptional bite erupting with sweet flavors and sumptuous texture. I lean toward him, our heads barely touching, and we make "*mmmm*" sounds to each other.

"Just so you all know," Glee says, glancing toward me and Maury, "I've used politically correct chocolate from beans grown in Africa that have eighty percent cacao."

I expect Flora to jump on anything that's politically correct but she's surprisingly quiet. Worse, I'll be up all night. I don't sleep anyway. No sleep will be worth every morsel. I close my eyes perched on the bar stool visualizing chocolate mountains.

Steve, ever ready for a legal opportunity, asks Stavros, "So you think our little Glee here can write a best seller?"

"Absolutely," says Stavros, sipping from his demitasse cup. He licks a little foam from his top lip. "All successful books are non-fiction. Self-help is a big arena. With our society in a mess people are hungry for advice. They search for solutions. Glee has experienced so much."

Glee, her hands busy creating silky chocolate desserts, gazes at Stavros. A look passes between them. She trusts him.

I nudge Maury, hovering over his second dessert. He gives me a "what?" look. I know what he's thinking. He can spot a con.

"All she needs is an outline, some personal stories, an empathetic absolute uplifting conclusion and *opa!* She has a book. Promotion is more important than the book. With Glee's agreeable personality and the right author endorsements, it could be spectacular."

"Like who would she need?" Steve asks.

"With a quote from Deepak Chopra or Dr. Wayne Dwyer, the book is a winner."

Maybe Whoopi Goldberg could help me. I've been working on a novel about an early feminist firebrand's struggle to get women the right to vote for years. Twenty million single women haven't even registered so I think it's a hot topic. If I got that going, people like Flora couldn't get elected. I glance in her direction. She's spooning chocolate into her mouth.

The group absorbs Glee's possibility of fame. Bertram turns around and scowls at me, as though he can read my feminist thoughts.

The doorbell rings. Amanda, who has faded against the wall, cat eyeglasses propped on top of her head, springs into action.

Now what? Flora's husband, the blind sheep infector himself?

Glee stands to maneuver center stage, a fresh margarita in hand. "Our entertainment has arrived. Please welcome The Mariachi Mavens!"

Six short and chubby musicians parade into the room dressed in black. With their heads down they strum guitars and sing, "*Besame Mucho.*" Silver buttons trail down the sides of their tight pants. With colored ties at their necks and over-sized sequined Mexican sombreros, the kind you're sorry you bought on vacation, they glimmer in the candlelight.

Maury whispers in my ear, pointing. "Look at the *guitarron*, the six-string instrument with the rounded and humped swollen back. You don't see those much anymore."

His description reminds me of the *fakrimpt* ladies at my mother's place. That's why I love him. Who else would have such obscure information about a musical instrument? I enjoy the entertainment but my mind wanders to Flora a few feet away.

After five or six songs they offer a red rose to each of the women. They swoop off their sombreros, take a deep bow and make their exit with an extended serenade to Glee.

After the musical interlude two couples bid good-bye with apologies for being the first to leave.

Glee urges us to join the circle around the warm, dripping chocolate fountain now that there's space on the sofa.

I salivate. I don't want to dribble down my chin. Plates are whisked from our hands. Men sit on one side, women on the other except for Flora. She stays with the men. Steve throws his head back on the sofa, his eyes fluttering. I sit at the edge of the women in between the men. Flora is a few seats away from me.

The rest of the women, acquaintances of Glee, refer to themselves as "the girls." Spa treatments dominate the conversation.

"There's a special over at the Four Seasons—a reflexology foot massage with a simultaneous facial for three hundred dollars," says a plumped, tightened blonde. She adds, "I met Donatella in the Jacuzzi last week."

I eavesdrop. Maybe the men are talking about something more interesting. Uh-oh. Maury's broken the cardinal rule. He's discussing politics. Damn. And he was worried about me making a scene? I can't leave him alone for a minute.

"Look, the election's ten days away. Environment's the main issue. If we don't clean up our air, no one's going to want to live or vacation here. It'll kill the economy."

"Every time an ecology issue comes up, it makes my blood boil," says Bertram, spreading his arm around Flora and tapping her shoulder.

"Why?" asks Maury.

"Because the environmentalists put too many restrictions on how a city can develop."

Oh no. Flora won't be subdued for long.

Maury responds with a clear, level voice. "Look, there are great inequities. Some restrictions have to apply, especially to manufacturers who dump toxic waste and developers who churn up the earth. Otherwise, polluters would take more advantage than they already do. We've seen the effects on people's health."

My stomach flips. I inch closer to the men's group.

Bertram shifts on the couch, his right hand searching for a pillow behind him. He finds one and positions himself to look taller. Leaning forward, arms on knees, he says, "Once the polluters pay high fees, you hamper the economic viability of certain industries. Like developers who want to build houses so people have a nice place to live."

Oh no. Oh no! I know Bertram's comment will elicit a response from Maury. I can't say anything. I have to behave. Maury can handle him. I hope Glee doesn't take us off her A-party list. As long as Flora stays out of it he'll be okay.

I tune back into "the girls." A heated debate ensues about the merits of a lavender loofah scrub as opposed to a tea tree body polish. Why would I want to smell like my grandmother's linen closet or medicinal herbs?

It reminds me of when I tried the pumpkin facial at the beauty school and smelled like a pie for twelve hours.

I go back to eavesdropping on Maury. Is he going to take this guy on?

Maury's got that intense, go ahead just start up with me, look on his face, one I only see before sex.

"I understand raising fees is unpopular but Arizona is leaving a million dollars in emission revenue on the table. Under federal law we could collect much more."

Bertram waves his hand in dismissal.

Flora pipes up, "Oh, you sound like one of those Robin Hood's who want to take money from the rich and give to the poor. You probably think global warming is changing the weather too."

Frustration creeps into Maury's voice. Now he has both of them in the fray. I'm amazed at his capacity to speak with calm authority.

Maury gives Flora the eye. "Green issues affect everyone, our health, our food sources. They need to be foremost so we can preserve and improve the world we have."

Bertram harrumphs and folds his arms tight across his chest. He's silent for a moment perhaps deciding how to handle this confrontation.

"I am so sick of you greens who want to shut down government. Bidniz runs this state and what's more. . . ," says Flora.

She said bidniz instead of business. I want to correct her.

Maury jumps in. "In our Valley it's not just the carbon emissions choking us. Its particles created by construction. We have one of the dirtiest cities in the nation."

Does he know what Bertram does for a living? Is he baiting Flora?

She pipes up. "Hey—wait a minute. I'm tired of you people dumping on developers. Are you trying to blame the pollution problems on the people creating the jobs? Have you ever been out to our great planned community fifty miles west of Phoenix? Even have wi-fi in every home."

They're plowing down the desert to put up thousands of homes with identical red roofs. I'm burning up.

Flora positions herself so she can wag a finger at Maury. "I'll have you know my husband is a responsible developer. Why, people from California and Colorado fly in here to purchase multiple lots."

"Which is why we have blind bighorn sheep," I add.

"You lefty Communist tree hugger," says Flora, leaning in at me with her wagging finger.

A poker of anxiety moves to my neck positioning itself for a boulder-sized headache.

"Ahem," I say, addressing Flora and clearing my throat. "My own mother can't go out half the time because of our high pollution advisory days. You are destroying our environment."

"Now Jean," says Maury.

Flora's body language makes her aggression apparent. Her hands are balled into fists, the cords of her neck stand out. "Now your feminazi wife thinks that's my fault too? I'm serving the public so people can have jobs and live decent lives."

Maury knows Rush Limbaugh's offensive term drives me wild.

"Just a minute. Don't speak about my wife in derogatory terms," says Maury in my defense, leaning forward. "Let's be civil here. Name calling doesn't address issues."

I sputter, interrupting my erupting husband, "Clean air and water are basic. If you think you're going to win the next election with your attitude of screw the little guy, you—"

"And now, for our grand finale. Amanda?" Glee, our effervescent hostess, has rescued us from the hostility. Maury and I lean back. The confrontation has ended for now. I'm steaming. I glance at Flora. She stands up, gathers her purse and heads toward the door. Kelly Hershman breaks away and chases after her.

Amanda, Personal Assistant Extraordinaire, eyeglasses on the bridge of her nose, carries in an easel with a canvas hidden under a black cloth. She wears a floppy straw hat with a large yellow flower in the front and lots of feathers.

Flora appears and addresses Glee. "Thank you for including me in your evening. I must leave to pick up my daughter Tiffany who's coming back from Vegas on personal bidniz."

I'm not finished with her yet. Did she throw Tiffany's name out there just to make me more irate?

"Your daughter has no integrity," I sputter.

Flora turns to address me. "How dare you cast spurious doubts upon my daughter's character. I should've strangled you the first time I met you."

"What?" You threatening me?" I stand up. Maury's hand is reaching for my arm.

"Now, ladies," says Kelly, our mediator, guiding Flora toward the door.

Flora has the last word. "As for your inconsequential opinions, my victory party is at the Ritz. The people of my district know who they want representing them. Where's yours? McDonald's? Oh, I forgot. You greens don't eat meat."

I look down to see if I can manipulate myself around the cocktail table and everyone's feet. I am going to kill her. I'm going to get my hands in that rat's nest of hair and start pulling and then I'm going to . . . "Aargh!" I am out of words and I'm trapped where I'm standing. I start to stammer and sputter. "How-how-how dare you b-bait me? You've got a helluva nerve."

"Jean," says Maury, standing up next to me and giving me a bear hug.

Amanda takes the opportunity to guide Flora to the foyer. We hear the door close. I sit down. Usually I'm a sissy but that woman makes me so mad. Then I eye the chocolate fountain. I should have poured the whole thing over her. But Glee would have banned me forever from her parties.

Maury and I sit down with Bertram glaring at us. Kelly squeezes in next to him.

Glee addresses the group in measured tones reading from an index card. "Jose Guadalupe Posada, a famous wood-cut artist who lived in the early 1900s and died in poverty, was an amazing engraver and illustrator. He popularized the *calaca*, the most famous of which is Caterina."

Amanda whips off the black cloth. We stare at the head of a skeleton wearing a large hat decorated with feathers carved into a thick wooden plank.

"I present a linoleum cut of *"Calavera de la Caterina"* in her *pacheco*," says Glee in a *ta-da* voice.

Steve's eyes are closed. April tilts forward and squints. She never puts her glasses on in public. Her brows can't scrunch or raise, but her mouth drops open a bit.

"What does it mean?" she asks.

"Aah," says Glee. "She's the messenger of mortality, the symbol of death, an artistic expression."

"But what's the point?" April asks, wriggling a little to get closer.

Glee looks puzzled. I think it looks like the velvet stuff stacked in stores at the border. Fine art? Really? Okay. More like folk art. Maybe.

"What is the point of any art? Self expression, beauty," says Glee.

Maury offers, "Posada did many versions of Caterina because he satirized the life of the upper classes. He saw the disparity between them and the poor. A Mexican middle class didn't exist in those days."

It's silent, except for a few guests chomping on candy sugar skulls they've taken from the table. Did Glee know that? I give Maury a slight jab in the ribs with my elbow for his ironic observation.

How does he remember these things instead of where he put his keys?

"Well, it's been a lovely party," says a botoxed blond as the women gather their evening bags. It's a quiet exit.

I think Maury killed the party. Satirizing the life of the upper classes? Dear God.

Glee sees people to the door among exclamations of what a fabulous night it was and how much they enjoyed the food and the uniqueness of the "dead" theme.

Maury, always a gentleman, stands to shake Bertram's hand. "Consider a vote for Craig Burton, our Green Party candidate November seventh. He could make a real difference."

"Over my dead body." Bertram mumbles as the door closes.

Our hostess slips off her shoes, settles in, tucking her feet under her and sighs. The last hard core partiers, Glee's nearest and dearest friends, join her for the after party re-hash. Maury, April and I spread out on the sofa while Steve snores softly.

Ted, Glee's ex, slips into my mind. He used to be in our tight little circle with his overblown gruff style. I don't know about Stavros, who stands behind the bar mixing another drink. He makes my friend happy, but is he for real? She dives into relationships with such abandon.

April stares at the new art work. "I don't know if I'd want a skeleton in my home," she says.

My sentiments exactly.

Glee responds. "I wasn't sure either. I'm going to live with her for a while. If I change my mind, I'll take it back to the gallery. I thought she'd be great for tonight."

Maury shifts. "Wait. You bought art just for tonight's party? And you might return it?"

"Some women in town do that with expensive dresses. Ask the saleswomen at Saks," says April.

"It's not as bad as purchasing a painting to match a sofa. Why not a fiesta? Women change their minds all the time." Glee shrugs.

I tread with deference because Glee's my friend but those types of generalizations disturb me. "It's sexist to say that women change their minds. Men do too."

"Oh, Jean, don't take it personally. Besides, we all learned something about the artist."

Glee says, "Think about all the people who benefit when we celebrate—musicians, bartenders, caterers." I nod in agreement. I never looked at it that way before.

Steve snuffles like Amber when she's having a bad dream.

April says, "He's been working so hard. Plus there's all this upset with the police, the insurance company, setting up a new security system. I'm still afraid to stay in the house alone. I make the dogs follow me everywhere."

We nod in support. I try to envision April's dog dust- mops, six inches off the ground with bows from the groomer, scaring anyone.

I change the subject. "So what's the deal with Bertram and his mediator wife bringing Flora? Couldn't you have warned me?"

"Honestly, honey, I didn't know. Kelly said she had a friend who she thought would enjoy our evening and asked if she could bring her. I had no idea. And she was late! How weird."

"Not as weird as having Flora as a friend."

"Listen, Kelly and Bertram are a fun couple. They have a ballroom. It's the newest rage. Turn part of your backyard or pool area into a dance parlor with hardwood floors, preferably recycled maple, put in a sound system and sexy lighting. They're learning to salsa."

I'm so conflicted. Part of me wants to dance on their private ballroom floor and the other wants to know if they destroyed rainforest trees to build it. No wonder I'm on the edge of insanity.

"They had a terrible time getting it installed. I can't believe they want to move."

Maury always reminds me that rich people's problems are different, like when they go ballistic because the gardener doesn't show or the cleaners ruin their leather pants.

April nibbles sensuously on a chocolate, "Where did you find these?"

"At a specialty shop. They're from São Tomé, an island off the coast of Africa."

"I just thought of something," says Maury. We look at him with interest. "There's a *calavera* in an adult comic book series who's a female Mexican assassin with razor claws."

"How did they base a comic book on Flora?" I ask.

"Oh, Jean," says the group in unison. Steve elicits a few snores.

Stavros clears his throat. He is not going to let politics

distract him from his purpose. "For our final surprise, Glee has signed a contract with Acropolis to publish her first book."

Glee smiles, getting up to hug him. She could write about a lot of things. For three chapters maybe. *Women who Date Younger Men: the Cougar Movement Up Close* or *Coaching for Love: Erotic Art for the Bedroom* or *Yoga for the Inept* or *How to Divorce Well in Today's Economy.*

"I don't have a title yet . . ." She gives us a quick wink. ". . . but it's about how women can possess more sex appeal." She adjusts the elastic on her off-the-shoulder blouse.

"That's a great topic. If anyone can do it, you can. Can't wait to read it," April says, worrying the same chocolate.

Stavros briefs us on why Glee and her hot topic are just what America needs. I can't underestimate Glee, but publishing a book and getting it to hit number one? Sure, the original Chicken Soup guy broke all sales records, but Glee?

Maury touches my arm. He's pointing to his watch, his not so subtle signal.

All couples have those. Steve usually gives April the circling finger which means wind it up. My father's two short head jerks to my mother meant let's get out of here. When we first got married Maury was anti-social and wanted to arrive late and leave early. The man would be a slug if it wasn't for me. I'm feeling woozy anyway.

Glee walks us to the door.

"Thank you," I say kissing both of her cheeks. "It was wonderful as always."

"My pleasure."

"Uh, listen, I got a little out of control. I hope we didn't offend any of your guests or commit a *faux pas*."

With a wave of her hand she says, "Bertram? He'll get over it. Flora? She's used to it."

Glee hugs Maury, then me. She has moved on to the next event. "You have to come to a writer's conference with me so we can finish our books."

"Maybe." I can barely sort out my life.

"It would be good for you. Stavros says I'll get some feedback and crystallize my ideas. There's one coming up."

I shrug my shoulders. Finishing a novel I began years ago with my manic life? Sounds great but what are the possibilities?

On the way home Maury reaches for my hand. "You okay?"

"Don't I seem okay?"

"Just a little belligerent maybe."

"Why?"

Maury hunches over the wheel. "You're testy."

I wrench my hand away and cross my arms over my chest.

"I am not." My heart races faster.

"So we're still a good team, eh, Babe?"

I don't respond. Maury doesn't get my frustrations.

"Oh, by the way, Lara called earlier when you were getting dressed."

My body language remains in a tight, closed pose.

"And?"

"She wanted to know what we're doing Tuesday and Wednesday nights."

"What did you tell her?"

"I told her we're free."

"Maury! Why did you say that? You know I need some space to catch up with everything."

"She and Gus want to drop the kids off for a sleep over."

I get out at our house and slam the car door.

19

STRESS RELIEF TIP: Irritability is a known side effect of stress. Relax often.

—Tension, Trauma and You

THE DETAILS OF MY LIFE HAVE OVERWHELMED ME. After entertaining the adorable but demanding grandkids, I rushed to my client's to meet his deadline. We're implementing a new program to prevent against sexual harassment.

I stopped short when the car in front of me braked for a yellow light and I plowed into the back of a Toyota. I got out of the car relieved no one was hurt. The vehicle's bumper was mangled and askew. The teen professed in a high pitched voice that his father was going to kill him. I offered to drive him home and say it was my fault. He declined. Death was worse than driving with me so we waited in silence for a tow truck. I glanced with sadness at the dented fender of the Volvo and called Maury.

I didn't admit to anyone except him that I was texting while driving. Maury was waiting for me in the kitchen.

"Jean, don't you know you shouldn't be doing any other

activity when you're operating a vehicle? What's wrong with you? Nothing is that important."

"I was letting Lara know Macy's is having a sale on steamers," I respond in a small voice.

"Jean! That's nonsense! You could have been killed. Or worse, killed someone else."

"She has a lot of laundry. Besides, I wasn't going very fast. No one was hurt. Insurance will cover it. Wait a minute. It's worse if someone else dies instead of me?" This *must* mean he's having an affair.

"You are the most frustrating woman I've ever known. I don't get mad at you often, but now I'm angry."

"You're mad at me over a fender bender?" I put my hands on my hips to defend my position of incompetence.

"Someone is going to be harmed by your incessant multi-tasking!" He steps toward me and puts his hands on my arms, staring into my eyes with concern.

"It was a sale. Steamers cost a hundred dollars."

"JEAN! You're impossible." With that he grabs his keys, baseball cap and iPod, the door slamming behind him.

I feel terrible. Maury and I rarely argue.

My life is unraveling. I'm miserable. Besides my stiff neck from the accident, Maury and I are not speaking. I stay in bed snuffling and patting my tears with a crumpled tissue. Maury's at the office. I wander downstairs after he leaves without brushing my teeth or combing my hair and eat cookies for breakfast.

Then I crawl back into bed and stay there for three days. I'm on strike. He manages the inconvenience of multiple phone calls from the insurance company. I hear the frustration in his voice. "Are you sure we had a thousand dollar deductible? What about our rates?"

What repeatedly comes up for me is the confrontation with Flora at Glee's party and how badly I handled it. I made a fool of myself. I should have limited my alcohol intake. I should have told her off. I should have kept my mouth shut. Flora represents a significant constituency who have a different vision for our state and that frustrates me. I sink into a depression. I'm in the traffic jam of life experiencing a meltdown.

I doze, sleeping to escape. I can't face anything. After the mini-stroke scared me I made an effort to take better care of myself. I took my supplements and showed up at the gym. But the rest of my activities didn't change. Now I can't get a handle on anything.

I try to self-talk myself out of a chasm of despair. Things aren't so bad. Life is good. Maury's still here. But it doesn't work.

My problems may not look terrible to other people who aren't having their basic needs met. I'm not in Darfur caught in a civil war or an Afghani woman being punished for going to school or someone dying of AIDS because there's no money for medications. But in my world right here, right now, I feel like an exploded balloon, the kind where the skin's stretched thin and the air's sucked out. I'm deflated, torn, used up, a discarded condom in a park. I feel immobile and lumpy.

I stay in bed with brief forays into the kitchen. I eat all the wrong things thanks to a stocked pantry. I bring snacks to bed. I'm lolling on crumbs from cheese Danish, cashews and peanut butter crackers.

Finally, Maury and I start to communicate again. He checks on my status, either chiding me to get out of bed or coaxing me with sweet words to take action. He even confesses he'd welcome back the multi-tasking Jean.

But I've given up. He sighs and goes to work or plays golf, brings home Chinese food and pizza for dinner, all the while admonishing me to call my cardiologist or a mental health counselor.

"You're going to have another stroke if you keep up this kind of behavior," he tells me.

However, he doesn't mention the other catastrophe's enveloping our lives like Amber's multiple accidents on the foyer rug because she's not being walked regularly, or my cancelled car insurance because I have too many points, or the downstairs toilet that's overflowed, or the ever-present threat of roof rats. Or Rivka's infertility hysteria or Tangie's chomp on her brother's penis in the tub or the terrorist threats and child abductions reported on CNN or my technology ineptitude.

I can't follow up with everyone about everything. I want to show I care, but I've run out of empathy genes. Worse, the paperwork and calls about the fender bender make me want to hide, a reminder of my ineptitude.

I don't check messages, ignoring the *glub-glub-glub* burp

sound the machine makes. I'm not checking anything anymore—my cell phone, e-mail, fax or snail mail.

Maury suggests I go to my stress self-help group after Facilitator Bob calls. On the ten-point stress continuum with one through three being vegetable calmness and nine to ten high anxiety, I'm in the nine zone.

I'm not a ten because I haven't freaked out, screaming and flailing my arms so a straight jacket is required. But I'm not managing that well either. My frustration makes me want to give up.

The phone rings. Dreadlocks from my support group. I pick up to tell her I'm a drop out.

"What are you doing?" she asks.

"Lying in bed eating bon-bons."

"Sister Jean, go outside, take a walk, smell the flowers, look at the beautiful blue Arizona sky."

"No. I like wallowing in self-pity. Please don't call again. I'm not coming back."

"Go outside. For five minutes. I promise it'll help.

I can come over and soothe you, talk it out."

"Thanks, but no thanks." I hang up without returning the phone to the cradle. Maybe the battery will run down.

After the next trip to the bathroom I creep downstairs, look out the glass doors to check for dead roof rats and slide one open. Amber's tail wags. She's thrilled to be let out.

I try. I really do. Dreadlocks suggestion hasn't been lost on me. I stand outside my house, looking at my wilted flowers that didn't survive the extreme heat, the sky that's grey with pollution and take a deep breath of dust. I come right back inside.

Dejected, overwhelmed, hair uncombed, face unwashed, I climb back into bed and stare at the rotations of the ceiling fan. I can't bear another day.

It is in this state of inertia on day number five that Maury finds me at four in the afternoon. He stands at the end of the bed, reading glasses perched on top of his head.

"Jean, this is supposed to be the best time of our lives. I've slowed down to three days a week. Our bills are paid. No one's been diagnosed with a serious illness. Why are you falling apart now? We live in Scottsdale for Chrissakes."

As if living in Scottsdale will solve all the world's problems. What about all the conspicuous consumption, the plastic surgery slaves, the high percentage of two people wandering around 10,000 square foot houses?

I close my eyes. I can't look at him. I've failed everyone including myself. I pick up a pillow and hug it.

He comes over to sit next to me, pulls the pillow away and takes my hand. "What are you so busy with? Is it all necessary?"

"I've got so much to do and I don't think I can get anything done anymore." I frown, croaking at the same time. Then I break down in tears. I look really ugly when I cry so if there's a shred in me that wants to keep my husband, this won't help.

"What's on your list that's so urgent?"

"The car and all the insurance paperwork."

"I'm helping you with that."

I roll over and bury my face. I can't stop crying. I'm muffled, but I know he can hear me between heaves of sobs. "I-I have all these people to take care of and they're draining my energy. The kids and my mother and my friends with their problems and you . . ."

"Me? I'm not a problem. I'm considering medical missionary work in a third world country."

"That's the point. You'll be fulfilled and I'll be left behind to manage the house, the kids, the rats."

"What do the rats have to do with this?" Frustration rises in his voice.

"Because your stupid chart on the front of the refrigerator declaring war on them shows there's only two taken in battle, including an unsuspecting bird. You're losing!"

I turn over. Do I tell him lost keys, misplaced glasses, unfinished home projects and a political campaign with a red-haired ectoplasm are adding to my unhappiness too? Yes. I verbalize it in a torrent of hurt and accusations. By the time I finish my litany, I'm spent.

He comes closer to the bed, his eyes melancholy.

"You're cracking up, Jean. Compose yourself and listen to what you're saying. You're screaming at me. I'm you're biggest supporter."

"I AM NOT SCREAMING."

Maury sits on the edge of the bed next to me. He puts his hands on my shoulders. "Maybe you should try some meds. Like Lexapro for your nerves."

"I DO NOT NEED MEDS. I AM CALM." I take in a deep

breath through my nose, hold it and then let it out, unclenching my fists. Doctors always want to prescribe.

"What's stressing you out the most?"

I cover my face with my hands. "Everything. I can't do it all. Even the little things are setting me off. Like the mail. All those solicitations for money from Democrats, Libertarians, pro-choice groups, environmental causes and Al Gore. I'm not sure I like Al Gore since he got fat. It takes me an hour to sort mail and I don't even work for the post office."

Maury stands up. "I'm capable of sorting mail."

"No! You'll throw away my favorite catalogue or send money to Siberian orphans or forget to pay a bill. You don't make four piles like I do for household bills, charities and stuff to shred. I sort your ACLU, Southern Law Poverty Center, Simon Wiesenthal solicitations, Greenpeace and Doctors without Borders mail into piles. I keep the restaurant coupons, endangered animals and feminist causes for myself, making another pile for bills. That's besides the stuff I shred."

"Why are you shredding?"

I remove my hands from my face to enunciate my words, my voice louder. "Everything has to be obliterated because of identity theft. We're living in an insane world where people go through garbage to steal credit card applications with free checks attached. They might even sign us up for a magazine we don't want."

Just the thought of *Sports Illustrated* with a bikini-clad model on the cover arriving unsolicited makes my heart beat faster. I'm panting.

"Jean, this is ridiculous. I promise you the Super Scottsdale Identity Thieves are not searching the Rubin garbage. When did you get so neurotic? You've never been like this." Maury's exasperated tone riles me.

He doesn't get it. "When life became so complicated. I can't stand it when you humor me."

Maury sees the upset on my face and tries to soothe me with conciliatory words, stroking my arm. "It's only mail."

I feel angry, belligerent, annoyed.

"Jean, it's self-created stress. Take things in stride. Look how mellow I am. Nothing bothers me."

Maury's lack of understanding makes me berserk. "Of course not! You work part time, play golf, change a few light bulbs while I work, shop, chop, cook, run a household, take care of my mother, buy birthday presents. Why can't you pick out an ecologically sensitive, politically correct present for a kid?"

"You're in a chronic state of stress. It'll kill your brain cells. I'll help with your mom. We get along great. We're a team, remember?"

"Right. You'll help? I show up at her place to check on the placement of the hideous gold chair and you're watching a baseball game, beer in hand, and my mother's wearing your baseball cap. Backwards."

"C'mon, Jean. She likes the Phillies."

"You were supposed to be hanging pictures."

"Okay. I'll do that next week. Do you know where my tool box is?"

"See what I mean?! You don't know where anything is." I smash my fist against the bed.

Maury's phone buzzes. He stands up to dig it out of his pocket, squints at the screen and clicks it off.

"That was Starr, wasn't it?" He looks sheepish. "I know it wasn't the office because you would've taken it."

"The election's in a few days. It's crunch time at campaign headquarters," he says in a conciliatory tone.

Now I'm really pissed. "You're texting with that eco-warrior and oblivious to my needs?"

Is there more to this relationship than particulates? Something holds me back. Maybe I don't want to know.

"Look, we've got some important pieces in place. Sunday's paper will have an editorial about the effects of dirty air on the population's health. It implicates the developers because of all the dust they kick up. Starr and I have been interfacing with the writer on pollution issues."

I give him a disgusted smirk.

20

I REMAIN IN MY BED WHICH HAS BECOME MY FORTRESS. Maury has taken over mail duty and cooking. Lara and Michael have come to visit with spouses and kids.

Tangie asks, "What's wrong with Grandma?"

"Shush. She's not feeling well."

"Oh." She puts her thumb in her mouth.

I do too.

My mother calls. She assaults me with, "Honey, I know you're feeling down. I've been depressed most of my life but especially since your father passed away. But I get up every day, get dressed, put on my make-up and face the world."

"Mom, I'm just not in the mood to do anything."

"Why not? I need you. When are you coming over?"

I switch the phone to speaker so I can nibble string cheese

and drink Kool-Aid. "Mom, I don't feel competent to drive."

Her voice echoes around the room. "Jean, I didn't raise you to be a wimp. Get out of bed this minute and come over here! There's a whole mall waiting for us."

"Mom, you don't understand. I can't. I'm not functioning right now."

"Well, neither am I! Unless you get out of bed and come over, I'm going to take a cab to your place. You cannot ignore your mother," she shouts at me.

That is a serious threat. The thought of my mother marching into my bedroom, criticizing my hair and sloppy food-stained nightgown upsets me.

"Mom, you can't do that."

"They don't have taxis in Scottsdale? I'm hanging up and calling one right now."

Oy. Just what I don't want. "Mom, listen. I'll send Lara or Maury over to help you."

"No, I want you. And unless you get over here in twenty-four hours, I'm going to take that as a sign you need my help. I'll pack a bag and have it ready. Is the guest room clean?"

Maury opens the bedroom door gingerly. The air-conditioning is running at full blast blowing the papers from the bed onto the floor. A pile of newspapers and magazines sit next to me.

"Jean?"

I look up.

"Feeling any better?"

No response.

"I have some upsetting news." He walks around to my side of the bed.

"I do too. What's yours?"

"The kid from your accident? His dad is suing us. Got the letter from his attorney today. Found out I'm a doc and he thinks he's going to get big bucks."

"But no one was injured," I say, agitated that I have to be bothered with this. My foot starts to shake.

"I know. You happened to run into someone's car whose uncle is a personal injury attorney."

"What's his grievance?"

"Says the kid has suffered emotional trauma and has broken out in boils. Can't go to school."

Both of my feet are on a tremor march. I push myself to sit up better. "Are you telling me we're being sued for pimples?"

"Yup. People can sue for anything."

"That does it. I'm never going out into the world again."

"What's your bad news? Maury asks, placing a hand on one of ankles to stop the shaking.

"My mother is packing a bag and moving in."

Maury's face falls. He digs into his pockets, pulls out a folded piece of paper, walks around the bed and crawls in close to me.

"Jean, you have to do something. This flyer came to the office. Thought it might help you. Mayo Clinic is promoting 'mindfulness' for healing stress. It's a combo of Eastern meditation and western psychology called MBSR."

"I'm not interested in some nutty course with strange

initials."

He puts on the readers hanging from the front of his shirt. "'Mindfulness-based stress reduction' bolsters health, helps you focus and inhibits worrying about the past or the future. It's called 'Reduce Stress Now!'"

"Since when are you the guru on stress?"

He reaches out to stroke my arm. "Since I want to keep you around for a long time. My first choice is to have you talk to Adolph Scheiner, the new psychiatrist. He can put you on some medication."

"I am not going to talk to anyone named Adolph!"

"Then if you don't want to take meds, try this."

"It sounds like another mumbo-jumbo discipline."

"No, I don't think so. Says here it was invented by a molecular biologist named Jon Kabat-Zinn in 1970 who founded the Stress Reduction Clinic. He's proven stress batters the immune system. It's implicated in diseases from hypertension to cancer. You're going to get yourself sick again if you don't break this cycle."

I'm glum. I know what he's saying is true.

"Come on, hon. Be proactive." He leans over and kisses my cheek. He smells like a clean bar of soap.

My cell chirps with a text message. I check it.

"Who is it?" Maury props himself on his elbow.

"The organic dry cleaner. Wants to deliver our clothes. Glee told me to switch. Said the toxins and plastic bags would morph in our closets and attack us."

"Doesn't the trēo help?"

"No, it's making my life worse."

"Use the different features. Snap pictures, take video, check the weather—"

"Are you kidding me? I can barely manage to turn it on. No more cords, buttons or headphones! I can't remember to synchronize it with my computer. A few weeks ago I lost all my appointments."

He shakes his head. "You're trapped in cyber-hell."

I am not amused. I grab a pillow and throw it at him. He chuckles, gets up and ducks out the bedroom door. His head peeks around the corner.

"If I can get the old Jean back I'll make eggplant parmesan tonight and call your mother and tell her not to come."

He knows that's my favorite dinner.

I fold my arms across my chest and harrumph.

I stew a while longer so I can finish a box of Cheez-Its, roll out of bed, head to the shower and "get off it," a term used often in my group. The Great Bed Rebellion is over. I have way too much to do.

21

THE DEMISE OF THE DEMOCRATIC CANDIDATE changed the tone and
texture of the race. With the ballots printed and an unknown
added as a write-in candidate, Craig Burton's chances have
improved. People who would never have endorsed a Green
Party candidate now endorse Craig.

Personally, I don't think he has a chance against Flora, but
Maury gives it his all. He's been at headquarters every day for
the last week making calls on his days off and evenings after
work. They're trying to bring in money for a television blitz to
air in the final hours. I've been asked to make calls too. I am
back in action.

"Hello, this is Jean from Craig Burton's headquarters. He's
running for state senate from your district."

"Is he one of those Washington insiders?" asks an elderly
woman.

"No, ma'am, he does not live in Washington. This is a local

election."

"What's he going to do about my taxes?"

"Ma'am, he cannot do anything about your federal taxes."

"Well, that's rotten."

"May I ask, have you sent in your mail-in ballot?"

"Why do you want to know?"

"If you haven't, may I take a few moments to explain the importance of this election and the worthiness of our candidate?"

I pause.

"Craig Burton is a former ecology professor well-versed in environmental issues affecting our state. He wants to reduce our high-pollution days by passing legislation to regulate industries that create brown haze."

"It sounds like you're reading that."

"Well, yes ma'am, I am. But I want to get it right."

"Denny died four years ago. Couldn't breathe."

"I'm sorry to hear that."

"Passed away from emphysema."

"So you understand our need for clean air. Can we count on your vote Tuesday for our Green Party candidate?"

She didn't have to hang up on me.

The League of Women Voters sponsors a panel a few days before the election. All the candidates running for state office in the Scottsdale districts show up at the Mustang Library auditorium.

The auditorium, a well-lit circular room with graduated seating and a full apron stage in the front, holds a sparse audience scattered throughout the rows.

The female moderator, a round woman in her seventies with reading glasses on top of her bobbed silver hair, rotates each person through a five minute cycle. They come to the podium, many awkward, to explain why they've taken the risk of running for office in today's climate of political suspicion.

Maury and I slip in late knowing the state senate candidates will go last. I fidget.

Starr's in the front row. She turns around when we come in as the doors slam behind us, motioning to Maury. I scowl. There's only one seat next to her. I am not amused by her interest in my husband. I lead him to a row half way back on the right side.

Even though I've made some improvements after my breakdown, I'm still fragile. I've curtailed a few activities, meditating every day. I feel I'm flying solo without a self-help group. I consider the Mayo Clinic seminar, going over the scientific credibility of the inventor of the process. Maybe. But I have to schedule it between my mother, a bone density test and a Pap smear.

The moderator calls the candidates in alphabetical order by districts. Finally, it's Flora's turn. She strides to the podium in her Ferragamos and navy dress, grips the sides of the podium and waits for absolute quiet. I spot her broad-shouldered daughter, Tiffany, next to Starr in the front row. She's sitting forward in her seat, clapping with enthusiasm.

The buzzing and coughing stop. Flora's hair, pulled into a bun, springs from the top of her head. The high color of her rouged cheeks enhances those wild eyes. When she speaks she uses measured words and doesn't sound volatile at all.

"I know there's talk of change in the world but not all change is good."

Tiffany whoops and punches her arm in the air, drawing attention away from her mother. I don't know what she's like now, but that kid was unbalanced when I taught her. She was athletic, but now it looks like she's beefed up even more. Her arm bulges in a sleeveless top.

Flora smiles like a White House press secretary, making eye contact around the room. Does she know I'm here? I slink down in my seat. Maury leans forward in his.

"In these trying times with our state budget crisis, it is imperative to keep our tax base the same. Average citizens feel the pinch of accelerated economic blows."

Maury leans over and whispers, "The 'average citizens' she's talking about all have 401Ks, pension funds and multiple assets."

"Sshhh," I tell him with my finger to my lips.

"In actuality a reduction of taxes is what we need. That stimulates entrepreneurs and creates more jobs. Scottsdale is made up of small businesses. Recently *Fortune Small Business* magazine ranked our fair city number 25 among 'The 100 Best Places to Live and Launch.' What a superb atmosphere to grow our economy." She leans in with intensity. "Let's not ruin the progress we've made in the legislature. A vote for Flora Beaudreaux is a vote for stability and continued prosperity without raising taxes."

"She didn't attack Craig once," I murmur in Maury's ear during her applause. I can envision how people would think she has a sensible platform. Change threatens some people, especially if it's going to affect their pocketbooks. A dozen more people straggle in filling up seats.

"Yeah, well, that's because we've made some serious inroads in these last few weeks. Notice she didn't bring up the environment? She knows the Greens have appealed to a segment of the population concerned about air and water." He leans back.

Maury says it's possible for Craig to win but I'm a realist. I'm amazed at her change in tactics from the speech at the Scottsdale Babes and the debate. No ranting or raving. A bit haughty, yes, but not an attack dog or banner-waving right-winger either.

Her "not all change is good" statement makes her message seductive. She's obviously wants to appeal to the middle of the road voters with economic concerns. She may look maniacal but her righteous dignity for our city will pull voters. She makes it seem as though her silky positions are in everybody's best interest.

My trēo beeps. A text message from Lara: Buzz has green diarrhea.

Now? Maury elbows me to pay attention. I show him Lara's message. The good thing about being married to a doc is nothing grosses them out.

He whispers his medical advice in my ear.

I hold the trēo down low, pull out my stylus and tap back:

Lots of fluids. Dad will call in a script soon.

Craig Burton enters the stage. It's the first time I've seen him without notes and not disheveled. With combed hair, new rimless eyeglasses, dressed in a shirt, tie and brown jacket, he looks impressive.

He forgoes the podium. Instead, he reaches up to remove the microphone. He stands center stage.

"Good evening, my fellow citizens. My name is Craig Burton and I'm running for the Arizona State Senate."

"Wow. Someone's been coaching him," I whisper.

"We hired a consultant," says Maury.

"My number one issue is the environment. What makes Scottsdale special is the respect for our desert which gives us a balance of business and recreation. Without state legislation to ensure preservation of land trusts our city will not be recognizable in ten years. Do you want the developers to be in a land grab to destroy our trails, wild flowers and few blue sky days we have left? Are you concerned about air quality for seniors and children who are vulnerable? People lined up to receive clean bottled water last year because leakage from our sewer systems brought E.coli and other dangerous contaminants into our homes in the most innocuous way—our tap water. It posed a potential health risk to all residents in the area."

He takes a breath and dives for the finale. "Charles Dunn, the husband of my opponent and developer of Los Robles Properties, agreed to pay a record $12.1 million dollars to the state to settle a lawsuit that accused him of polluting Arizona water, bulldozing protected land and destroying archeological sites for a 67,000 person density development. An environmental villain, he set up a scheme to attract buyers by setting up a bucolic meadow. He imported goats and bighorn sheep that became infected and are now impaired. You have a choice. Let Arizona be a clean, green state. Pick Craig Burton. I want your vote."

There's scattered but firm applause. The moderator winds it up reminding us this Tuesday is Election Day. I get into the aisle, moving toward the door. I don't want Maury to have a chance to talk to Starr. Without warning someone punches me in the back, taking the steps two at a time.

"Hey!" I shout out.

"What happened?" asks Maury at my side.

"That person slammed me." I point to a retreating figure. "How rude."

"Did you see who it was?"

I think. "Yes. Tiffany. It was deliberate."

"You okay? I can try to chase her down."

"Nah. But it was a thwack. Took my breath away."

"Maybe it was accidental. She was in a rush."

"I don't think so."

Starr tags Maury in the lobby.

"Hey, are you going to be at headquarters on Tuesday?" she asks him with ga-ga eyes.

"No, I work Tuesdays, but Jean will be there. You remember Jean, don't you?" He places his hand in the middle of my back to inch me forward. Starr acknowledges me as though

I'm an inconvenient intruder from another planet. I give her a tight smile.

"Wasn't Craig great tonight? I thought he covered the issues so well," says Starr, nuzzling a little closer to Maury to let people get by.

"Yes. The policy paper we worked on together gave him lots of ammunition," says Maury.

Wait a minute. I'm the one who did the research on Los Robles and the blind bighorn sheep. Should I interrupt and point this fact out now or just watch this unfold?

"You know if Craig wins we'll have to be on his environmental board to keep up the pressure. He'll need steady PR until the next election." She says this as she takes her auburn braid from the back of her neck, throws it over her shoulder and strokes it.

My mother used to do that when she'd be going to a fancy bar mitzvah in her mink stole. It's an unconscious self-admiration done with the fingers.

I clear my throat. "Uh, it's getting late. Why don't we see if Craig wins this election before we plan the next one?"

Maury checks his watch. "Geez, I've got to be up early for rounds tomorrow. Have a few patients in the hospital."

On the ride home Maury says, "You're awfully quiet. Everything okay?"

"I don't like the way that eco-twit hangs all over you." I narrow my eyes at him.

"Who?"

"You know who."

"Starr? Oh, she's harmless."

"She's practically throwing herself at you."

"Where? When?"

"At the meetings. Tonight."

"Me?"

"Don't act so oblivious. You know she has a crush on you."

"Well . . . maybe a little. But it's just because I know how to communicate about green issues."

"Men are susceptible to women who think they're smarter, stronger."

Maury has a satisfied grin on his face. "Aw, what would she want with an old guy like me?"

I don't respond because we're back in our driveway, but I am not above snooping. I'm going to monitor his emails. Some skinny broad without enough *tush* meat to sit in a folding chair is not going to steal my Maury. More to worry about.

The day of the election I stop by Craig Burton's headquarters to drop off unused posters and make a few last minute calls. It's crazy with activity. Some of the staff hunch over with phones pressed to their ears, others consult demographic charts and Adrian, the corpulent office manager, has her hand in a box. It's filled with Cheetos, Pringles, Raisinettes, Ding Dongs and envelopes of popcorn, ready to be micro-waved. With a robotic motion her hand reaches her mouth in a steady rhythm. She directs volunteers pondering maps to figure out where to pick up elderly voters and get them to the polls.

We didn't raise enough money for a television blitz, but

Maury feels the kind of voter we want wouldn't be watching TV. They'd be reading the newspaper. Or out hugging a tree.

I pull up a chair at the conference table. Posters taped to the doors and walls have notes written on them, phone numbers for Domino's pizza and bumper stickers bought from the head shop downstairs: *Legalize Mary Jane Today—She's only a Plant* and *Old Hippies Never Die—They Just Smoke Away.*

Volunteers tiptoe as they weave through the room to step over phone wires and computer cables.

Despite my reluctant involvement in the campaign, I feel committed to the blind bighorn sheep. I can't tolerate cruelty to animals. Kind souls adopt dogs and cats. Who takes in handicapped sheep?

"Still kinda hot today," I say to Adrian who hasn't stopped chewing. I scrunch my curls to get them out of my eyes. "November seventh and the weather has finally shifted to a cool ninety-eight degrees." She nods to me, ripping open the Ding Dongs. Maybe I should tell her about my addiction group.

Snarling bear guy shows up in a long-sleeved shirt and tie. He pulls out the tails of his shirt, opening a few buttons to reveal his bear. He joins a group in the corner abuzz with a story leaked from political spies on Flora's team.

I can't see who's speaking but I hear, "Okay, guys, this is big. It has to do with Flora."

"What? She took advantage of one of the blind sheep?"

I can't wait to know the scoop, especially if it involves an animal. I lean in to eavesdrop.

Brian Depalma breaks up the gabfest by throwing his arms

over the shoulders of two guys. "Let's not start rumors. Unlike Flora, our campaign deals in facts."

"But, there's fund raising improprieties. She might get indicted," says the bear guy.

"Get busy on the phones reminding voters the polls are open until seven o'clock. This is not a big election year. Low voter turn-out from the other side can work in our favor," says Brian.

All the phone lines buzz. Adrian stops chewing to answer some of them. I assist by taking calls from people who want to know the location of their polling place, what the candidate's stand is on right to choose and other pertinent issues.

"Craig Burton's campaign headquarters. Jean speaking. How may I help you?"

"This is Linda 'Bumblebee' Schwartz."

I recognize her name. "I've heard of you. You're the lady who goes around in the bee outfit."

"Right. I'm raising community awareness about bees. If there's no pollination, there's no food. The planet could starve itself to death. There's twenty-five percent less bees than last year. The price of honey has gone up."

Serious data, but would I be committed enough to wear black and yellow tights in public? Horizontal stripes make my thighs look really fat.

"Listen, Jeannie, I got the name of the guy who owns the fancy water company in town to donate fifteen cases. They'll be delivering them in a few minutes."

"Terrific. We're always parched here. I know the Greens

holding signs outside the polls will really appreciate it. Thank you so much, Bumblebee. Keep up the good work."

I announce to the group, "Hey, everyone, we're getting a big donation of bottled water."

"Oh, that's great. I'm mummified over here," shrieks one of the workers. "I'm dehydrated," says Adrian whose lips are blue from drinking a giant Slurpee. Two empty Coke cans sit on her desk.

"No," says Mr. Preppy. "We can't accept it. Cancel it."

"Why?" I ask with a chorus of staff and volunteers.

"But I'm going to be *schlepping* seniors all day," whines one long-haired guy with a faded green backpack strapped onto his shoulders.

"Because we don't use bottled water. Period. Plastic bottles are not bio-degradable. They rot in the landfills for a thousand years."

Boy, am I bummed my coup is a bomb. Greens are weird. I crouch under the table to take a big gulp from my water bottle, pushing it deeper into my bag.

A uniformed man arrives with the water. He's sent away with a dismayed look on his face, especially since he just carried two of the flats up the stairs.

I leave to meet a new client who wants better integration of women and minorities into his business. I also have an appeal for Michael to work for him marketing technical support to foreign countries. Why not? He's married to someone from another country. That has to qualify him for international relations.

It turns out my client wants Michael to be part of his multi-level marketing team that sells a caffeine-laden, sugar-drenched juice drink that requires finding thousands of people who are willing to pay eighty dollars for a bottle of the elixir that claims to boost energy and cure cancer. I tell him I'll pass along the information.

Maury calls me on my drive home. "Where's the election party?"

"I told you." I try to be sweet when I say this because he's been trying hard to remember keys and events.

"I forgot. You know I'm on a need-to-know basis."

"A vegetarian sports bar on Mcdowell Road. Look for big hairy guys screaming at hockey on TV and munching tofu lettuce wraps."

"Jean, don't make jokes. It's the only place we could find for the vegans that we can watch the election coverage."

"I'll meet you there at seven for tabouli and faux chopped liver. Let's hope it's a victory party."

I arrive at Cabbages and Corn a little early to stake out a spot. Starr comes over and asks, "Hi. Where's Maury?"

"He'll be here." I smile, the kind where you want to stab a person in the heart.

"Well, I've got something important to tell him."

Over my dead body will I pass him any messages from her. I stifle a curse. I hate her and her skinny thighs.

I've covertly checked Maury's emails over the last few days. None were from Starr. If only I was more tech saavy to check his text messages. Am I making things up? No matter what, the election's over tonight.

Maury arrives. We share artichokes and edamame humus while drinking beer at a high-topped table. Some of the Greens join us. Bear guy turns out to be an engineer who constructs cell phone towers in Africa.

Craig Burton shows up with his stunning 5'11" red-haired wife. We stand up and applaud. He makes a brief speech thanking everyone for their hard work, then joins Brian and the inner circle in the back of the restaurant underneath large oil paintings of cabbage and corn.

Soon Starr heads our way. She greets Maury with a hug and me with a nod, leaning in with a conspiratorial manner. "I spoke to my source at the newspaper and she says that whether Flora wins or not, there's an investigation starting." She has our attention. "I can't say what it is but it's going to be big."

For any media to investigate an issue it would have to be huge, scandalous or politically advantageous.

I examine Starr. I have to admit she looks very cute tonight with her jeans, boots and big-scoop eyes.

She continues. "Scottsdale passed an ordinance this year that requires dust to be kept out of the air."

Maury and I nod because we know about it although there's been no enforcement. I can't help but be interested, but why do I have to get my information from her?

She licks her lips. The only other person I know who could make dust sound suggestive is April. "Well, there's an opposition group forming to overturn it. They say it'll keep

Jeep tours and dirt bikes out of the desert."

"Then the Greens have to form an opposition group to the opposition group," says Maury banging his fist on the table. He's passionate about dust.

I, on the other hand, have so many other priorities I let him worry about particulates. I want to appear intelligent and involved so I don't give her any hint that I'm not keeping up on the environmental front. I put a look on my face of, tell me more, I'm fascinated.

"Are you talking about the Granite Mountain area? Those twenty square miles northeast of Pima and Dynamite roads?" asks Maury.

"Yes. They're afraid that since we're mobilized now we'll put enough pressure on the city and state to close all the unpaved parking lots. Maybe restrict trail access to hikers, bikers and equestrians."

I break in with authority, "That's a terrible idea. If we don't leave some land open for recreational use it'll cut into tourism. As much as I'd like that, it's not a good idea. Too radical. People here like a walk in the desert even if there's dust."

It's a practical approach. Otherwise, I envision hikers, bikers and horse-back riders with gas masks.

"You mean you're not on our side?" Starr asks me. She gives Maury a knowing look, like your wife isn't a true green; she's a nincompoop polluter.

My hands go to my hips in my best don't you mess with me pose. "You can't make so many restrictions that people can't enjoy where they live."

Starr leans close to my face. "Yes, but if Scottsdale doesn't set the standard, who will? It's people like you who compromise our positions."

Maury jumps between us, his hands on our shoulders backing us off. "Ladies, please. We have to find solutions to these problems, not create more of them. We're all on the same side."

I'm fuming and I let Starr know it with a nasty frown.

Maury says, "The Granite Mountain Multiuse area has eighty-nine miles set aside of trails for all-terrain vehicles, mountain bikers, hikers and equestrians. For recreational use. Scottsdale would have to pave or treat all of it with dust suppressant to keep it open. Never going to happen."

"But-but if we're true to our cause of clean air we have to champion what's right," stammers Starr.

I make an angry noise. I might scratch her eyes out for messing with my man.

Cheers erupt from the back of the room. We turn our attention to the nearest television set hanging from the ceiling. I can't hear anything except yells and the clinking of glasses. The first election results are about to come in. We have a long night ahead of us.

We watch the fuzzy cable channel until late when most of the districts have reported. They show a picture of Flora with her monkey-hair and a studious one of Craig. It doesn't look like Craig's going to be victorious. They predict another win for the incumbent, Flora Beaudreaux. I'm not surprised. Maury, on the other hand, remains more optimistic.

"Ah, but the Green Party's made a good showing."

Chin in hand, I sigh in relief. At least the campaign's over. I gather my things.

I put his arm through mine as he walks me to my car. "I know you're bummed about Craig's loss," I say to him.

"Sure, I'm disappointed, but we have so many possibilities. The environment will be an issue in every campaign. Detroit's been ranked greener than Phoenix. That'll be great ammunition the next time around."

"I'm happy you have a good attitude about it," I say.

Maury opens my car door, smiling, his mind someplace else. "Did I tell you The American Heart Association says that for every ten microgram increase in particulates there's a three point four percent increase in heart attacks?"

"Fascinating," I mumble. I remind myself that if I don't appear interested, my competition will.

"That could be a talking point in the next election. Greens have to figure out how to make that information attractive to voters."

Not a chance.

22

APRIL AND GLEE ENGINEER AN INTERVENTION. They hijack me for a day at the spa. They claim it's to relieve terminal crabbiness, but I know it's their way of telling me I'm not making enough time for them.

April's horn toots early. She waits in the car while Glee comes in juggling an armload of books.

"Jean, you have to read more about your condition."

"What condition?" I race around looking for my tote, fill my politically-incorrect water bottle, let out Amber for a last pee and tie a gauzy scarf around my neck. I leave my planner behind. I'm flying solo with the trēo.

"Anxiety is a scourge. Look, I've brought you these books. I've read all of them."

"Now I've got a scourge too?"

Glee places a stack on the table. She shows me the titles while I stand near the door waiting for Amber. I pray Maury's poisons and cages have done the job on the roof rats. I don't want Amber to gobble down a killer tablet.

"*Full Catastrophe Living* is about luxuriating in the moment. It reinforces giving up fat, sugar and caffeine to detox your body."

"What would I eat?" She doesn't respond and Amber's taking forever.

"This one's *Wherever you Go, There You Are: Mindfulness Meditation in Real Life*. It has a chapter on cleaning the oven while listening to Bobby McFerrin. *Coming to Our Senses: Healing Ourselves and the World*. This one's great because the author blends personal experience and science. With meditation you have to let go. When you get to the zone it'll lower your blood lactate levels. The exercises want you to listen to classical music, smell spices and flowers . . ."

"You have to be kidding. I don't have time to sit and inhale oregano."

I check on Amber, tapping my foot hoping she'll stop sniffing and pick a spot. Any spot. At least before Glee brings in more tomes on "my condition."

"And, this one is my favorite. *Releasing Burdens through Breathing*. Stress causes changes at the chromosomal level. High levels can invoke ten years of aging. I want you to pay attention."

Glee wanders over to my refrigerator. "What's this?" she asks, pointing to Maury's rat chart.

"Maury's tracking his roof rat progress," I say. Waiting for Amber to poop is giving me anxiety.

I call Amber.

"Two dead rats and one bird?" asks Glee.

"Never mind."

I thank her for the books, pile them on my kitchen desk, pat Amber's head as she ambles in, fill her dishes with water and kibble, then make a hasty exit before Glee starts to read me the back covers with endorsements from Deepok Chopra.

April's examining her lipstick in the flip-down mirror with the motor running. I get in the back, leaning over to give her an air kiss. She backs out of my driveway and steers her gleaming black Mercedes in a leisurely fashion, creeping along in luxury, a German tank invading the Champs Elyseé.

We catch up on the Pet Luncheon as I settle into the back seat. They raised $50,000 for the no-kill shelter. We discuss the Heart Ball, where some of the women, paranoid about the Rock Burglar, arrived sans jewels, their bare necks and lobes exposed for all to see. And finally, we talk about the deviant burglar who has disappeared without a trace.

When we arrive at the spa they give us keys to our lockers with a plastic card holder containing lists of our treatments. I get excited when I see I'm scheduled for a massage after lunch.

Glee announces, "First we have Ratango. Jean, you'll love it. I took a workshop when I was in Marin a few months ago. Change into your workout clothes."

I have no idea what Ratango is but I'm sure it will be beneficial. As I stuff my tote into the locker I read signs reminding us to turn off our cell phones. I put the trēo on vibrate.

In a few minutes I've slipped into a large "Go Green" T-shirt that swims around my neck and donned faded black tights with scuffed sneakers. I think there's a small hole under my right bun.

I grab a fistful of hair and make two unruly, fuzzy bunches, one over each ear. Glee and April are decked out in gold-patterned leotards, colored tights, black ballet slippers with metallic scrunchies pulling their hair off their faces. They look hot. I look like a refugee from an eastern bloc country.

We enter a room with a mirrored wall and polished light wood floors. Rubber yoga mats, giant elastic bands, stair-steps, giant red, blue and yellow balls and barbells are stacked at the end of the room. There's a water cooler, paper cups and small white towels at the other.

The space fills up with women, some professional looking with no-nonsense haircuts, a few who have been tightened and lifted and a group of young African-American women in stylish work-out clothes. No one looks like me. We all get mats and place them near our spot. Glee and April head for the front row. I secure a place in the back.

A tall, buffed blond with bare feet wearing grey pants and a tight pink shirt, crosses the floor with wide strides. *Namaste* is scrawled across her chest in script. She speaks with a well-modulated low voice at a slow pace.

"Ladies, we have a real treat today. If you have any conditions, remember to take it easy. This is heart-fluttering, death-defying awesome. Straight from California we have the creator of Ratango, Billy Tuesday Munkee!"

A tanned six-foot man, his mustache and goatee trimmed to perfection, hair scooped back into a pony-tail, bounds into the room with a gold hoop earring and a sleeveless black T-shirt. It shows off his cantaloupe biceps and hairy untrimmed armpits. The blond hits the music on a stand in the corner. He's off, jumping and clapping his hands over his head to the music.

"This is your warm-up, ladies. Let's see what you've got." He starts suggestive hip thrusts.

I look around. The babe next to me is jiving away; April and Glee in the front row swivel their hips; and I'm stunned. What have they gotten me into now? I try to move the lower half of my body in a circular fashion but it's more like a square. And my back hurts.

"Move it," Billy Tuesday says as the music slows down and the circular hip swivel becomes racy. "Cure that pelvic paralysis and tune into the primordial rhythms of our ancestors."

My ancestors? Bubbe Rose with a come hither look on her face? Shifting her hips under a flowered dress with suntan-colored stockings rolled to her knee? Horrifying.

I look at the mirror in the front to see everyone's reflection. We look like a smutty band of aging strippers.

"You, in the back row, put some grind into it." Of the few women near me, one has her eyes closed in ecstatic energy and another gyrates with enthusiasm. He's talking to me. Oh God. This is humiliating. I'm going to kill Glee. I close my eyes, stroke my mid-section with snaky hands and torture myself into wild circular motions.

"Do you want to be a better lover? I can't hear you."

"Yes," yell a few women.

"I said do you want to be a better lover?" He cups his hand around his ear for our response. The room erupts in screams. One women's enthusiasm turns into a coughing fit. I yell too. I don't want him to single me out again.

It goes on like this, one song blending into another, until the room is writhing in prurient agitation. A silver-haired woman with a spiky crew cut swings her body around emitting slight moans. Glee is, of course, a show, using provocative motions toward our instructor while he encourages us.

"Turn me on. Turn me on," he says over a drum beat.

April looks like a Las Vegas show girl, strutting in a circle with pooched lips, one hand on her hip.

Turn him on? If anyone saw this display they'd call an ambulance with strait jackets.

We continue like this through so many songs I think I'm going to fall on the floor in a heap.

"And now for the finale and my favorite exercise, the one that will enhance sensuality, increase passion and improve intimacy. Here comes the Bad Kitty! Let's go, girls." The Joe Cocker song, "You Can Leave Your Hat On" begins to play.

If I thought I had seen it all, this beats everything. Women get down on their mats, roll around, hips thrust into the air, simulating sex. Anything goes. Many of the women reach out their arms and hands like claws, uttering guttural meowing sounds. It is a display of ribald activity and agitation that could compete with the best pornography.

Since I'm the only one left standing and don't want to draw any more attention to myself, I get down and crawl in a circle. I give a weak meow once or twice. I can't wait to demonstrate this for Maury. If I can get down on the floor again. Hell, if I can get up! Wait 'til I get my hands on Glee and April.

Afterward, when we're all out of breath clumped together in the front of the room, Glee says to me, "Wasn't that terrific? It's just what you needed. Billy's philosophy imparts such wisdom. We don't have to age or get old. Look at me. I feel thirty-five." She thrusts her arms into the air and shouts, "Ratango's a fountain of youth that teaches you to live in the moment. Don't let your mind run you, take control of your destiny." Then she leans in with confidentiality. "I'm thinking of financing a school for Billy in Scottsdale. Won't women just love this?"

Maybe. If she can get the Babes away from their guns.

Glee expounds as I try to catch my breath and rub a few sore places. April looks in the mirror admiring her perfect body. Billy Tuesday Munkee does too. He has a towel around his neck as he approaches her.

"Hey, gorgeous, you did a terrific job today. Can I interest you in teaching a few Ratango classes? I could use instructors in Arizona. I'll show you my curriculum during our training sessions."

April, who's used to male attention, says, "I don't think so. I'm way too busy. Thank you for the opportunity." She sidles over to us with a smile that acknowledges she's flattered.

Billy Tuesday, eyeing April up and down, goes to the other

end of the room to pack up his CDs and gear. The blond appears to check on how the class went and to flirt.

"Glee, who is that guy?" I ask in a whisper. "He could be a charlatan. Have you given him any money yet?"

"He's perfectly reputable. Amanda checked him out for me. He trained as a boxer in Guam before he became a Chippendale dancer. He knows what men want from women. Besides, everyone can use a little training in becoming a better lover." She raises an eyebrow at me.

"Who says I need instruction in that arena?" I catch a glimpse of myself in the mirror with the silhouette of my two fuzzy bunches sticking out of my head.

Glee gives me a know-it-all look. "Didn't you mention you were worried Maury might be interested in a young woman working on the campaign?"

April leans in with interest.

"Well, yes, but . . ."

"But, nothing. Sensual movement heightens romance."

"Glee, this was obscene. I can't believe you dragged me here. Besides, you're sharing personal information."

"Since when did you become so prudish?"

"I'm not prudish. Just reserved. And private."

"We thought it would help loosen you up," says Glee adjusting her straps, a bit annoyed.

"You always have these crazy ideas and drag me into strange situations like that afternoon in the nudist camp."

The two of them glance at each other remembering that trickery. "And you," I say turning and pointing at April who opens her eyes wide and pushes out her bottom lip in an innocent baby pose, "go along with it."

"We thought it would be good for your soul," says April.

"My soul? I'm going to need my back adjusted."

April and Glee glance at one another and give a slight shrug as if to say, *We tried. She didn't appreciate it but we tried.*

This annoys me. I decide not to make an issue of it. Besides, all this activity has made me hungry. We never love everything about our friends even if we remain loyal and steadfast.

"I'm sorry I was crabby. How 'bout lunch?" I ask, looping their arms through mine. After all, my friends want the best for me. And I am a bit cranky.

We walk down a long hallway that opens into a contemporary restaurant. Men and women in various stages of undress sit at wood tables decorated with small cactus centerpieces. Copper lighting fixtures and sculptures decorate the walls. One side is a glass with a view of Camelback Mountain, its famous humps enlarged because we're so close. I can even spot the praying monk rock formation, a small shrouded figure that tops the camel's head.

We order a spa feast. Two butter lettuce leaves with fresh basil and an organic cherry tomato the size of a pebble arrive. Everything's drizzled with balsamic vinegar and imported Mediterranean olive oil. All for $18.95 a person. We refuse dessert.

"It's time for our treatments," says Glee.

In the locker room Glee emits a throaty few bars of music

as we mock strip out of our Ratango outfits. I show off the best moves I've learned. I thrust out a final hip before donning a beige terry robe. They laugh.

We move to a soothing room with leather recliners. A breakfront displays pitchers with water. One contains lemon slices, another cucumber. There's one with something I cannot identify. It's small and brown and could possibly be rabbit turds. Glee tells me they're baby organic red grapes. Clean glasses are stacked in the back. A tray of freshly polished apples sits next to the pitchers in case two leaves of lettuce didn't fill you up. No one touches the apples but a few women help themselves to the various waters.

About fifteen women wait in the lounge area stretched out in fluffy robes and plastic slippers. Some have their wet heads wrapped in towels. We look like classic "before" pictures.

At first I think no one except April is wearing any make-up, that we're all equal save for my friend who has on waterproof mascara. She's an exotic princess with her towel swirled around her head.

The rest of us are stripped to the essentials—wrinkles, lines, no eyebrows except for . . . the tattooed ladies, which, when I glance around, realize is almost all of them. Their eyebrows are arched, plucked and permanent.

When I examine Glee, I realize her eyebrows are medium-brown and uniform unlike my sparse, faded ones. I squint and peer closer. She also has charcoal eyeliner, pink blush and berry-stained lips executed with perfection even though we've showered and washed our faces. Glee has spent some time in a tattoo parlor.

My eyes browse around the room at the lounging women. I am the only one with a naked face including flaws and original eyebrows.

"Ms. Rubin? Ms. Barstow? Ms. Lefkowitz?" Therapists in light blue scrub tops and white pants are ready to take us to our rooms. April's having an herbal wrap with ingredients from the forests of Romania, Glee's signed up for the organic strawberry soak with a Watsu water treatment and I'm having a Swedish massage. Since I don't have a weekly masseuse visit, this will be a treat.

"Hi, I'm Ingrid and I'm going to pound you today," is what I think I hear her say with her Scandinavian accent. No matter. It's my turn to melt into the table listening to New Age music and breathing citrus scents from a lemony candle.

After an hour of Ingrid's man-sized hands pummeling my Ratango-ed achy body, I mush out of the room to meet the girls.

"It's time for our hand treatments," says Glee. I make my hand into a fist. My nails are terrible. I didn't want another Asian assault so I haven't had a manicure in ages.

We shuffle behind Glee in our plastic slip-ons down a hallway to another part of the facility. She guides us into an organic nail spa. There's no list of charges on the wall like the places I go to so I pick up a standing card. A manicure is one hundred dollars.

Glee grabs it out of my hands. "Never mind. It's our treat. This is very special. Haven't you asked yourself why they're wearing surgical masks in those other places? Toxins can kill."

"Glee, April, it's very generous of you but I can pay for my own manicure." *Even if it is five times as much.*

April stands in front of a display to pick out a color from the selection of polishes. She turns around with a few in her hand. "None of these have formaldehyde."

Glee adds, "It's your influence that has enticed us to go green. They don't use acrylics or perfumes either." She takes a deep breath. "See? You can breathe. The air's clear enough to do yoga."

Manicurists lead us to their stations. I might as well give up. They're determined to give me the full spa experience. My mother taught me to accept gifts graciously.

"My name's Heather." I nod and smile. I hope she's not a talker who says "like" in every sentence. I have a sudden longing for the snide Asian ladies who make no effort to communicate, deriding my needy nails in another language.

"I'm going to be soaking your hands in pure distilled water and organic oils and wrapping them in a one-hundred percent organic towel. We use only sterilized surgical instruments," she says reaching for something to push back my overgrown cuticles. If she says organic one more time I'm going to scream. "The purpose of a natural manicure is to rehydrate and seal in moisture." I lean my head back and let her organically adjust my hands.

"Have you picked a color?" asks Heather massaging each finger with studiousness.

Color? I'm in a bathrobe covered with fragrant oil, paralyzed with relaxation. I can't get up. I look at the young woman's hands sitting next to me. She's having them painted a pale pink with an iridescent flash.

"I'll have what she's having," I tell Heather nodding to my next door neighbor. She hears me.

"This is a great color. It doesn't show so much if I chip it. I work on the computer all day."

"Oh. That'll work for me." I won't mention that I unpack boxes for my mother, clean up dog doody, cook and change the grandkids diapers besides working on the computer.

"What do you do?" I ask, assuming she has a job in technology.

"I answer two hundred emails a day plus Twitter and Facebook."

"You get two hundred emails a day?"

"Yes, and I have at least nine hundred saved for reference." She seems very self-satisfied splaying her fingers for examination.

I repeat my original question wanting to know what occupation keeps her so entrenched in her computer all day.

"Just answering friends. MySpace. Facebook. JDate."

I'm flummoxed as I trade hands for Heather. She wraps the one that's been soaking in distilled water in a one-hundred percent organic cotton towel. "But can't you call people and talk?"

"Oh no. That interrupts. Besides, I've never actually met most of them. We're just cyber friends. Hey, are you on any social sites? You can join my network."

"No thanks. But I appreciate the offer. I'm pretty busy."

She says, "I understand. I've got to get home. There will be at least a hundred emails waiting for me. Whoops! Someone's twittering me right now." She motions her manicurist to reach into the red Kate Spade purse next to her for money, credit card and keys.

The manicurist warns her, "Remember. No BlackBerry, IMs, texting or Game Boys for at least thirty minutes. Your nails need to dry solid."

Ms. Hi Tech whines, "I can't drive unless I'm texting." She slips her purse over her arm, fingers spread apart, and sashays out in rhinestone flip-flops.

I finish my manicure in silence contemplating what will happen to society when we no longer speak. Will my multi-tasking evolve into mobile perpetual-tasking? Will we all be in a constant state of communication?

I'm already annoyed when my kids text when I'm speaking to them. As if I don't notice their hands under the table. Do we all need blow-by-blow descriptions of every activity dissected? I feel myself getting agitated so I concentrate on the top of Heather's head. She's a brunette with blond streaks.

Later, Glee and April are dressing in the locker room. It's empty except for the three of us.

"Honey, we have to talk to you about something," says Glee.

"What?"

"Get ready and we'll talk."

Uh-oh. Do they really think Maury is having an affair? Or

maybe I've been too much of a pain-in-the-ass. Is it another activity so I can make a fool of myself? Could it be I have bad breath or body odor or some other physical malady I haven't noticed and only best friends tell you?

I hustle to re-dress myself in shorts and a T-shirt re-creating the fuzzy bunches on either side of my head. I plop on a canvas hat. I pack up my tote and sit down on a bench facing Glee. April is re-applying make-up in the mirror next to us.

"You know we love you, right?"

"Right."

"You know we've been friends forever. We respect your intellectual curiosity and interest in social change, right?" I'm getting fidgety. Where is this going?

"Right." Although I don't know how great my mind is.

"April, get over here." She sits down. "You tell her," Glee says with unusual abdication.

This must be serious.

April places both manicured hands on her knees. She examines me with bright blue eyes. "Glee and I think you need a style intervention." She leans back with relief.

"What's wrong with me? I've got a no-nonsense look. I'm busy. I don't have time to think about fashion."

Glee takes the reins with sincerity. "Jean, you look like a toddler. No one your age should be wearing pigtails or buns except Frida Kahlo and she's dead."

"But I'm okay with the way I look," I say, feeling self-conscious, adjusting the buckles on my shorts.

Glee holds my wrists. "It's time to update your look, get a

new style."

"What's my old one?"

"Most of the time you're dressed as a left-over folk musician/hippie. You can't stay trapped in the Seventies forever." Glee says this with concern for my well-being.

"Why not? Wait a minute. I can be upscale if I try." I think about some silk blouses and a really cool pair of black shantung pants I have in the back of my closet.

"We're trying to help you," says April sensing my upset. As if changing my appearance is going to solve my problems.

I think for a moment. It's true, Glee does have an upscale artsy style and April is glamorous perfection. I look at what I'm wearing—lime shorts, T-shirt, sandals, bunches and a hat. I left off my scarf thinking it might be too much. I look like my granddaughter, Tangie, only older.

"What image should I have?"

April offers an initial suggestion. "Get a tan. Everyone looks thinner with a tan. Look at the Scottsdale scene in the magazines."

"I do look at them. Those orangey women wear clothes that are too tight with their cleavage spilling out. It's not for me."

"I have a few suggestions," offers Glee.

She takes out pictures torn from magazine society columns and passes them to me. One's a picture of a woman with jet black hair wearing tight jeans and cowboy boots, another's in a strapless dress with little fat pads hanging between her arms and her boobs and in the last one a blond with huge implanted breasts in a halter top carries a studded purse.

I stare at the pictures. "No one over fifty should wear any of these. If someone's buying a size fourteen sundress, I think they haven't looked in a full length mirror for a while. Besides, they're way too young for me. I'm an adult. I try to be age appropriate. Despite today's outfit."

"You still need 'a look'," says Glee. "Like sophisticated doctor's wife."

I point my finger into my mouth and pretend to gag.

"Or prosperous intellectual."

"You can't be serious. How do I pull that off?"

"We could get you big tortoise shell framed glasses. You could wear lots of black with big chunky silver David Yurman jewelry," says Glee.

"And boots," adds April. She and Glee catch each other's eyes. Glee nods in agreement.

"Cool boots," says Glee.

"Uh, ladies. I appreciate your interest in my appearance but it's not any of these," I say, handing back the pictures. "Besides, my feet sweat and swell in boots."

"Well, you have some nice pieces. Wear them. Put some effort into your appearance," offers Glee.

"You need a little sex appeal," says April, wetting her glossed lips with her tongue. "I'd be willing to do your make-up."

I narrow my eyes. "Wait a minute. Do you do think Maury's having an affair?"

"No," they say in surprised unison.

"This is for *you*," says April.

"Besides, think how happy your mother would be," says Glee.

Yes, my mother would be thrilled if I fixed myself up. Maybe what they're saying is true. I should be paying more attention to what my image projects. Maybe it'll help my business. "Okay, I'll try a little harder."

April says, "Spend at least an hour getting ready before you leave the house."

"I can't do that." She looks disappointed. "How 'bout a compromise? I'll contemplate my closet for five minutes and study myself in the mirror for another two."

They get up and hug me.

"Come on, it's time to go home," says April. "I have a super busy day tomorrow."

We all stand to gather our belongings.

"What's going on?" I ask.

"The security people are coming to test the alarm system."

23

THE GLOW FROM MY SPA DAY WITH THE GIRLS doesn't last long. I laugh about Ratango, especially demonstrating my best "Bad Kitty" for Maury. He snickers then goes back to viewing the bombing of Dresden.

I'm back in my harried life, bouncing around like a ping pong ball in a losing match. The mangled, massaged and mushed places in my body return to knots. My digestive system is in an uproar. I decide to attend my stress group. Maybe I can absorb more now that I'm not so distracted with the people and their stories.

"Hi, I'm Jean and I'm a stress addict."

"Hello, Jean," the group says in unison.

"I'm doing better since my breakdown. I still feel rushed. But I'm not saying yes to everything. I'm taking better care of myself by guarding my time." I feel satisfied with this last statement.

"It's an accomplishment not letting your life run you. Guard your time with a jealous fervor," says Bob, our facilitator. "Prioritize what's important. In your case, you. Set a schedule with time allotments for your family and follow it."

Okay, he just lost me. Cutting off my mother, Lara or Rivka because they're only in fifteen minute time slots isn't a possibility.

"What are you doing for Jean?" he asks, crossing his leg, his head bending forward with interest.

"Haven't thought about it."

"What dream have you always wanted to pursue and have never given yourself permission to do?"

I think for a moment. I'm not used to focusing on my needs. "Well, maybe I'd like to write. I haven't given myself permission to pursue that."

"What kind of writing?" asks Bob.

"I'm not sure. I have a novel languishing, but I think it would be healthier for me to let out the sardonic side of my personality.

"What would it take?" Bob's eyes bore in on me from behind his glasses.

"Time. Lots of time. An impetus to start."

"We give you permission. If not now, then when? Right, group?"

There's a murmur of "Yes, you go, girl, do it now."

I nod. They're right. It's time.

After I leave armed with positive thought ammunition, I call Glee from the parking lot. My trēo does automatic dial very well.

"When did you say the writing conference in Sedona was happening?"

"Next week. Why? Are you coming with me?" Her voice rises an octave with anticipation.

"Yes. Yes, I am."

Glee and I drive to Red Rock country on Highway 89A in her silver BMW convertible. She sings along to Amy Winehouse's "*Rehab*" thrilled to have company. She'll be in the non-fiction group and I'll be in beginning fiction.

I have Maury's blessing to explore what I've been talking about for years. He can play golf, eat popcorn and watch TV all weekend while Dresden will undoubtedly be bombed again.

We check into the Sedona Southwestern Lodge late Friday morning. A packet of materials awaits us. The general session starts this evening with individual workshops scheduled the next two days. Saturday and Sunday nights are reserved for authors and poets to read from works in progress.

My anticipation flies high. I'm a little nervous. What if I'm a complete amateur and embarrass myself? What if the lectures and exercises are over my head? What if . . .

I stop myself and remember advice from my support group. Not all stress is bad. Some can be thrilling. Couple it with relaxation. Search for balance.

Glee drops her belongings in the room we're sharing and says, "I'm going to find some people in my group."

"I think I'll prepare for the conference and look through

the literary magazines I brought with me," I tell her, fanning out copies of *Poets & Authors*, *The Sun*, and *Lilith*, on the bed.

"Okay." She ties a bandanna around her hair, slipping out of her Tod's, leather driving shoes with pimply soles. She slides into a pair of strappy silver kitten heels.

Instead of reading magazines or laboring over my laptop and portable printer with six pages of instructions and multiple wires Maury has given me, I pull out the conference schedule. Curled up on a chair near the window with a view of Cathedral Rock, I figure out that three of the seminars I want to take are at the same time. Will it be rude to walk out if I don't like one? My mind wanders and I gaze outside. A magnificent red sanctuary looms. I could be on Mars.

Glee returns in an hour bubbling with excitement. She's met everyone and knows everything.

"Jean, you're just going to love it. You're in Birkenstock country. I met fabulous people. You're going to learn so much."

After a dinner of organic greens and trout fished from Oak Creek Canyon, Glee and I attend the general session in a mini-ballroom. Sconces light the room. The carpet's a dizzying floral print of turquoise and mauve. While we wait for everyone to file in Glee tells me about the people she's already met. She's like the mayor of a small town who knows everyone and we've only been here four hours.

"Magda's writing a Jewish da Vinci Code," she says pointing to a woman wearing a muu-muu and a Hawaiin lei.

"What's she calling it? *The Teplitsky Sign*?"

She smiles and gives me the elbow.

"Those two guys are writing a sex thriller." She's motions toward two chubby men in writing conference T-shirts. They take seats in the front row.

"Isn't all sex thrilling?" I ask.

Others file in. I am not alone in Birkenstock country.

A petite woman with long grey hair, over-sized pink framed eyeglasses, wearing a shapeless beige skirt and blouse buttoned to the neck approaches the podium. She has red canvas flats on her feet. She adjusts the microphone to her height.

"Welcome to Sedona Writers for Change Conference." For the first hour we are instructed on rules and procedures. "Please show up on time. Doors will be locked to late-comers. Eating is not allowed in the sessions. Water's okay. If you must smoke, do it away from the building. Any change in your instructors has to clear through me. Please get permission from your new teacher first. The restrooms are located in the hallway but there will be no bathroom breaks. If you have to go, just get up and go. We start at eight a.m."

I'm overwhelmed. "I thought this was creative camp. This woman makes it sound like we're going to prison."

Glee says, "I'm getting up at six to take a yoga class. Want to join me?"

"Six a.m.? To twist into a pretzel? You sure you're not trying to trick me into another bout of Ratango?"

"Oh, Jean." She smiles at me, touching my arm. "Come with me. You'll join your female and male energy."

I despise getting up early. But . . . I'm making a supreme

effort to turn my life around so I say yes.

"Let's go to the bar for a drink. That's where all the real writers hang out. A glass of wine would be good for you."

"Can I pass tonight? The three hour ride has me aching for sleep. Besides, I don't know enough to ask anything yet."

"Okay, I'll see you back at the room," says Glee. "But you've got to learn to network." Grabbing the arm of a sophisticated woman in a man's shirt, she takes off.

It's chilly in the morning at the yoga class on the terrace. We pull on sweat shirts. I'm amazed other people are up at this hour. A motley group of sleepy writers spread out their mats. Glee has one for me. We all arrange ourselves facing the instructor who sits with his legs crossed.

I am inspired by the magnificent scenery. The rocks cast a variety of pinks, reds and blues in the early morning. Saguaro cactuses stand with outstretched arms guarding the unique landscape.

The instructor, a black athletic man with a velvety voice and shaved head, says, "*Namaste*. I'm Thomas, author of *Yoga for Yogis*." He guides us through some familiar poses like downward dog and cobra, his seductive voice urging us to focus on our breath.

Glee glances at him often. I concentrate on breathing, absorbing his instructions for inhaling and exhaling with a slow rhythm. After a while we move to some excruciating poses which I've never mastered and probably never will in this lifetime.

Glee, one knee over the other, twisted around to look over her shoulder pants at me. "You can do this."

Instead of twisting my back I sit on my heels, knees underneath me to bend forward into the child's pose, my hands stretched forward. I repeat the affirmation, *I am here, I am right here, right now.*

Soon we're all stretched out on our mats. Our instructor's mellow voice guides us through a relaxation meditation. I feel my body flow into a river. When it's time to open our eyes I'm happy to be alive. We leave satiated, moving at a snail's pace for a breakfast of whole wheat toast and fruit.

We stop at the room to gather our notebooks and purses and head to the first seminar. Glee hugs me goodbye.

"I'm so glad you came. This is going to be great for you. It'll turn your life around."

The nearly full room buzzes. No one's sitting in the front row. I'm a teacher. That's where I head.

Our instructor, a short, wiry guy in tight jeans and a plaid cowboy shirt, sorts hand-outs at a table. He glances at his watch and walks to center stage, swaying with the motion of someone who's been on a horse too long.

"I'm Harry Frommage. I'm going to give you a short bio about me. I tell it like I see it. Don't want you to have any fancy expectations about being discovered. I've had twenty-seven novels and short stories published. Won over thirty prizes. I may look like a ranch hand because I am one. Been rustlin' cattle since I was a kid and writin' at night. You want this life? Listen up. I'm going to give you the crux of dialogue. It's the key to a good story after character and plot."

I hold my pen a little tighter and wipe my hand across the clean page of notebook paper on my lap. My eye level is at his crotch. I raise my gaze to his weather-beaten face, deep lines tracked across it like irrigation ditches. He's got all the tell-tale signs of a heavy smoker—yellow fingers, brown teeth and the aroma of an old ashtray. No wonder I'm the only one sitting in the front row.

"Want your characters to sound real? Take out the beginning of sentences. People speak in fragments. Don't have them repeat phrases. Give the reader clues to their motivation. Make sure your characters don't sound the same. Give them distinctive voices."

The stink of cigarettes makes me sneeze. He ignores my fumbling for a tissue. He goes on in his pithy style for thirty minutes, glances at his watch and says, "It's time for a break."

A woman in the back calls out, "We're not supposed to have any breaks."

"Lady, I need a smoke. I don't care what that Nazi woman says. Anyone care to join me?" He heads toward the door in the back. I turn around, amazed to see a dozen people following him.

A skinny woman wearing a newsboy cap, glasses and dangling earrings moves up and scrunches next to me. Her cap perches on the crown of her head instead of low on her brow. She's carrying a newspaper.

In a conspiratorial whisper she says, "That's how they get in with the instructor. Smoking's intimate. I used to indulge.

Quit a few years back."

"Why do they want to get *in* with him?" I stare at the puckered vertical lines around her mouth.

"Maybe he'll read a few chapters of their book or refer them to his agent or publisher if he likes their work." She sits back satisfied, opens her newspaper and reads the obituaries.

"Oh." I feel enlightened.

"I always check these in case someone I know expired over night."

"Mmm. I'm a horoscope reader myself," I say.

Mr. Frommage, whose name means cheese in French, comes back and smells worse than any Limberger I've encountered. I can't breathe. My new buddy folds up her paper, drops it under her chair and presses up against me. "Watch who he picks to share their work."

He continues to lecture us, challenging the class with assignments. We're supposed to write dialogue between a mom and her child who doesn't want to go to school on the first day. It's a boring topic and I get stuck on *Johnny, you're going to grow up to be an ignoramus like your father.* The next exercise we're trapped in an elevator with five people. Who are they and what do they say?

He addresses the student smokers who followed him out of the room by name. They volunteer to stand and read snippets of what they've written. A few of the humorous lines of dialogue make us laugh. A couple of them are stilted and awful. He's gentle with his critiques.

Finally, his hands shaking a bit, he passes out the papers

stacked on the table. "This is a list of situations that promote dialoguing. Practice free writing with them. Just imagine two characters and let them go at it. Conflict is the nucleus of a good story. It advances the plot. Your assignment for tomorrow is to go to a restaurant or coffee shop and listen to peoples' conversations. Make up a scenario with conflict. What's their life about? Who are they? What can be revealed about their character?"

A flutter of panic waves over me. My creative juices can't just be called up like whistling for Amber. Besides, with my luck I'll get stuck next to a table of senior citizens out for the early bird special discussing Medicare supplements and hemorrhoids.

My front row buddy hands me her card. "You look worried. Call me on my cell if you need any help with the assignment." She pats her cap down on her head.

That evening, after dinner, where I forgot to pay attention to dialogue at the next table, Glee and I attend a reading by a married couple who are both famous. She's the poet; he's the novelist. I've read both their work.

Their black and white portraits, displayed on corkboard and posted outside the mini-ballroom on easels, reveal a glamorous couple. She appears intellectual with a pair of glasses in her hand seductively teasing her lip, long dark hair and large hoop earrings that accentuate a dark turtleneck. He's handsome with unkempt hair and bushy brows, a knowing look in his eyes. I can't wait. They're formidable, serious writers. *Real* writers.

Inside, Glee and I find seats in the middle of a row halfway back. I can't see very well because of all the heads in front of me but the point here is to listen.

Our severe director taps the microphone a few times to get our attention.

"Recording and video devices are not allowed. Please turn off all cell phones."

A flurry of activity and beeps fills the room as people scramble though bags and pockets for the devices they can't live without. I don't have to worry. I forgot to turn my trēo on today after class. I haven't missed it.

"And now it is my distinct pleasure to introduce a couple who need no introduction in the literary world. Winners of the Peabody Prize for Poetry seven years in a row, short-listed for the Orange Prize and author of twelve best-selling novels, please welcome, Linda Harris and Andrew Studder."

Two large figures with grey heads maneuver with deliberation toward chairs behind a long table in the front. She walks with a cane and his shoulders are stooped, his wild hair forming a halo around a significant bald spot. It takes a few minutes for them to settle into their seats. They position the microphones in front of them.

I whisper to Glee, "They must have taken those pictures when Nixon was in office."

"Sshh," she says.

Linda Harris speaks first with a tremulous voice reading a poem that starts with, "I come from witches and playwrights and healers and storytellers." It's a masterful piece that she reads with expression. We applaud, invigorated by her words and images. Poetry speaks to the soul.

Next, her spouse reads a chapter from his soon-to-be released memoir. He sets us up. "Most of you know Linda and I met when she was married and I was merely a struggling actor fifteen years her junior. This chapter reveals what's happening a few weeks into our relationship."

No, I didn't know that. The blurb about the author on a book jacket doesn't tell you the good stuff. Glee squiggles next to me. She loves personal, inside information.

It takes me a few minutes to grasp what's going on. It sounds like he's reading pornography. It's an explicit sex scene that borders on kinky.

I look around.

Glee is captivated as are others in the audience. His wife, who looks like she hasn't seen this kind of action in twenty years, grins. She's not embarrassed at all; she's delighted.

I have a hard time following the arms, legs, wetness, slippery sheets and various lips. Mostly I'm uncomfortable with people's prurient details except for maybe mine and Maury's. I shift in my seat and close my eyes. Maybe it's almost over.

Soon there's enthusiastic applause and when I open my eyes, they're receiving a standing ovation. The audience responds with "Bravo!"

I hope writing a novel doesn't require sharing my sex life.

Afterward, they're mobbed with people thrusting copies of their books at them to sign. They sit next to each other and smile with pride.

"I had no idea writing conferences were so explicit," says Glee. "I could write something hot. Maybe I'll switch over to fiction."

I roll my eyes.

Later that night I sit at the enameled desk in our room working on my dialogue assignment. So far I have written two lines. They're not very good.

Glee, on the other hand, propped up in bed wearing a leopard silk bathrobe, a green mud beauty treatment masque on her face, scribbles away.

"Listen to this," she says. "'I rolled over on top of him. He turned me on. He grabbed both nipples and pinched.' What do you think?"

"Well, I'm not a critic but I think sex scenes have to be more sensual than mechanical. Besides, only fourteen year-old boys attack both nipples at the same time."

She looks disappointed, biting the eraser of her pencil. "I think I'll read it in class anyway."

"Right. See what the instructor in non-fiction says."

Glee has few self-doubts, but I can see she's contemplating sharing this with her group who express themselves writing about problems, nature, family or their pets.

At our Saturday morning class I expect the smelly ash tray guy so I sit farther back. People talk quietly as we wait. The few women around me complain about the difficulty of eavesdropping on people's conversations. I had no problem with the assignment because I scrapped the seniors' conversation. I imagined the writers from last night who shared their sex life after it was over:

"You think the audience bought that?" she says slamming her cane across the bed.

"Who knows? Who cares?" he asks, running his hands up and down her muu-muu. "They bought our books."

We check our watches. It's past the starting time for the session to begin. A compulsive woman who has designated herself the leader checks the hallway. Soon the door opens. Instead of the short, wiry guy we get a female football player dressed in khaki safari garb with an Aussie hat turned up on one side.

Even though I can't see all of her I can hear the instructor clomp down the side aisle, probably in hiking boots. My body jerks when metal pails drop to the floor in the front of the room. I hear a splash of water and loud slurping.

"Anyone afraid of dogs?" she asks. The room hushes. Who would admit it?

"Boris is my one-hundred-ten pound Wolfhound who goes everywhere with me. Say hello, Boris." I hear panting and a tail hitting the wall.

When we're settled down she introduces herself as Savannah Kaye, author of *Cowgirls Always in the Saddle*, a *New York Times* best seller. "It's fiction based on true experiences from my years of self-discovery. I've been working on the sequel for ten years. It's almost ready to send to the publisher. I expect great reviews. Y'all know I won the Short Story Fiction award, right? Never mind. I want to know all about you," she says.

We start a tedious process of everyone introducing themselves. After they say their name some state they have a goal of being discovered by an agent, having their book go to auction, getting published, making a lot of money and becoming the next rock star of the literary world. Some are brown-nosers who say all of the above but add that they want to be just like her. One guy wants to know if she'll be taking any smoke breaks.

She says, "No, but I walk Boris every hour." Oh no. That'll waste time.

As the introductions come down my row we have a few writer conference groupies, the people who follow certain authors or enroll in every workshop no matter the location or cost. How do they have time to write?

My news cap buddy sits next to me. She can't decide whether to write anything at all. "I like the camaraderie of the conferences," she says.

For my introduction I state my name and say, "I want to tell stories." The teacher nods in approval.

After we finish with introductions and two dog walks, we have fifteen minutes left.

"I want you to do a free writing exercise about being in the woods, remembering a childhood incident or anything about an animal." As if on cue Boris begins to slurp with his ten-pound tongue.

Some of us stare at the ceiling and others scribble with

frantic abandon. The minutes pass quickly. I can't think of anything to write. Writing about my childhood can give me a headache and, although I love Amber, she's not that interesting.

"Okay, writers, let's wind it up. Finish this tonight. Bring copies for everyone tomorrow so we can critique your work."

"What about the dialogue piece we wrote last night for the professor we had yesterday?" asks the compulsive self-appointed leader. "I was up until two a.m. polishing it."

"File it away for future use. Frommage's emphysema is acting up so he won't be back."

The second day passes with speed. I go back to the room in the afternoon to contemplate a childhood incident. I'm torn. Should I write about the time my brother lost three gerbils in the house or when Lara and Michael dragged in the garden hose to fill the bathtub? Neither seems to have much literary merit. I'm stumped.

Glee insists we go to dinner and the reading afterward. "We can't miss a poet reading his own words. They have such passion."

"I don't know. I should call the kids, check in with Maury and my mother, outline a new proposal for a client. I've left so many things unfinished. If I don't work on the proposal tonight, I'll be jammed up next week. Plus, I haven't even started tomorrow's writing assignment."

"Jean, that's the reason you came this weekend. To get away from it all. Before you know it you'll be all worked up again. Stress is an option. Besides, it causes the body to store belly fat. Look at my middle." She strokes her flat stomach. "No stress," she says, raising a knowing finger at me.

I look down at my pudgy belly.

"Train yourself not to think about all those aggravating details that drive up your pulse rate and come with me."

I know what she's saying is true. And, she did have liposuction. I push back my chair at the desk. "Okay, I'm ready."

Glee gives me a look of disapproval. "Remember we talked about image? If you want to be a writer you have to dress like a writer."

"What does a writer dress like?" I'm thinking about glasses, dangling earrings and a news boy cap. "What's wrong with what I'm wearing?" I ask, pulling my baggy purple yoga pants out at the sides.

"If you're a writer you wear black." Glee does look creative in a tight black T-shirt with POET scrawled on the front in white, fitted black jeans and lizard cowboy boots. A Kanga hat perches backwards on her head with the kangaroo logo plunked between her eyes. She's accessorized with silver and turquoise jewelry.

Maybe she has a point. I change although I still lack style. My black T-shirt's a bit baggy, my Dockers jeans for Middle-Aged Women with Wide Asses are not very cool. I slide into suede beaded moccasins, brush my hair, add lipstick and spray a little cologne. I'm ready for anything.

"Here. You need this," she says, tying a black and white scarf with skulls around my neck.

We join writers from Glee's non-fiction class for dinner in

the motel coffee shop. All three women are in therapy and want to write about it.

One has been seriously damaged by a bad boyfriend who dumped her. She emphasizes the word "sociopath". The second is in love with two men, her husband and a lover who are aware of each other. She's documenting her schedule and douches.

The last woman explains she used to be 300 pounds but chose gastric bypass surgery over ice cream and doughnuts. I'm touched by her story. She orders a small salad, dressing on the side. I wonder if she's wearing Spanx to suck up the extra flesh.

Glee hands her a business coaching card.

"What do you think of the conference?" I ask the jilted woman.

"I'm enjoying it. I didn't know what to expect. My dream is to go to a liberry and see my books."

Glee chimes in. She knows I might correct the woman's pronunciation of library. She steers me in another direction, putting me on the spot. "What do you really feel about what's going on here? What are your observations?"

"You want the truth?" I ask.

"No, lie to me. Of course I want the truth." She turns to the others. "Jean's had some issues lately with her family and job. I thought the conference would be good for her. She's got keen insight. I know there's a writer in there."

With her fork stabbed into some iceberg lettuce, the gastric bypass lady says, "You can do anything you want if you're determined enough."

"Jean, what do you think?" asks Glee with her usual attitude of pursuance.

"Okay, you asked for it. First of all, let me say I've met some lovely people, present company included. Secondly, I am absorbing information in the workshops. I don't know when I'll use it. As of now I have no immediate novel writing plans."

"Now, Jean—" says Glee.

What I love about Glee is she doesn't cringe even though she knows I'll tell it as I see it, never trying to censor me. She's all for self-expression. Whatever is coming next she's open to it, even if I step on some toes. I begin with what's formulated in my mind from my observations.

"Okay. As far as I can see there are four types who attend writing conferences. "First, there are the exposers, the ones who want to share their sex lives. They relish words for shock value like vagina, penis, hard, wet. A lot of them spend time in a pot haze, which, I might add, does not enhance their writing ability."

I stop. Everyone at the table is enraptured. I continue.

"The second group wants to scandalize. One guy read a piece about shooting a Mexican near the border. He had sex with his girlfriend afterward. Even the instructor expressed horror when he told us it was a memoir."

Two of the women gasp.

"Why that's a crime," says the one who knows a sociopath, her glasses hanging on a turquoise and silver chain around her neck.

"It's a moral and judicial nightmare," I respond. I'm on a roll so I continue. "Third, there's the pushy writers who think they should be famous now. One of them gave me her card with the title of her book, *Sugar Bitch*, on it. Then she grabbed it out of my hand. She even tried to pawn off her eight hundred page manuscript on the instructor who couldn't take it because her dog pails were too heavy. Sugar Bitch offered to carry them."

Glee puts her chin in her hand. "This is the Jean I love," she says.

"Finally, there are the ones who want to talk about themselves all the time. They think we need to know every detail of their life thinly disguised as fiction. A lot of the ones with broken hearts write romance and dream of Fabio sprinting across the cover of their latest novel."

The group remains silent. I don't know if I identified some of them. Maybe I'm way off mark. I skipped the leftists, the left-overs, and the left-outs.

"I don't think I fit into any of those categories," says the gastric bypass lady eating her miniscule salad. The rest of the table agrees with her.

Realizing I might have hurt some feelings, I back pedal. "Well, I wasn't talking about anyone here, of course."

There's a sigh of relief.

The waitress drops off the check. After scrambling in our purses we put our share in the center of the table. The one with the hanging eyeglasses stares at the bill, counting the money. "Everyone has to put in seventy-five cents more for the tip."

Glee dips her hand into her metallic feedbag purse, pulls

out a ten and tosses it on the table.

"But now we'll need to wait for change," says our self-appointed accountant.

"It's covered. Let's go. Come on, we want to get good seats for the reading," says Glee.

The evening part of the conference we hear from the two guys who have written a series of sex thrillers. Their books make the best seller list every year. With wit they describe how they choose character's names, develop sinister plots and create unusual settings. They receive a standing ovation, hold hands and thrust them into the air.

One of the male instructors introduces our next author. "Let's welcome Boyd O'Harlan, winner of the 1989 Scrud Award for Outstanding Literature. He's a prominent writer whose work is based in fact but elaborated with fiction. Let's welcome my great friend, Boyd O'Harlan!"

The audience claps with enthusiasm. A disheveled man with stringy black hair walks unsteadily to the front. He looks like he needs a shower to sober up and get clean.

He searches for reading glasses in his pants and shirt pockets. When he finds them he places them on the end of his nose. He licks his lips, surveying the room. With an Irish brogue and a baritone voice he begins an esoteric reading, slurring his words, swaying away from the podium.

A young woman rushes forward with a glass of water. He staggers toward her with a lecherous grin. He takes a sip, placing it on the podium. His hand shakes. He begins again.

I can't follow what he's reading. It's obvious he's had too

much to drink. I tune out and think about the drive back and my lists.

Andrew Studder, the author who shared his sex life on the first evening sits in the back without his wife. Glee keeps glancing at him. She hunches down to get out of our row to stand in the back of the room.

She stands behind him during the question and answer period, while the inebriated author clings to the podium. Answers to questions about his writing technique are met with slurred derision.

The woman in charge interrupts him, ending the evening with an abrupt, "Well, we've had enough of that, haven't we?"

I head for Glee who's wormed her way into the row in front of the author. She pushes aside a few chairs and sits backward, her chin on her hands, in front of him. I take a seat nearby, tuning into her approach.

"I'm not trying to flatter you, but your acting background made your delivery exceptional," says Glee.

"Really? What else did you enjoy?" He tosses his arm across the empty chair next to him, leaning back with pleasure.

"What happened to acting?" she asks.

"It went the way of my cocaine habit. Whatever happened thirty years ago is way more fun to talk about than anything in the present."

"I assume the cocaine habit is over."

"Regrettably, true."

Glee sits a little taller and smiles. "Come on. You want to be addicted to something at this stage of life."

"No way. Except sex maybe."

Uh-oh. I'd better get her out of here. Glee could get her head bashed in with his poet wife's cane.

I make my move. "Sorry to interrupt but we have another early session. I'm heading back to the room."

"Sure," says Glee. The author rises, fishes in the back pocket of his jeans and hands her a beat-up business card.

"I'll be happy to read your manuscript when it's ready," he tells Glee.

We walk out together.

"He doesn't even know what you're writing about," I say with irritation.

"What difference does it make? I've got his card."

As we walk through the loggia lined with pink bougainvillea, the stars appear crisp and clear in the inky sky. The red mountains, outlined as black monoliths, have their color absorbed by the night.

"Jean, you should network more. Someone like that can help you get discovered."

"Network? You practically threw yourself at him."

"Maybe. But I don't have to follow through, do I? Create more options for yourself."

On our last day the morning session, devoted to student readings, seems interminable. One plain young woman, mousy brown hair parted in the middle, holds up a paperback with a nude woman on the cover. It's a frontal shot, arms overhead, nothing hidden, her triangle bush very visible.

"I want to read a selection from my first novel, *Confessions of a Southwest Slut*." She pushes back her chair to stand, the book cover prominent.

The group nods in approval. We want to show we're open-minded, creative, liberal in ideas and non-judgmental.

Boris, our wolfhound class mascot, slurps.

While she drones on in a monotone voice reading poorly written salacious words, I realize she's the one who posed for the cover. When a few others get it, a buzz starts.

She gazes at the front of the book. "Oh, it's me on the cover. I love this photo."

Everyone's quiet. The instructor says, "We've run out of time. Thank you so much. And now I'll pass around a sheet for you to sign with your name and email. We all want to stay in touch."

One young woman in an MFA program announces, "I feel bonded with all of you forever. I've never made such close friends."

Oy. I don't think I'm tortured enough to write. I need more neuroses. Being stressed doesn't cut it. I have to get a little crazier.

24

I'VE BEEN PREPARING OUR THANKSGIVING DINNER for a week. The aroma of a slow-cooking turkey permeates the house. I ordered a kosher twenty-pounder to respect Rivka's dietary considerations.

The house has been meticulously cleaned, Amber's been bathed and wears a new orange collar, the places at our dining room table have been set with my best dishes and silver and an autumn arrangement of yellow chrysanthemums enhances the ambiance.

I start at seven a.m. to prepare a casserole of yams blended with pecans and marshmallows, garlic mashed potatoes made from scratch and stuffing with celery and nuts for crunch. Butter-laden crusts rolled out for two apple pies are complete. The gravy, from the turkey drippings with mushrooms and onions, bubbles on the stove. I've shopped, cooked and prepared for days.

Guests arrive at noon for our feast. The women come in first, arms laden with their contributions to our meal while the men stroll in behind them.

Rivka's brought homemade organic cranberry sauce, Lara's responsible for green bean almondine, Glee's loaded with gift bags of wine and April carries pumpkin pies from AJs on a silver tray. My mother, dressed in her beige shantung suit, make-up applied with perfection, has dibs on criticism, interference and unsolicited advice.

"Hi Mom," I say, bending over to kiss her as she comes in with Lara and Gus. She places a shopping bag on the floor. "What's that?" I ask, holding the spoon I've been stirring the gravy with away from my body.

"Something you can use." Uh-oh. I'd better check it and see if I can pawn it off on the kids before they leave. Maybe it's a white blouse, Asian figurine or an elaborate ash tray.

She looks around at the dishes, pots and casseroles. "In my day we opened a few packages of Lipton onion soup, poured it over the turkey and roasted it. I don't know what this gourmet fuss is about."

One of my new techniques is not to react to everything my mother says. "Lara honey, get Grandma some wine and take her into the dining room. Thanks." I roll my eyes. "Then come back and let's get all this on the table."

Maury's in charge of carving our divine bird. He attacks it with surgical skill after sharpening his knife. I scoop stuffing into a bowl.

We carry a platter of white and dark meat, drumsticks,

wings and the wishbone into the dining room. The table looks inviting with all its abundance as we find our places and squeeze into our chairs. The table is crowded with so many places. Maury and I head up each end of the spread.

"It smells great," says Lara.

"I'm starving," Michael adds.

"Are we eating yet?" asks Tangie.

Maury says a brief prayer of thanks. Lara and Rivka take care of the kids, wine and water are poured into glasses, napkins snap onto laps. The dishes fly around the table, some being passed for additional servings, others so people can help themselves. The energy of a family holiday begins.

And, as with most meals, it takes hours of preparation and fifteen minutes to gobble it up. We sit around what was moments ago a very elegant table. Now the lids from the casserole dishes are scattered among gravy stains, blobs of dropped food, spilled wine and crumpled napkins. I open the top button on my pants with discretion. We'll have great sandwiches tomorrow.

"I ate too much," moans Gus. The kids fidget in their seats.

April's still cutting her single slice of turkey into tiny bits. "Don't mind me. I adhere to the rules of the Slow Food Movement."

After seconds and thirds have been offered and accepted by most, I say, "Let's go around and say what we're grateful for."

"I'll start," says Glee who's sitting in the middle. She positions her used silverware across the corner of her plate, surveying the table. "I'm grateful for wonderful friends who have included us on this special occasion." She touches Stavros's arm. "And an important man in my life. I hope this is an appropriate time to mention I'm changing my focus to be a stress coach. I want to help people enjoy the sanctity of the lives they have."

Our group, used to Glee's capricious pronouncements, nods or smiles with encouragement.

She adds, "Why, you can't even get pregnant nowadays if you have tension."

I glance at Rivka. Her eyes water.

Glee continues. "Of course I've changed the title of my book to a new working one, *An Unstressed Life—A Guide to Women's Mental Health.*"

I clap my hands in approval; Maury gives me a blank stare, his mouth open in amazement. Stavros beams. The kids blink.

Stavros picks up where she left off. "I'm grateful to find enlightened, intelligent people far from my home. America is the best country in the world." He drapes his arm around Glee. "Where else could a folk dancer from Greece become a publisher? *Apolanvano tizoi!*"

"What does that mean?" asks Lara.

"I'm thankful for life!" says Stavros.

We offer acknowledgement. It's Lara's turn.

Lara pushes her plate back a little with her thumb and says, "I'm grateful to have a wonderful husband and two beautiful children." She leans over and whispers in Tangie's ear.

Tangie, who's playing with her fork, says, "I'm grateful for my brudder." She makes a face.

"Buzz? It's your turn. Do you want to say what you're grateful for?" I ask. He shakes his head no and puts his face into his hands.

Gus pats Buzz on the back. "I'm grateful for being able to hang out with such a cool family and play my guitar every day." He looks around. "Uh, I have a new business idea."

Maury and I look at him with expectation. We've been waiting for something to happen. He takes a deep breath.

"I'd like to open kiosks to help anyone who's technically challenged. They could bring their electronic devices to me like computers, phones, VCRs, cameras, iPods and I'll show them what to do. I'll give them clear printed out directions, tech support, organize their passwords, get them on social media sites. I could even make house calls."

Maury gives me a look. I laugh. He's kidding, right?

April looks at Gus and says, "I'll be your first customer. I'd like someone to show me how to Tivo so when I want to watch a show, I don't have to bother Steve at work. I want my iPod programmed with Beyoncé."

Steve, a stitch between his brows, says, "Hey, Buddy, let me know when you're looking for financing. Lot of people could use some help. Especially April." She gives him a light punch on the arm.

Michael's turn comes next. "I know I'm not supposed to make a speech but listen, guys, I'm grateful for my new business. But I could use a few more customers."

"What does he want?" my mother asks, blinking with confusion.

"More customers," I whisper.

"What's he selling?" she asks.

"Grandma, I'm marketing supplements. The company I'm with has a patented process. These vitamins are guaranteed to make you feel younger, put a spring in your step and a bounce in your walk."

"That's all I need with my terrible feet."

Glee offers, "I'll be one of your customers. I'm always open. Do they have antioxidants to fight free radicals?"

Michael's arm plunges into the air. "Yes! Now I only need nineteen more clients before the end of the year." Then, turning to Glee, he says, "We have antioxidants, fish oil and ginko biloba."

"What happens when you have twenty customers?" I ask, saying a silent prayer he can pay his mortgage.

"Then I move to Super Diamond Executive Presidential status and get a big bonus."

"I can't wait," says Rivka dryly. She's heard all this before. She turns to address the table. "I am so happy to be part of this welcoming family since mine is in Mexico. I also want to thank God I am . . ."

"Pregnant?" asks Lara in a small voice. Rivka nods.

Lara screams, pushes back her chair from a tight spot, gets up and hugs her. "I noticed you didn't touch your wine."

Everyone at the table bombards Rivka and Michael with questions after saying congratulations and *mazel tov*. "When are you due? Do you want a girl this time? Have you picked out names?"

Michael leans back in his chair buffing his nails against his shirt. "I did all the work."

My mother leans over and asks me, "They didn't need a fertility vacation or the shots?"

"No, mom, it was the old-fashioned way."

"Thank God. A good *schtup* never hurt anybody."

"Grandma!" says Lara.

"What? You nut," says Rivka, smiling and throwing a roll at Michael.

"Wait a minute. This holiday dinner can't deteriorate. No food fights," says Maury with the knowledge of how unruly our kids can get even though they're adults.

Stavros interrupts and offers a toast with his wine glass raised. "To babies. May you dance through life."

"*L'chaim*," say a few of us.

I'm teary eyed because I know how hard they've tried and how worried they've been. I look at Maury at the head of the table. We exchange smiles. I'm so happy I'm going to be a grandmother again. Maury's also probably grinning because skipping IVF just saved us $35,000.

Next it's Lara's turn. We look at her with expectation. "Okay, I'm grateful for healthy children and a wonderful family. And that my kids are going to have another cousin." She claps her hands.

I get the group back on track. "Let's move along. April?"

"I'm grateful I've learned what's important in life. I can live without jewels as long as we save the cats and dogs in the no-kill shelters." Amber barks at this appropriate moment. We laugh.

Steve leans back, smiling for the first time since I can remember. "I'm grateful I have a beautiful wife and a law practice that affords me luxuries."

"Maury?" I ask.

"I'm grateful for my intelligent, attractive, sometimes-harried wife who pulled off this great meal. And a wonderful family."

"Aaaaw," the group around the table says in unison.

"Wait. I'm not finished," says Maury. "If we're doing a few commercials, I want to add that I'm on a steering committee for the Green Party. We plan to have a viable candidate on the ballot for governor in the next election. Contributions of time or money are welcome. Our issues have come to the forefront, especially since the EPA has found elevated levels of arsenic in Scottsdale and Paradise Valley water."

Michael, with the consciousness of a new baby on the way, turns to Rivka. "Don't drink the tap water no matter what." She nods.

"Jacob, it's your turn," says Rivka, leaning toward him. "Say what you're happy about, honey."

"I'm happy I have my mommy and daddy and that we're having a baby."

"Grandma?" says Lara.

"I'm grateful to be with family but I miss Pop-Pop. He would have liked the kosher turkey. It melted in my mouth."

I reach out and touch my mother's arm. "We miss him too, Mom. Dad was such a fine human being."

A sad smile crosses her lips as she looks down, her eyes filling with tears. "He was a wonderful companion and the most elegant gentleman I ever met."

Michael says, "Yeah, and he was the sharpest dressed grandpa ever. I loved all his jokes too."

I'm overwhelmed. I realize the people whom I'm closest to and that I care about the most surround me except for my dad. Life is very precious. We're going to be welcoming a new one soon. Maybe Rivka will consider naming the newest addition after him.

"Mom, what about you?" asks Lara. "What are you grateful for?"

I swallow. I haven't thought about it. My words tumble out. "My family, being a grandparent, good friends, an understanding husband, surviving Thanksgiving." I take a deep breath and release it. "A Universe that supports me."

Our group smiles at me. I take my mother's and Lara's hands. Everyone reaches for the person next to them. We look around the table cherishing the moment.

"When do we carve the pumpkin?" asks Jacob.

"That's Halloween, honey. This is Thanksgiving," explains Rivka.

"Why don't we have any Pilgrims?" he asks.

"I'll explain later," says Michael.

I clap my hands together. "Okay, before we have dessert, let's clear the table. Lara, you carry in the big plates. Rivka, please gather the silverware. The guys can bring in the platters." We ease into motion.

"Maury, take everyone else in the family room. See if anyone needs more wine. They're running a repeat of the Macy's Day parade. The kids will love it."

Gus asks, "Can we do pix-in-pix so I can watch the game?"

Sure," says Maury. "I love that. I watch the golf tournament and the history channel at the same time."

I don't try to clean up completely, but I get the counters under control and start a load of dishes. Rivka peels off the plastic wrap covering the pies and gets out the ice cream.

Lara pulls me aside and says, "Mom, I have to talk to you about something. Gus is driving me crazy. He's so disorganized. He doesn't complete a simple errand."

"Honey, your father goes to Home Depot, gets lost in there for two hours, comes home and then goes out again to the hardware store."

"Mom." She slaps her hands on her legs. "I can't stand it. He wastes time, energy, gas."

"Sweetheart, that's just what men do. They're a human toothache sometimes." I touch her cheek.

"You mean I married my father?" asks Lara, shocked with the realization.

"Yes, dear."

I set out the pumpkin and apple pies, plates and clean forks. "C'mon, girls," I say to my daughter and daughter-in-law, hugging them. "Let's sit with our guests. This time next year we'll have another baby. I'm so thrilled. This is special."

In the family room the guys gather at one end of the sectional while April, Glee and my mother perch at the other. April has her shoe off and is showing it to my mother. The kids sit two feet in front of the TV. They're fascinated by giant balloons of their favorite cartoon characters among flurries of snow in New York City. The guys concentrate on a touchdown in a small screen inside the parade.

Our local suntanned anchor appears with a breaking news story. "We interrupt this programming for a special announcement." Bright blue messages scroll across the bottom of the screen—Breaking News Breaking News Breaking News.

"Oh no. I hope we haven't invaded some foreign country again. It puts Wolf Blitzer in a terrible situation," says my mother.

In his best broadcaster voice the announcer says, "The notorious Rock Burglar has been caught. After seven years of terrorizing Valley residents an arrest has been made."

I sit down, grabbing April's arm with an inhalation of breath. Everyone in the room sits frozen, transfixed at the screen, except for Tangie whose *tush* is in the air. She's demonstrating a somersault for the little boys. I think I can hear my wrist watch ticking.

"In a high profile stake-out, Scottsdale Police have arrested a suspect known for bold finger puppetry at security cameras."

Footage we've seen before of the suspect plays again with the hand and its prominent finger blurred out. It makes no sense to me they can show war on TV but not someone flipping a bird.

"The perpetrator, seen here being led away in handcuffs, has been identified as one Tiffany Beaudreaux."

I gasp. Tiffany's wearing a dark baseball cap and a black jogging suit.

April screams. "Her?"

The announcer continues, "She and her boyfriend, Rich Gunby, and several other suspects who have not yet been apprehended, have been accused of robbing some of the most prestigious families in the Phoenix area with smash and grab tactics. In many cases they entered while people were at home."

A shot of Flora's headquarters flashes on the screen.

"Tiffany is the daughter of legislator, Flora Beaudreuax, under investigation for campaign funding improprieties."

"What happens with an indictment pending?" Maury asks Steve.

Steve answers casually. "Flora's in office until they case comes to court and they cart her off to prison."

"Does that mean Craig might get appointed?" I ask.

Steve shrugs. "The judicial system has to play itself out. I don't know what the election statutes state."

It's the first time I've heard Steve say he doesn't know something.

The screen flashes back to the male newscaster, showing off his million dollar smile, stacking his papers.

"Looks like a bad day for the Beaudreaux family. And now back to the Thanksgiving Day parade recorded earlier."

"Wait. Does this mean I get my jewelry back?" asks April.

Steve leans forward, his arms on his knees. He shakes his head until his forelock comes loose. "That SOB stealing my wife's yellow diamond. That family has assets. I'm gonna sue."

Maury and I are stunned. Maury jumps up, grabbing my hands to pull me up. He dances me around the living room as I spin in his arms. He sings, "Good things are happening in Scottsdale. Good things are happening now!"

The Rock Burglar's been caught. Flora's almost washed up. Life has shifted in a few minutes.

"See? I told you there were robbers and dangerous thugs out there," says my mother, sitting back.

Spontaneous cheers come from the others. It seems we're all talking at once. I can't wait to get the full story.

Maury pulls out his phone to text message. Starr? Everyone important in our lives is right here. I'm deflated. I have to get to the bottom of this.

April follows me into the kitchen to cut the pies. She's a head taller than I am because she's put her stilettos back on and I'm in flats.

"That's a shock, isn't it?" she asks.

"I'm angry at myself that I didn't suspect Tiffany sooner with her athletic build. She could pass as a man. She has access to all the society people, knows how to run and probably has a luxury vehicle to cruise the neighborhoods."

"I can't believe I never saw her when I walked the dogs. I wonder what kind of car she has," says April.

"Wait a minute. She's the one that stole my parking space. The Hummer Hogger! She gave me the finger too."

"Figures she'd be rude," says April.

"An impolite crook!" I say.

"How 'bout her mother, Flora?" asks April. "She's been around for years attending events, raising money."

"She's a villain. Maybe now she'll be off the political scene."

"Just a sliver of apple for me," says April, pointing to the pies. "No ice cream."

We bring slices of apple and creamy pumpkin pie with vanilla ice cream to everyone in the other room.

Glee, cozying up to Stavros, says, "I'm so glad they caught the burglar. It's really bad karma to steal. I think I'll celebrate with another dinner party. Maybe with costumes."

Maury groans.

"Everyone can come dressed as the person they've always wanted to be."

"I'm coming as a veterinarian," says April.

When we're seated again I relax into the sofa. With the preparation of such a large meal behind me, I look around at my beautiful family and friends. Some anxiety can be exciting. It's not all bad. It just needs to be coupled with periods of relaxation. I'm taking the day off tomorrow. Balance is the key to rejuvenation.

Maury and I could use a vacation at the beach now that the campaign and Thanksgiving are behind us. I doubt we'll do that, but I'm going to make exercise a regular part of my day. Ratango may not be the best choice but going to the gym has to be a habit. Of course when I'm there stomping and sweating on the treadmill, the irony that I'm working hard and not going anyplace, will not be lost on me.

25

THE DAY OF NEW YEARS EVE I'M TRAPPED in a shopping nightmare.
Rivka wants my expert advice in picking out baby furniture.
She's convinced that the best place to find what she wants is
IKEA, an enormous store located in Tempe off the freeway.
After a harrowing ride down I-10 past semi-trucks and crazy
speeders, I'm in a consumer's paradise. Except I'm not a big
consumer. I get overwhelmed with too many choices and too
much stuff.

It's Sweden's answer to Wal-Mart—miles of merchandise
at bargain prices. The biggest differences I can see are the
attractive displays of merchandise and no senior citizen
greeters in blue vests.

Instead, we have peppy people in yellow shirts who hand
out maps. I marvel at the floor plan and the acres for household
items, furniture, kitchen gadgets, the warehouse and check out
area.

Aware that all their furniture requires assembly, I have a commitment from Michael that he'll complete the projects with Maury's assistance. That will take a few days of reading instructions, losing screwdrivers, interpreting assembly drawings, mild cursing with a few nuts and bolts left over.

After five minutes I realize I'm the oldest person in the store. Yuppies with round glasses, cool haircuts, Izod shirts, pushing strollers, cruise the packed aisles. We've left Jacob with his grandpa for the afternoon which means he's watching golf and eating rice cakes with peanut butter. On my sofa.

I've never had the kids over where I didn't have to fumigate the living room and clean every glass door of multiple fingerprints. The joys of being a grandparent.

With map in hand we walk around the perimeter of the store looking for children's furniture. We can't get there until we pass through myriad departments.

Ikea wants us to pass every item of inventory before we find our destination. Bargains distract us. Who can resist a rainbow of plastic utensils that will last five years for $5.99?

We wander but can't find what we're looking for in the tall displays that climb to the ceiling. There's a method to this consumer madness. They want us to get lost so we view more products and buy more stuff.

"Excuse me. We're looking for a youth bed and a cradle. Can you tell us where they are?" I ask, approaching two yellow-shirts conferring about which party they're going to attend tonight.

With a cheerful smile he and his female cohort buzz

together and say, "If you follow the signs you'll come to it. Here's another map."

Rivka, who's three months pregnant and looking peaked, drags behind me. Her morning sickness has depleted her energy.

I'm determined to find the right department. I'm wearing my best Birkenstocks so I swing my arms and pick up the pace. "We must be getting closer," I tell her.

She gives me a weak smile.

Just as I'm sure it's around the next corner I find the food court. "How 'bout some refreshment?" I ask Rivka whose thick hair has fallen out of her banded ponytail. It hangs in front of her ears.

"Okay," she says putting her hands on a table and sitting down in slow motion.

I'm not sure what she's hungry for so I order their specialty at the counter, a mound of Swedish meatballs, fries and a drink for under five dollars. When I bring the tray back she has her eyes closed. I remember that early pregnancy exhaustion.

"Here, honey, you need sustenance for both of you."

She takes a few bites of a meatball when I do. They're awful. And this is their specialty? She eats one, excuses herself, claps her hand over her mouth and runs toward the restroom. Uh-oh. This may not have been such a good idea.

While she's gone I think about her. We had our differences in the beginning, especially when Michael brought her home to live with us because she was pregnant. That had its challenges;

however, in recent years with her family far away, she's bonded with me. She's a good momma to our first grandson.

For her recent birthday we gave her a gift certificate to a day spa that caters to pregnant women, baby sitting by Maury and Jean included. She loved it.

When Rivka opened the brochure, she said, "I've heard about this. The massage table is designed for pregnant bellies and the pedicure chairs are wider."

After her appointment she told us, "Everything's decorated in subdued colors to make a pregnant woman feel relaxed. I loved the quiet with bubbling fountains and soothing lighting." It sounded so good I considered being pregnant again so I could receive a little pampering. Of course that's not possible but Maury shows me articles about pregnant grandmothers in foreign countries.

Glee gave Rivka a belly cast appointment so we'll see a plaster belly hanging next to the framed ultrasound picture of baby number two soon.

We're grateful things are looking up on the home front. Michael's committed to his new business. Everyone in the family uses his nutritional supplements, including Glee who has wrangled all her health nut friends into the program too. I have to admit, the vitamins have enhanced my energy level.

Maury's scientific skepticism precludes an all out endorsement, but he encourages Michael. "The research backs up their claims," he tells me.

Michael attends rah-rah meetings and has reached Double Gold Bullion Level Four, whatever that is. It's close to his goal.

He wears his acknowledgement pin with pride recruiting every breathing soul who crosses his path. What matters is he's finally earning a living that has potential. He reminds us with frequency," There are seventy-six million aging baby boomers." Like I didn't know.

I dial Michael to let him know his wife's not feeling well. He doesn't answer.

It drives me crazy that neither of my kids have a land line. They say their cell phones work just as well. Between fuzzy reception and dropped calls I don't think so. Or maybe they're avoiding their mother. With my slow thumb I send a text message.

Rivka returns from the bathroom paler than before.

"Maybe we should give up on this and go home," I tell her.

She nods.

As we drive home Rivka's quiet. She opens the windows for air. The Volvo vibrates. I wouldn't have been able to fit those huge boxes in here anyway. It may cost more, but I think we'll do better at a nearby Punch and Judy store that caters to moms and sends the furniture over assembled.

My mind races over what I have to do this afternoon before we report to Lara's for baby sitting on their special night out. Our kids are still at the age where New Year's Eve is a big deal. We're satisfied to veg out after reading *Winnie-the-Pooh* and watching the ball drop down into Times Square.

I plan to write down my goals for next year after the kids go to bed. I'm integrating information from my self-help group and advice from the book I've been reading that Glee gave me, *Coming to Our Senses: Healing Ourselves and the World.*

Glee's suggested I follow Buddhist principles. "Be a Jew-Bu and chant too."

I don't know about that. I am committed to living a healthier lifestyle, eating more fruits and vegetables, taking vitamins, exercising and walking Amber. I'm also going to schedule more time for me.

After my collapse I attended the Mayo Clinic seminar Maury suggested called "Reduce Stress Now!" Aside from the title that gave me anxiety it did give me the facts and momentum that I needed to make some changes.

They showed a picture of the brain on a screen in the front of the room. With a laser the nurse, a calm woman with glasses and a navy suit, said "Stress causes cortisol in the adrenal gland to age the brain, shrinking the hippocampus, the part used for memory and thinking." I can't afford to lose either of those.

I took copious notes to learn what I am doing to my body when I run around like a hamster. Cortisol regulates blood pressure and cardiovascular function. The body can handle short metabolic bursts but chronic cortisol in the blood stream weakens the immune system, affecting brain function by interfering with dopamine and serotonin.

That got me. Stress affects my heart, raises my blood pressure and leaves me susceptible to getting sick. All the daily short term anxiety makes the long term worse. I can no longer subject myself to high levels of stress.

I don't want to forget or lose one more minute of this

glorious life. I've been meditating in the mornings forcing my brain to clear its debris and focus on a single thought. Some days I'm not so successful but many times I reach it.

At least once a day I enjoy an herbal tea, choosing from a cherry wood chest. Chamomile calms nerves, peppermint's for digestion and passion flower relaxes the body and mind. I take the time to let it steep, adding honey, savoring each sip, while I read the paper.

I believe if less stress extends life span, April's going to live to be 102 and Glee's going to be around forever.

Glee dumped Stavros. "I think he was after my money," she told me. "I want to keep coaching. Look how much *I've* helped you over the years."

In the evenings I shut down early after working on my novel for a bit, listen to classical music, drink more herbal tea, journal, read and ignore the phone. I've slowed to a snail's pace in order to find my peace. I want a low maintenance life.

I'm still taking clients but only after they've been screened not to have a high PIA factor. Pain-in-the asses are not good for my equilibrium.

I've quit my self-help group because, although they were supportive and assisted me in reaching my goals, it was too much pressure getting there. Fewer appointments means less to do.

Have I given up? Given in? No. I'm just content to enjoy life with Maury and appreciate my family. So if things don't get finished, or even started, and my living room looks like an aging boy's fraternity house, so what?

I peruse my cook books, decide what to eat, shop for food and wine and whip us up some wonderful dinners.

We set up some family rules. One Sunday a month and one Saturday night babysitting services. Visits welcome. Just don't expect us to host all dinners and holidays, although we'd like dibs on Thanksgiving and Passover.

We have plans to enjoy foreign films and attend a few lectures at the art museum. Maury's considering a *locum tenems*, an opportunity to work in another doctor's practice in a cooler clime in the summer. We can do that together rather than a solo sojourn to a Third World country which would require me to get umpteen shots. He's even researched hanging out on a Mexican beach. Without kids. Just the two of us.

When Maury comes home he finds me with the radio tuned to the classical music station, a Telemann flute concerto playing. Amber's on the floor, thumping her tail when she sees him. She doesn't rise from her splayed-out pose. A few magazines surround me. I'm mellow and content. He crawls into bed next to me and reaches for my hand.

"Where have you been?" I ask.

"Test driving a Prius. Time for a new car."

I have mixed feelings. "It's always so complicated to change cars. I'm used to mine."

"Jean, I'll take care of it. That ancient Volvo has a permanent oil leak and the Prius can take you all over town on a gallon of gas. You'll love it."

"What color is it?" I ask.

"Your favorite. Beige so you don't have to clean it after the dust storms."

Instead of anxiety bubbling up I relax and decide to let Maury handle it.

"What time do we have to be at Lara's tonight?" he asks.

"Eight o'clock. We have plenty of time."

I turn to face him, glancing over his shoulder at our bedroom, the things that make our lives distinct—books, bathrobes, the bathtub.

However, I feel incomplete about Starr. I never questioned him about her. I'd like to know the truth. Should I confront him? Show my insecurities?

"Maury, something's bothering me." He turns to prop his head on his elbow looking at me with the best coffee-colored eyes on the planet.

He strokes some curls out of my eyes.

"Sure, what is it?"

"Well, I'm uncomfortable."

"What about?"

"You'll tell me the truth?"

"Of course. Jean, you look worried. What is it? You've done so great calming down your level of activity, shifting your attitude. I feel I have my old Jean back."

I'm silent for moment, biting my lip.

Maury pulls back. "We've always been up front with one another. You're my best friend. And lover. We're soul mates. Tell me."

"You're not interested in Starr, are you?"

"Starr? Why would you think that?" He looks surprised and hurt at the same time.

"Because she's pretty and knows about eco-everything. She already has her doctorate."

"Honey, I love you. Starr's an orthorexic obsessive." He pulls me close to him for a hug.

I look at my husband's inviting eyes.

"What's that?"

"It's those people who do coffee colonics and read labels and only eat raw food. Everything's organic."

"So?"

He falls onto his back. "Echhh. I love corn dogs, a thick bloody steak, butter popcorn and real ice cream, not that non-fat yogurt crap. Some skinny broad's not for me."

"Really?"

He nods with affirmation.

"I like a woman with a *tush* you can *knip*." He reaches behind me to give my slightly well-proportioned one a squeeze.

"Does that mean you're not on a diet anymore?"

"I'm still going to try to eat a little more sensibly because that's the healthy thing to do, but I want to enjoy my culinary pleasures. If I'm a few calories out of bounds in the sand trap of life, so be it."

"Does that mean I'm still your one and only?"

"Always have been, always will be."

He reaches for me. The concerto we're listening to reaches a crescendo like a 1950s Technicolor film as his lips lock on mine. The evening has just begun. Ecstasy hovers nearby. I have to keep dancing even if I don't know the steps.

Omm ommm ommmmm.

ABOUT THE AUTHOR

Marcia Fine, an award-winning author, grew up in South Florida and now resides in Scottsdale, AZ.

She is determined to keep her sense of humor.

To Purchase Other Books By

Marcia Fine

Please Visit

www.MarciaFine.com

Want to know

what Jean's thinking now?

Visit www.JeanRubinBlog.com